I0666572

Prison

Grits

By

Jean Bell

Southern Sass Publishing Alliances

Southern Sass Publishing Alliances Sumter, SC

www.SouthernSassPublishingAlliances.com

This book is a work of fiction. Names, characters, places, and incidents either are products of the author's imagination or are used fictitiously. Any resemblance to actual events or locales or persons, living or dead, is entirely coincidental.

Copyright © 2015 Jean Bell

All rights reserved, including the right to reproduce this book or portions thereof in any form whatsoever. No part of this book may be reproduced or transmitted in any form or by any means, except by a reviewer who may quote brief passages in a review, without permission in writing. For information, address, Southern Sass Publishing Alliances, 19 Courtney Court, Sumter, SC, 29154.

Cover Design by Holly Holladay
Author photo by Brent King
Printed in the United States of America

Trade Paperback edition ISBN 978-0-9987387-0-3

Dedication

To the many honorable employees of the South Carolina
Department of Corrections

Acknowledgments

For many months, my friends in the Sumter Chapter of the South Carolina Writers Workshop critiqued drafts of *Prison Grits*.

Under the leadership of Sandy Richardson, grammarian-in-chief, their suggestions were always helpful.

All remaining improper verb tenses are the sole responsibility of this author and the misspoken/outspoken voices of my characters.

Dirty Rice

Mrs. Kelly's Story

Every day's not Sunday.

Prologue

We locked the meat freezer from inside. We didn't want the inmates to push in after us. When the other cooks and I rushed through the door, tall shelves of Sunbeam bread fell to the floor. Slices broke loose from their bags and got trampled under our feet. They looked like cotton scraps after the harvest. It was so quiet in the freezer we could have heard an ant pissing on the cotton.

What was I thinking when I took this job?

One

Curled up in my dear dead husband's raggedy recliner, I checked my bank statement for the second time. The ice pack on my knee dribbled on the living room rug. When I bent to pick it up, the television remote fell and jammed in the chair's metal brackets.

I couldn't move the chair down so I climbed over the side to get out. When I landed on my bad knees, I slipped in the puddle of melted ice. Biting my lip to keep from crying out, a little blood dripped on the collar of my good blue jacket. It landed right above the tear stains that fell at the surgeon's office that morning.

It hadn't been a good day.

Then the phone rang on the table across the room. Since I couldn't get up, I gave thanks for my plump rear end and scooted over to answer it. The search for grace in the midst of this mess was either God's challenge... or his crazy humor.

"Mom, is that you? You sound winded." My daughter Sharon shouted at me over the phone, as if my arthritic knees deafened my ears.

"Hi, hon, no, I'm fine. I just rushed to catch the phone." I still hadn't decided how much of my predicament to share with her. She tended to assume that my previous sixty years were not relevant now that she was grown and more knowledgeable about every damn thing. She loved me, and I loved her, but our love was like a wide field of yellow daisies with unexpected sink holes of quicksand hidden beneath the blooms.

"Oh, okay. Tell me what the doctor said this morning about your knees. I've been so worried about you. I really wish I could have gotten away from work to be there with you." Sharon earned her law degree last year and finally found a job here in town. Since she's the newest person at her office, it wasn't easy for her to get away.

I propped the phone between my many chins, and pulled up onto the couch. "Well, it's not really good news. He said both knees are grinding bone on bone and need to be replaced. When he suggested we try more shots and pain pills, he agreed those would buy a little more time but not much more than six months." I didn't tell Sharon how upset I got when he said those words, or how embarrassed I felt when I cried in front of him.

"Oh, Mom. I'm sorry. I know how disappointed you are. I wish it could be postponed for a couple years like you hoped. But I hear the rehab won't be so bad, and then you'll be fixed and out of pain. Did you set a date for the surgery?"

So now we came to the second part of this problem. And truth be told, a problem bigger than pain or surgery. The problem was money. My husband's social security death benefits covered most of the month, but no way did it stretch for a big hospital bill. Even though I was sure feeling old, that precious eligibility date for my Medicare was still five years away. When I was young, becoming a senior citizen seemed too far away to worry about it. Now that I had turned *almost* old, I worried I wasn't old enough.

My mind flashed to a fantasy that made me smile. Me in a USA swim suit, my hair as red gold as it was back yonder, but with knees twisted and lumpy, so bowed that they about touched each other. Good grief. How weird was a life where turning sixty-five in order to have your knees cut felt as exciting as a daydream of standing on an Olympic box, waving a gold medal.

"Mom, are you still there? I was asking about your surgery date so I can block it off on my calendar. When is it scheduled?"

"Yes, I'm here." I took a breath. "Sharon, this is my plan. I'm going to limp along taking the meds and find a job with medical insurance to help pay for most of the surgery. I can't afford to have it done right now, and I'm just not comfortable having such big debt afterwards. So that's my plan. It will work out just fine."

"But, Mom, your knees are so bad. I hate for you to stay in pain any longer. How about we charge the hospital on my credit cards, and you can have the surgery right away. And then when you get another job after rehab, we can pay it off slowly."

That was my girl. I sure did love her for making such an offer. But owing her money would be one of those sink holes. The quicksand of that debt would suck the joy right from us.

"I love you for thinking of that, but you know how I hate debt, even to family. Besides, you've still got a wheelbarrow load of student loans to pay off. Adding more debt would mess up your credit. I watched Suze Orman on television the other night, and she had a whole segment on student loans. So don't worry, you know I never have trouble finding a cooking job. My plan will come together. But I've gotta go now. I need to call around to see who's hiring. Talk to you soon, love."

I hung up quickly to avoid more of Sharon's logic. I walked back over to the recliner, smiling since I kept one big secret from her. Even before this morning's appointment with the doctor, I checked around town to see which cooking jobs carried good medical benefits. I already knew that McDonald's and Hardee's didn't have the type I needed, but I hoped that a more upscale place like Cracker Barrel would be my answer.

When I went out there to check, Chris, the manager, was nice as could be. He graduated from high school with Sharon, so we'd met when they were on the debate team together.

"I'm so sorry, Mrs. Kelly, but the kind of insurance you're looking for is just not available from us."

As we talked, he finished putting the leftover pancake batter into the fridge as the staff started prep for the lunch crowd. It was the perfect time of day for a cook. The smell of breakfast sausage mingled with the sizzle of a basket of fries hitting the oil. What a beautiful combination. Chris looked over his shoulder as he stored away the jugs.

"You know, for what you need, I'd look at working at the new prison. After just a couple of months there, a worker is eligible for some really good coverage. You know how government has all of our tax money to play with." He laughed a little, not sure of my politics. "I thought of it myself, but I decided I wanted to work in the commercial market." He turned all the way toward me and straightened his tie. "If I show a good profit margin at this location, there's a regional manager's job opening up." His tie must have been a treasure, the way he stroked it. "So, by the way, I hear Sharon's back in town."

Well, I thought, not seeing a wedding ring on him, *they did like arguing together on that debate team. Maybe they could live together happily ever after, proving each other wrong over every little thing.* I sighed, imagining decades of Thanksgiving dinners with him at the head of our family table. The thought made me tired. I figured I'd have to take some leftovers and leave early. Surely some body part would give me a good excuse. But, please Jesus, at least my knees would feel good. And maybe I could scoop away some grandbabies under my arm, just to give Sharon and Chris time to enjoy another good round of dissent.

"Yes, she is back, Chris. She finished school and just started a new job. I'll be sure to tell her that you asked about her."

"Great, thanks, Mrs. Kelly. I gotta tell you, that girl has a logical brain. We sure had fun together. Tell her to stop by for a cup of coffee if she gets a chance."

"I will for sure. By the way, do I just call the prison to apply for a cook's job?"

"That's what their personnel director said at our last Chamber of Commerce meeting. He said they were hiring for security jobs mostly, but also cooks and plumbers. It sounds like a good fit for you, but I'm not sure about the safety issue out there. It might be too much for you. You probably want to check with Sharon before you look into it further."

He smiled at me, not at all aware that my own smile no longer showed the pleasant sparkle of teeth, but was now a closed mouth grimace. His opinion that I might not be up for the job, plus his advice to check with my daughter, were two big negatives on the scorecard for future son-in-law. At my imaginary Thanksgiving table, his pumpkin no longer carried the fresh smell of fall. I caught a whiff of something not so pleasant. And his polyester tie had an old grease stain on it.

But still, it was good to be polite. "Thanks for your help, Chris. Good luck with your job plans." As I walked out of Cracker Barrel, I regretted my short term memory glitches that would keep me from delivering Chris's message to Sharon.

Hmm, let's see, someone said to say hello, but no, I can't quite remember who it was.

Driving down the highway toward home, with the radio blaring "Born in the USA," I sang along with my boy Bruce. I giggled about Chris's idea to discuss the prison job with Sharon. If she had any notion of it, she'd have me declared insane by some of her lawyer friends. Then she'd strap me to the surgery table herself. I'd be hollering, and she'd use that "logical" voice that made me cringe. "Now, Mom, you know this is for your own good." We'd fuss right up until the anesthesia shut me up, just before the shiny scalpels did their magic.

Thinking of Sharon's call to me today, I didn't feel at all bad about keeping the prison part of my plan from her. I loved her for calling me to check on the doctor's appointment, and I loved her for offering to pay for the medical cost herself, and I loved her enough to not tell her that I had an interview tomorrow at the prison. If I got selected for a job out there, then Sharon and I could have our fuss, but for now, it was too early to disturb the daisies.

What I needed to do now was sit some more in Tom's recliner with another ice pack and take a few too many of those pain pills that let my mind wander in any direction except down towards my knees. I didn't even want to watch the QVC channel to see what I couldn't afford to buy. I just wanted to time travel to the early days of our marriage, surrounded by the smooth comfort of Tom's fake leather.

Two

Counting my blessings usually eased me right into sleep, particularly when jump-started with pain pills. As I snuggled in the recliner, my prayer was one of thanks. My marriage was a blessing, even though it had been too short. My daughter was a blessing, even if we didn't always get along. I had also been blessed with an ability to work all my life. Some jobs took a while to learn, like my time in a cotton mill; but once I got the hang of the job, I was all into it, whether it was culling cotton or flipping hamburgers.

Tom teased me by saying, "Girl, it's a good thing the South don't have labor unions. I swear, you would be blackballed for exceeding production limits. Your bosses sure do get a lot for that minimum wage they pay. Do you not understand that word 'minimum'?"

Even with his jokes, I knew Tom was proud of me. And he didn't play that dumb thing men do, pretending my paycheck was just for extras. We put his money and mine in the same pot and hoped for the best. Of course, Suze Orman would not have approved of our money management, which was mostly 'payday better come quick'.

We just weren't good with all that planning stuff. The only valuable asset we developed was Sharon. We dug deep into our gene pools to produce such a smart daughter. No messing around in shallow, shadowy puddles. We reached back many generations to create her. She got the brains of her daddy's grandma, but a sassy mouth like mine. And now she was a lawyer with a closet full of boring grey suits.

I learned my love of work from my mama and daddy. They had a crop business when I was young. I liked following them up and down the rows of beans, picking until we stopped to put cool, oozing ointment on our fingers. We teased the person who got the first blister of the day, since the blister meant cash in our pockets.

When the three of us took a break in the shade, I had my own scotch plaid thermos of water that mama filled every morning. After I sipped some, she'd say, "That's enough, child. Save some for later." Then I'd curl up for a little nap on my Minnie Mouse quilt.

While I drifted off, I heard the voices of mama and daddy, laughing and joking on their own quilt spread under the tree next to mine. Daddy stretched his long arms above his head, and would give a big sigh, and say something to mama like, "I swear, woman, that blouse looks real good, all sweaty and stuck to you. Is that lace peeking out?" Mama would giggle and scoot away. "You hush, you'll wake the baby." We were a team, and I was proud to be included.

When we buried my daddy lots of years ago, mama joked with the undertaker that we only needed a short casket. By that time, daddy was so stooped from his years of row cropping that he was, as he put it, "the size of a giant shrimp."

When mama said this with a small smile in her easy manner to the man in the black suit at the mortuary, tears ran past her nose, and I handed her my own soggy tissue.

By the time it was mama's turn to go, Tom took me to pick out her box. We spent extra to get one with a fancy silver trim because my mama loved sparkly things. I guess I got that from her.

When we were in the casket shopping room, Tom saw one model with its lid propped open to show a satin lining with a drawing of a phone and the inscription, "Heaven Called." Tom laughed enough for me to hush him.

"Your mama sure enough loved to jabber on her phone. We should get her this one." Toward the end of her life, we talked every day on the phone, mostly about nothing. She'd tell me about her soap stories, and I'd tell her about stuff that happened on the job. It was our way of being close. It was why I love talking to Sharon, who of course doesn't jabber, but the calls still keep us close.

Lots of times I didn't tell mama about some things that happened at work. With all the jobs I'd had, I had not led a sheltered life. I dealt with some characters in my time. Many of the grills where I worked were attached to bars, so I listed calming down drunks as one of my work skills. And I learned the knack of not hearing obscenities thrown my way. My loose tongue did know when to lay low.

So it definitely wasn't the work itself that gave me doubts about the prison job. Instead, I worried that at my age, I might not be able to carry my share of the load. I wasn't really old, but I sure wasn't young anymore either.

I never wanted to be one of those people who used age as an excuse to whine. And, truth be told, I was proud of being so strong in my young years. I liked being able to unload supply trucks when they pulled up behind the restaurants with their pay clocks running. Of course, I also liked being able to boss around the young kids who worked in the stockroom, but they knew I'd unload boxes with them if the driver revved his engine as a warning that he was tired of sitting at the dock.

Shortly after Tom died, my knees got bad. It happened real quick. For the first time in my life, I felt old. I hobbled on the job and took to sitting on a tall stool in front of the grill, no longer able to race with the young stock boys to unload supplies. When I tripped and fell and couldn't get up, I quit that grill and talked to the surgeon.

Getting old scared me. My knees were the first sign of it, and I wanted to fix the problem. I wanted to be able to sleep because I was tired, not because pain pills knocked me out. And to me, solving a problem was like picking beans. In those days, I looked out toward the end of the row, bent down, and kept going. If a fire ant hill popped up in the middle of the row, I stopped for my gloves and worked around the little buggers.

Or sometimes when I cooked on the job and a burner went down, I double-upped a skillet and kept the orders going out to the customers. I expected problems to be part of the job. I never expected problems to stop the job from getting done. So now, when the doctor told me I needed surgery, I figured out the solution for affording it, which was to get back to work. Except this time, I needed to find a job with the right benefits.

My ramble down memory lane was suddenly interrupted by the phone, startling me awake. It was Sharon again.

"Hi, Mom, I'll ring your doorbell in three minutes to drop off some chow mein from Oriental Oasis, your favorite Chinese place. I can't stay because I have to get back. We're working late, but I didn't want you to cook tonight. So get your shuffle on to get to the door."

I loved my Sharon.

Three

Sleep came slow the night before my interview at the prison. Part of the problem was a nest of possums scratching and shredding insulation underneath the floor of my doublewide. Their rustling crept into my sleep, so I couldn't get comfortable. If Tom were alive, they never would have taken roost to worry me. Tom would have shimmied under this old trailer and run them off some kind of way. But then, if it had been one of his Pabst Blue Ribbon nights, he'd have run them off with a shotgun, and I'd been left with possum carcasses staring up through the holes in the floor. It was true that his take-charge ways frequently left me with a pay-later problem.

The second thing that kept me awake was puzzling out what to wear for my interview. I liked clothes more than a half-broke widow lady probably should, but if it sparkled or swished, it made me smile.

In my accounting, the guy who invented polyester that looked like satin was right up there with Einstein or Edison or George Jefferson Carver, the guy who figured out how to mash up peanut butter at his house in Monticello.

But if it weren't for yard sales and Goodwill, my life would be like a scorched earth, empty of the fun of the hunt. Us poor people have style and standards, too.

So for my interview this morning, I wore my next best outfit: a light green pantsuit. It was kind of like what Hillary Clinton would wear if she found it on the Walmart sales rack before I did.

The new prison stood right down the road from my house on the way to the bypass. Our town was so excited when the state chose our location. We thought it would bring plenty of jobs for our young people. But it turned out that a lot of our recent high school graduates couldn't pass the reading test, particularly the fellows. The prison people scheduled extra reading classes to give them a chance to improve their scores, but the classes met when hunting season opened, so not many guys attended. We were all surprised that our girls did the testing real well, so a lot of them were hired.

When I drove into the big parking lot at the prison, most of the spots were filled. A car ahead of me pulled into a space right close to the prison gate, so I started to drive on. I sighed, resigned to the long limp back to the gate. I knew I'd be tired and sweaty before I even got to the interview.

"Hey, Miss Kelly, you can have this spot. It's closer. Wait for me while I park yonder, and we'll walk in together."

Blessed be, it was my friend, Wilma Collins. Her trailer was a little ways past mine, and we'd known each other a long time. But I hadn't talked with her for a while and didn't know she was looking to work here, too.

"Thanks, Wilma, you are a sweetheart," I yelled out my car window. I took her space after she pulled out, just as the final screeching part of the Bee Gee's 'Staying Alive' ended.

Wilma was only a little older than Sharon. She had two kids that she was raising mostly on her own. Her sorry-ass drunk of a husband spent a lot of time locked up on small charges. A while ago, she told me, "You know, Mrs. Kelly, having Ted locked up is sometimes easier than having him home."

Ted would do his time, come home, and before long, he'd be back in jail. But the day she told me it wasn't so bad, she also admitted, "But, sometimes, I get tired of being alone. If it weren't for friends like you and the kids' grandparents, I don't know what I'd do."

For Wilma's birthday last month, I dropped off a pan of banana cream pudding at her house. She was so happy to get my surprise gift; I might well have been the front man for the Publisher's Clearing House Million Dollar Payoff.

"Oh, Miss Kelly, this is so nice," she smiled with teary eyes. "I was going to pretend to forget my birthday this year, but this morning the kids gave me cards they made and now here you are. What a day I'm having."

When she lifted the pan of pudding for a sniff, I was glad I left out the rum flavoring in the recipe. I didn't want her to take a sniff and have Post Disaster Nerves, like when you crawl under the table because of a flashback from a bad time.

Still smiling, Wilma opened her door wider. "Come in, we haven't visited in a while."

"I'd love to," I lied, "But I've got a bunch of errands to run. How about I give you a call and we'll get together soon?"

Wilma looked a little relieved that I wasn't coming in, but I felt guilty for the lame lie. I might just as well said I needed to get home to let my cat out. But the bruise under her eye gave us too much that we couldn't talk about, so it seemed better to leave our visit for another time. I'd heard Ted had started his latest sentence a week or so before. So the black eye must have been his going away present to her. With the fading bruise, it looked like another bad time had got added to Wilma's long list.

But now, as she hurried across the parking lot toward me, I saw that she also had given some thought to her interview outfit. And when she got closer, I saw with relief that her bruises had all faded.

"Wilma, you look really nice," I said, hoping I didn't sound surprised. She had on navy khakis and a blue dotted blouse. If she hadn't been missing a tooth, she could have been a model in a J. Crew catalogue. It was a long step from her usual style.

"Thanks, Miss Kelly," she laughed. "My mother-in-law, Delores, picked it out for me. I think she worried I'd wear my usual jeans and t-shirt." She looked down at her new blouse and gave a fake pout, "Judging from this, she really, really wants me to get this job." She laughed again with the good spirits of her sweet nature.

And, truth be told, Delores was smart to give her such a gift. Having seen some of the slogans on Wilma's t-shirt collection, I was glad to see her masquerading as a yuppie.

Once I ran into her at the post office. She wore a shirt from the county's last Peach Festival. On the front, right below the scooped out neck were two of the prettiest coral pink peaches, linked by fancy lettering that said, "Try me, I'm juicy."

I was glad Delores watched out for Wilma, but I wished she'd done a better job raising her son to be a good husband.

As I locked the car, I said to Wilma, "I didn't know you wanted to work out here, too."

"Yeah," she answered. "I need a regular job with benefits. Cleaning rooms at the motel doesn't pay much, and I'm sick of cleaning up other people's messes. I swear, Mrs. Kelly, when I change those sheets," she stopped that thought and instead said, "you should see the sticky toothpaste people leave in the sinks."

She glanced at me to see if I appreciated her revised description. I nodded back like a baseball catcher who saved the pitcher when he tossed a loose ball that almost got away. The catcher would pause, look at the ball like he'd never seen one quite like that; then nod to the pitcher as if to say, "We'll just let that mistake be hardly noticed."

Wilma grinned a little at me, and went on, "Also, the kids have lots of cavities, so I need dental insurance. I heard that you're looking for benefits, too. I ran into Chris at the Cracker Barrel, and he said you were thinking about it."

In a small town like ours, it was easy to know too much about each other's business. I only hoped Sharon had been too busy to tune into the town's gossip.

We walked toward the sidewalk leading to the entrance. But then we stopped, trying to take in the size of the prison that loomed in front of us. When it was built, the prison people had meetings with the town people to educate us about the prison. According to them, this maximum security prison held fifteen hundred inmates, most of them with sentences of thirty years to life. Since I'd never been this close to it before, its size was a sight to see. Just driving by it on the highway, I hadn't realized how large it was.

Looking at the size and thinking of the fifteen hundred inmates inside, my mind whirled, imagining all the sad stories that lived here. But I came here to cook, so I wasn't interested in hearing sad stories.

As Wilma and I stood and looked, a truck went through one gate, which closed behind it. As we watched, the truck stayed still while a uniformed staff person used a mirror on a long stick to look under the truck. Then he checked inside the cab. After that, he had the driver stand with the keys in his hand while he wanded the driver, like at an airport. Only when all that was done did a second gate open for the truck to go through.

"Yikes," whispered Wilma. "It's like you see on television. And check out that barbed wire on top of the fences. No one could get through that without winding up a bloody mess." Neither of us moved, still in awe of the seriousness of the place.

Then, as we looked past the double fences, we saw housing units that stood like college dorms. They were spread out across an open area the size of a double football field. All the buildings were made of cement slabs. None of them had any trim. Across the front and on the sides, narrow slitted windows provided what must have been the only source of light into the cells.

Suddenly Wilma giggled, "Miss Kelly, look at the guys at the windows." I looked to see what she meant, and in almost every window, an inmate stood with a body part pressed against the glass. I squinted, and then looked away.

"Come on, Wilma, let's go inside. I'm glad I don't have my glasses, so I can't tell exactly what's a tongue or what's a whatever."

Wilma laughed, and seemed to relax some, as if seeing men acting ridiculous made the place more comfortable for her. I didn't understand why it affected her this way. For me, I felt mad and sad at the same time. I felt disgusted that grown men thought this was acceptable behavior, like they had slipped into a band of aliens who did this instead of a handshake. I wanted to slap them upside their heads, to bring them back to their right selves.

But I also felt sad, in the same way I pitied the dogs chained in the yard of the trailer next to mine. They lunged and snarled as I went past, and I'd think, *"There's nothing I want that you're protecting."* But with them dogs, I might feel sad for them, but I wasn't dumb enough to get too close.

I tugged Wilma's arm. "The door over there is marked Visitors and Staff, so that must be the right one. Come on, we need to hurry up. I don't want to be late for my appointment."

Four

The metal detector buzzed and blinked when the young officer at the visitors' gate passed it around my body.

"Do you have on an underwire bra, ma'am?" she asked in a bored voice.

I blushed to hear the details of my undies discussed so casually. I probably looked pop-eyed with surprise because she added, "If we don't figure out what makes the machine go off, we can't let you pass through."

"Oh, my goodness. Well, do what you need to do."

The officer then ran her fingers along the gosh darn wire. "Yep," she said, "that's the problem." While she talked, she finished patting down the rest of me. "You'd be amazed what visitors try to bring in. Once we had an old guy hide a shank inside his walking cane."

She and another officer nearby laughed together, remembering, "It was a quiet Sunday afternoon. Visiting hours were almost over, and this old man shuffled in, looking all pathetic. He must have thought we would just check him and not bother with his cane, but when we shook it, there was a rattle and a loose handle. Sure enough, a knife was inside."

"My goodness," I said to them as I straightened my blouse and jacket. "He must have been really scared of the inmates to think he needed protection."

They looked at me like I just fell off the cabbage truck. "No, ma'am, his grandson paid him to bring it in." Then they added, "If you're here for the job orientation, you can go on through the door to your right. It'll take you straight to the Personnel Office."

Wilma stepped up to go through the detector. She passed through without a buzz. As she came through the other side, she joked, "I've got on a Victoria's Secret wireless model in purple."

They didn't respond to her joke. They just waved us along to the inside of the building.

As we walked, I whispered to Wilma, "I swear, if I get a job here, I'll never again wear an underwire to work. I don't care if my C cups drift under my armpits, I don't want to be patted down every day."

Wilma laughed and said, "Oh, Miss Kelly, don't worry so much. My pretty girls have had rougher treatment to pay the rent. You'll get used to it." I didn't know for sure what Wilma meant, but I knew I didn't want to know more.

At the hiring office, we joined about two dozen other people also there to apply for jobs. The man organizing us looked like he had spent military time before coming to this prison job. He had a gruff voice, and his uniform was starched and tailored. I noticed he walked with a limp, but it didn't seem to slow him down.

"Good morning," he said to our quiet group. We stood together in the hallway, waiting for directions. "My name is Sergeant Murphy. Here's what's going to happen today. You'll be assigned to a room based on the type of job you're applying for. If you want a security position, go to the room on the right. Everyone else who wants a non-uniform job in maintenance or food service or medical or education, you all go to the smaller room at the end of the hall."

He paused to see if we understood. When no one asked questions, he went on. "Once there, you'll fill out paperwork. Then each of you will be interviewed to see if you meet the qualifications for whatever job you are interested in. During the interview, you will also be evaluated for your suitability for working in a prison setting. When that is finished, we'll meet together for a more detailed orientation on prison procedures. At the end of that, you will be free to leave. Within a few days, you'll learn if you have been selected for a job." He paused and checked his clipboard. "Any questions, now?"

I wanted to ask him more about that "suitability for prison work," but it clearly was too late for that. No one else in the group said anything either. "Okay," he said, "Let's get started. By the way, no one is to leave the room you're directed to, and you are not allowed to find the rest room without permission." He looked toward a young man at the back of our group who was leaning against the wall. "And, sir, please do not leave boot marks on the baseboard. They're freshly painted."

Well, my goodness. I had never worked at a place with so many rules. With most of my cooking jobs, once they checked to see if I knew not to leave hamburger out overnight to thaw, they threw an apron at me and told me to get started. At the cotton mill, when the guy in charge saw that I was breathing, he put me on the line.

Wilma gave a little wave to me as she headed away with the security group, and I joined the others to go down the hall. I did my best to walk like a healthy person but felt reassured that Sergeant Murphy had a limp, too. Maybe not everyone had to be young and fully normal to work in this place.

From my side of the table, the interview seemed to go well. I told the cafeteria supervisor what kind of cooking experience I had. "So you have worked in commercial settings for twenty years?" he asked.

"Yes, sir, and before that, I waited tables and did prep work." I wasn't sure how much detail to give, but I definitely wanted him to know that I knew the hygiene rules of restaurant work, so I started to go into that, as well as menu planning.

"You won't need to worry about planning menus. All of that is done by the central office. They send us a month of menus at a time, and they do all the ordering for those menus. We have to cook and clean and observe basic nutrition practices." I nodded, since it did sound familiar.

"Probably the biggest challenge you'd have on this job is getting used to working with inmates. They can be difficult. Plus, we have to be real strict about following security procedures since there are so many things in a kitchen that could be used as weapons."

I hadn't thought about that. I'd never seen a fry cook go after the salad guy with a sharp knife. My world was definitely going to change. But I didn't want to ask the question that really worried me, which was about my age and keeping up with the pace. I didn't want to give the interviewer any reason to doubt my ability. I knew that there was a law that kept them from not hiring me just because I was old, but I didn't want to give them an easier way to refuse me.

"Yes, I understand there would be security procedures I would need to learn. Is there a lot of training for that?"

"I was just going to say, don't worry about that part. If you are selected, you will go to central office for several weeks where they teach you about prison work. Some of the training overlaps with the uniform staff and some is specific to food service." He looked at his watch. "Do you have any other questions?"

"No, I think it sounds like a job I would like to have." With that, the interview was over. For all the worry time I spent, it was almost too simple. I didn't know if this was a good or a bad sign.

I waited with the rest of the group while others were interviewed, then we all went back together to a large conference room. They gave us a stretch break, then Wilma and I saw each other and sat together. A girl who was part of my first group joined us. She sat quietly, staring at the empty podium. When she didn't say anything to us, I leaned over to introduce myself and Wilma.

"Hi," she whispered. "My name is Faith Miller. I interviewed for a librarian job." With her whisper and her black skirt and sweater, I wondered if she was a recent widow. But, of course I didn't ask. Wilma bent towards us and said, "Wow, you must be a smart person. I didn't even know the prison had a library."

Faith Miller didn't smile at Wilma's silly friendliness. She just answered, "The library is going to be attached to the school." Then I joked that the prison school had more resources than the public school, but she didn't smile back at that, either. But she did answer.

"They don't have the funding available yet. If they hire me, they said it would be months before I start work. They also said they might bring me on at some point at an older prison if a vacancy comes available."

Wilma said in a sincere voice, "It's too bad you won't know anything for sure for a while."

Faith Miller just shrugged, "I'll keep on substitute teaching in town until this permanent job is ready." She didn't ask about our situations. But then Sergeant Murphy walked up to the podium, and the room got quiet.

"Listen up, everybody. I'm going to go through some issues related to prison work. Some of the material will sound a little rough, but that's just the way it is. My remarks will be brief. If you are hired, you'll find out in a few days and then be scheduled for more detailed training before you actually start work in the prison. At that training, you can ask all of your questions. But right now, I'm just going to tell you enough so if it doesn't sound comfortable, you'll have enough background to turn down a job if you get the call hiring you."

He paused and looked around the room. Then he went on. "By state law, the prison's main job is to keep criminals locked up. While certain standards have to be met related to nutrition and medical care, even those vital services come second to keeping the community safe by preventing escapes. Other areas, like education or religious activities, help make a better prison, but they cannot get in the way of our main priority. And to repeat, our main priority is to keep inmates from going over the fence."

Sergeant Murphy paused again to be sure we got the message. He stressed it in kind of formal words. I wondered how he talked about the job when he was at the local beer joint with his co-workers.

"This prison is a maximum security facility. It holds the worst of the worst criminals in the state."

Oh, yes, he definitely had our attention now.

"In order to be sure none of them escape, we count inmates six times a day. Most of these counts are done by lining them up by name to be sure we eyeball them. Other counts, like at night, are done by shining a flashlight in cells to count heads in beds. That's all the detail you need at this point about inmate counts, but you do need to understand that while uniformed staff do most of the counting, if you work in an area like the cafeteria or library, where inmates are assigned to a job, it is your responsibility to keep track of the inmates detailed to you. And at count time, you will do the counting. It is not allowed for staff to use count time for a break, or to expect uniformed officers to do all the work."

Sergeant Murphy paused for breath. I almost smiled. He apparently got a little heated over this issue. It sounded like he might have had some problems with staff sharing the work load.

After just a moment, he got back into it. "As for the security here, remember, this is a maximum security prison. If an inmate goes over the fence, the officer who sees him is required to shoot him. If you think you might hesitate to do this, you do not want to accept the job. Weapons training is provided so you will have the skill you need. If an inmate successfully escapes, either over the fence or hiding in a vehicle, we have procedures to follow which again

involve both uniform and non-uniform staff. You'll be taught these in your training weeks. And again I stress, both uniform and non-uniform staff are equally part of security. Just because you don't wear a uniform does not mean that you are not responsible for practicing security rules."

An older man in the back of the room raised his hand to ask, "What if an inmate tries to escape by taking one of us hostage? What happens then?"

Sergeant Murphy answered, "While we don't want to get into too much detail before you all are officially hired, it's understandable that this is a concern. The short answer is that we have a special team trained to negotiate hostage situations when they do occur. Most of these negotiations are lengthy. But the bottom line is that we are not allowed by law to let an inmate escape, even if he has a hostage."

The man who asked the question looked like he hadn't heard correctly, but Sergeant Murphy again said, "More details will be provided in training. It is not appropriate to go into any

more detail at this time. Be assured, though, we do have snipers assigned to the emergency SWAT team."

Wilma and I glanced at each other. Neither of us had considered the idea of being a hostage in order to get work benefits. We heard others in the room whisper among themselves, too. Faith Miller maybe hadn't heard the question since she didn't respond at all. Her face stayed bland and she didn't fidget.

Sergeant Murphy rapped lightly on the podium, and said again, "Okay, listen up. We have just a few more things to go over. Then you'll be free to go. It was not my intent to alarm you about the reality of the hostage issue, but we have had hostage situations occur at this prison already. So you do need to know that such a possibility is part of your everyday work environment. If you think that you are not comfortable with following security procedures to minimize such a threat, then you do not want to work here." His pause this time felt like a challenge. No one walked out of the room, but I guessed that at least a few people decided to look for work somewhere else when they left here. Since they were already dressed for a job interview, they could go to Walmart to see if there were any openings. At least there, the odds of being taken hostage were significantly less.

"The next thing we need to talk about is gangs, which are the source of most of the fights in prison. Inmates who maybe had no interest in gangs while on the street, most likely will get attached to one when they get locked up. It gives an inmate some protection, and if he's interested in making money, gangs control the profits of contraband that comes into the prison. Contraband is defined as anything that an inmate is not allowed to have. This includes drugs, weapons, phones, alcohol, tobacco, pornography, and many other things. It's a very long list. At our prison, most of the contraband that comes on the yard is thrown over the fence. These throw overs are paid for and coordinated by gangs."

Someone from the group raised their hand to ask, "But if the inmates are locked up, how do they organize it?"

Sergeant Murphy explained the details. "Let's say Gang A pays up front to have someone from the street put a package together and throw it over the fence. The plan is for a Gang A member to pick it up, maybe at dawn when he's on his way to work in the cafeteria and most of the other inmates are still locked in their cells. But if a Gang B member sees the package first, then Gang B will make all the profit from it with none of the operating costs. That's what leads to gang fights. Think it through yourself. Gang A paid for all the contents of the package. They paid for someone with a strong arm to do the throwing over the fence. And they probably paid a little to the gang member to take the risk to pick it up. That's a lot of overhead. But if Gang B intercepts the delivery, the contents are still as valuable to sell, so Gang B makes all the money."

He glanced around the room to be sure we understood. I felt like I was learning a whole new marketing approach that had nothing to do with flea markets or double couponing.

"So, here's the next part of the contraband problem," the Sergeant went on. "The loss of profit and opportunity will lead to a gang fight, Gang A against Gang B. During this fight, it's not just for show, inmates really try to hurt each other. They may not particularly have it as a goal to hurt a staff member, but in the middle of such a fight, you, the staff person, could easily get hurt. Sometimes the injury happens when an officer tries to break up a fight between inmates who are slashing at each other with shanks. By the way, a shank is made out of metal or Plexiglass, or anything that can be sharpened by rubbing it for hours on the concrete floor. During this fight with the shank, an officer likely sprays the tear gas he carries on his equipment belt. If he is able to spray it in the faces of the fighters, most times that is enough to stop the fighting. But, as an example, the last time I tried to break up a similar fight, the inmates didn't get hurt. But I ended up with a sliced Achilles tendon because I got too close. I was trying for a better angle to spray the gas, and the shank cut me."

The room was absolutely silent. "Maybe you think you're tough like I did after two tours in Afghanistan. But things happen differently in a prison. Remember, staff do not carry weapons on the yard since the weapons can easily be used against them. All we've got are the chemical munitions and a radio to call in for help to central control. We rely on each other for help. And sometimes help doesn't come soon enough."

We all stared at Sergeant Murphy. He had not shown emotion when he told us about his injury, but his stern expression didn't seem to welcome any questions.

"If a regular fight like I just described gets out of hand and spreads to other inmates, we have a riot squad, the SWAT team, that responds with heavier gas. They wear protective helmets and body armor and carry shields. You will, of course, get more information in training about riots and situations in which the prison might get locked down. During a lockdown, no regular inmate movement is allowed. All meals are served in their cells, and all activities like school are halted."

The same man in the back who asked about hostages, now asked another question. This question was probably on everyone's mind. "What happens to a staff person who is injured on the job?"

Sergeant Murphy answered with a little smile. "Again, that's a legitimate question in terms of you all assessing if a prison job is right for you. The answer is that medical treatment is provided, separate from your regular medical benefits. When, or if, you are able to return to work, a position is made available somewhere in the prison system. It is usually best to be reassigned to another prison so you can start fresh, so to speak. Sometimes coming back to the site of the injury can create other problems. So usually the staff person is transferred to another prison nearby.

If you need time to recuperate from an inmate injury, you're paid while you are out. But be advised, sometimes people make fake claims. They may claim that a back injury happened while restraining an inmate, when really the injury happened water skiing on their day off.

So staff injuries are subject to investigation by Internal Affairs. If it's a false claim, the employee can be charged with fraud. If it's an injury caused by an inmate, the investigator will bring street charges against the inmate for this new assault, which will result in more prison time added to his sentence. Most of the inmates in this prison are already serving thirty years to life anyway, so additional time may not be such a deterrent."

My head was spinning. I literally felt like Alice falling down the rabbit hole into a world I never knew about.

Sergeant Murphy looked at his watch. "Okay, that's enough for today. Just remember, my purpose for this orientation was not to scare you away from taking a prison job. It's just that you need to know the dangers. If you decide that the benefits outweigh the risks, you may find it to be fascinating work. Some of the finest people I've met work in prisons. But it is true that a whole world inside the fence exists, which most people on the outside have no knowledge of. So on that, good luck to you, and I'll escort you out."

Wilma, Faith Miller, and I walked out with the rest of our group. None of us spoke until we were on the other side of the visitors' gate. Once in the parking lot, Wilma and I waved to Faith as she walked on to her car. Then Wilma gave me a big hug.

"So, what do you think? Are you going to take the job if it's offered?" she asked me.

"I tell you, Wilma, it does give me pause. To hear Sergeant Murphy talk about the dangers was like listening to a police show on television. But the fact is, my knees hurt even now, just from that little bit of walking. This is my best solution. So if they hire me, I'm taking the job. But you can be darn sure I'm going to learn all the safety stuff I can at the training sessions. How about you?"

"Yep, it's my best chance to get my family straightened out. I want to work for the government. I want my kids to wear braces on their teeth. I want to feel like we're not just winging it, week to week. I want to have a savings account. I want all that stuff that families with a future have."

"What about the danger piece?" I asked her.

"Mrs. K, I admit it was scary to hear about what goes on inside. As often as Ted's been in jail, he hasn't told me much about what it's like. But I guess jail is not the same as a prison." She leaned toward me and said in a low voice, "By the way, talking about Ted, there was almost a
hitch in my application. I didn't get a chance to tell you about it earlier because I didn't want to share my business in front of that spooky girl."

I probably looked surprised at Wilma's rude words, but she rushed on, "You know on the application it asked if a family member was incarcerated? Well, of course I had to say yes because of Ted. But during the interview they said that as long as

I disclosed it, you know, didn't try to keep it a secret, that it didn't mess up my eligibility. They also said it was simpler because he was at the local jail, and not in the state prison system."

I smiled inside at Wilma's new vocabulary words like *incarcerated* and *eligibility*.

"Well, that's good, that it didn't automatically eliminate you." Then I asked her again, "But what about the danger piece. What did you think about that?"

"Miss Kelly, I'm going to tell you a secret that I've never told anyone. When I was a teenager, every time there was a television ad for enlisting in the military, it made me tingle. I loved looking at the girls in uniform, lined up next to the men like it was no big deal. Like they had a space there, too. And I thought it would be so cool for the military to figure out what I might be good at, and train me for some job I'd never heard of. Because, frankly, I could never figure out what I could do once I was grown. So handing me over to the military seemed like a good plan. But then I met Ted, and within minutes I was pregnant. So the military plan was gone. But late at night, when I pigged out on ice cream while nine months pregnant, those recruiting ads still made me cry. This prison job feels like a version of that dream I had, two kids ago."

Wilma walked me to my car, and we gave each other a strong hug. I was glad I had gotten to know Wilma better. But as I drove out of the parking lot, I realized I hadn't asked her why she talked so bad about Faith Miller. I agreed she was strange, but I saw her strangeness as sad rather than spooky. But it didn't matter, since we probably wouldn't be seeing much of each other.

I felt relieved that my interview had gone well, and that Sergeant Murphy's story of his injury didn't trigger a hot flash for me. Sometimes when I got anxious, it made me sweaty and jittery, and my skin felt too tight. I respected Sergeant Murphy a lot, both for his military service and for his prison job. I wanted Wilma and me to be fine bureaucrats, too.

As I drove, I felt relieved that I had made a decision. Then Andy Williams started singing, "Moon River", which Tom and I liked to dance to out on the deck after Sharon was asleep in her crib. I remembered Tom's arms around me as he held me close. His hands liked to rest on my behind as we danced, and he always sung off key in my ear. I took the playing of our song as a sign that my brave possum hunter was watching over me. So I sang along on the way home, ready to stick close to the phone, waiting for good news about my new job.

Five

While I waited in the silence of the meat freezer for the riot squad to arrive, I thought of the changes in my life over the last few months, changes which had brought me to this freezer. It was a happy day when the prison's personnel office called to offer me a job in the kitchen as a cook and gave me the start date for my training.

I knew Sharon would be upset about the job, so I invited her to dinner at the Oriental Oasis down the road from me, so I could break the news in public. I would have preferred the Cracker Barrel, but I wanted to avoid any chance for us to see the manager, Chris. Since he had a crush on Sharon, I didn't want him to remind her of their fun times on the debate squad. Of course, he might have really laid on the charm and given us extra yeast rolls, but protecting Sharon's future made it worth the sacrifice of giving up free rolls.

She was not happy at my news and spent most of the meal saying, "But, Mom, what about this?" Or, "But, Mom, have you thought this through?" This one-sided discussion continued right up until the fortune cookies came with our pot of tea. When we shared our messages, hers said, "Beware of change," which she tossed in front of me like a trump card in a poker game. But my fortune read, "Everything will be all right," which spooked even me as I laid it slowly in front of her.

"Mom, I love you, but I think this job is a bad idea. So if you need me to rub your feet at the end of a rough day at work, I'll buy you a gift card for a pedicure." We laughed and hugged and agreed to stay family. I knew she still worried, but she knew that everything had been said, and my job plan was still in place. Of course, she also knew she'd have more chances to change my mind.

The weeks of training were full of surprises about the prison world, but the training wasn't physically difficult. For us non-uniform staff, we spent most of our time in a classroom at the central office complex out of town. Faith Miller, the shy librarian, wasn't in my class, so I guessed her job hadn't been funded yet. For Wilma, her training was very different. She got hired as a uniformed officer on the night shift, so she had hours of calisthenics and self-defense classes.

One morning at daybreak we saw each other pumping gas at the Shell station before we got on the interstate to head out of town for our classes.

She looked happy as she hollered across the service island. "Hey, stranger, how's it going?"

"It's good, except my behind is tired from sitting," I joked. "How about you?"

She laughed and said, "Mine is tired and sore from being kicked, but I love it. Look at my uniform, isn't it cool?" She looked sharp in her blue fatigues, with her boots shined. She didn't have on a single sequin. We agreed to meet for lunch once our schedules got set and followed each other onto the interstate. She had said her mother-in-law, Delores, was going to keep the kids while Wilma worked the night shift, then Wilma would pick them up for school and spend afternoons watching them do their homework. She'd sounded proud and happy that she was making her plan work.

Which was how I felt, too. I'd been on the job now for a little more than a month. Most of my shift was spent actually cooking, which was easy for me. As a new hire, I didn't have direct responsibility for inmates yet, but I tried to show a few of them how to scramble eggs without bits of shell left in, and how to time the rice steamer so the grains came out softer than gravel. My co-workers answered my questions, but kept their distance from me and weren't too friendly. I sensed they were waiting to see how I worked out before getting too sociable.

My boss, Supervisor Rabon, was not the best boss I'd ever had. He stayed in his office most of the time, evidently not too concerned about the egg shells and gravel in the food. A few times I thought I caught a whiff of rum coming from his direction, but I didn't want to jump to conclusions. I'd had good bosses, and bad bosses, so whichever he was, I'd be fine.

The inmates also pretty much left me alone. When I showed them how to follow a recipe better, a few paid attention, but most of them wandered off. My days at work felt like a dress rehearsal for a performance or a play. The inmates and the other staff all knew their dialogue and places but waited to see how I was going to fit in with them. If we lined up for the Macy's Day Parade, I'd be the one trusted to hold the extra shovel for the guy who walked behind the elephants, cleaning up poop. At least he could be trusted with his part of the job, but the vote was still out on me.

The morning of the riot started like most days. We cleaned up from breakfast, then a fight broke out between two groups of inmates on the wide grassy area outside our cafeteria doors. When our inmate workers saw the scuffle, some ran out to join. Sergeant Murphy's description about gang fights had been right. Not all inmates tried to join in, but enough did so that soon the group was very large. Some of the inmates had rakes and brooms, while others just tackled each other and rolled around on the grass.

The fight kept getting larger, so most of our staff left through a door headed toward the school building, which was more secure than our open cafeteria. I was confused about the best route to take, so when Supervisor Rabon yelled to follow him, I scuttled in his steps to the freezer like the scared lamb I was. He carried the walkie talkie from his office and moved fast for a chunky guy with short legs.

Ernest, one of our inmate workers, was already in the freezer, taking inventory. We crammed in around him and locked the door behind us. He didn't ask what was happening, so I guessed this was something he had seen before. He stacked up cartons of ten pound turkey logs for us to sit on, and squatted next to my shoulder in the corner. We kept silent, puzzled at the quiet outside our insulated walls. My boss didn't say anything to us, just toyed with the radio trying to get a signal. His eyeglasses kept slipping down his nose. If we needed reassuring words, his well was dry.

The only other staff person with us was Cindy, who sat across from me. She had worked in the cafeteria for about a year, so in my eyes she knew what to expect. When she saw me staring at Supervisor Rabon like a thirsty dog waiting at the gutter spout for rain, Cindy rolled her eyes and gave a slight shake of her head and a hint of a smile. Evidently rain was not in the forecast, but I felt better knowing I wasn't the only staffer who thought our boss was strange.

Suddenly we heard loud *bam* sounds, like a fourth of July cannon. Ernest leaned over to whisper, "Miss Kelly, them sounds mean the riot team just moved onto the yard. It sounds like they're right close to the cafeteria doors. The fighters are probably running now, looking for a corner to hide from the gas. They know it will drift their way."

Just then, several more bangs came from the yard. Ernest kept up his play-by-play like a know-it-all SEC announcer. Or in this case, more like a guy who whispers at golf matches. "Them bangs are flash-bang grenades. Man, they're using the big stuff. They must want to break this up before the boys have a chance to get organized." He smiled and went on, "Wish this freezer had a window. It'd be like watching TV."

Cindy smiled a little again, and I whispered back to him, "Well, thank goodness they're here. Now we can finally get out of this freezer. I swear, Ernest, maybe working in a prison kitchen is not the best job to have."

Supervisor Rabon seemed to regain his hearing at this treason talk and raised his eyebrows. When he did, his glasses slipped down his nose again. At the same time, Cindy gave another modified eye roll and head shake, as if to warn me to watch my tongue. I felt a little dizzy from all the movement of their eyes, noses, and heads. I squinted to keep focused on Ernest, who ignored them.

After another bam, he answered, "Yes, ma'am, you might be right. But, ma'am, when they open the door, stay close to the floor so the tear gas outside won't bother you so bad. Put your apron over your head."

"You sure do know what's going on. How many riots have you been in, Ernest?"

He smiled and said, "They probably won't call this a riot. They'll just call it a disturbance. It sounds better on the news. Please, ma'am, Miss Kelly, please remember to tell them I helped keep you safe." He stopped smiling when he added his request. He looked more like a guy asking a serious favor.

"Don't worry," I whispered back. "I won't forget. Maybe they'll do something nice for you."

His smile turned to a smirk, "Yeah, sure, like give me extra pancakes in the morning."

By now both Cindy and Rabon were trying to listen to our conversation. Their eyes were scrunched into similar frowns to help their hearing. I guessed my conversation with Ernest moved into one of those gray areas they talked about in training. They had a whole session on not getting too familiar with inmates.

While I waited for the riot squad to arrive, I gave myself a talking to, mumbling the word 'titanium' over and over. I sounded like one of those yoga masters on the travel channel, humming a mantilla, or mantra, or whatever the word is. Titanium is the Cadillac metal for artificial knees and the reason I took this job. When the surgeon slides that shiny titanium in place, I'll pay him like the bonafide bureaucrat I am, a regular state employee with full benefits. I felt proud that I had my plan in place and not even a riot was scaring me too much.

But the longer we waited, my worry list started to build. I worried I'd get a hot flash, since I felt the walls of this small freezer begin to move in on me. I worried my nose would soon be too close to Rabon's and our eyebrows would get tangled. I worried my butt was frozen to the carton of turkey logs. I worried the riot squad didn't know we were in the freezer, and we wouldn't be found until broccoli was on the menu next week. But before I was totally lost to my worry list, voices outside the freezer got louder. Rabon dialed in more static on his radio and suddenly a SWAT leader outside the door yelled to us.

"Staff can come out now. It is safe. Any inmates in there need to lay on the floor until we get to them." So, praise be, me and my new favorite inmate, Ernest, finally got rescued. I felt so distracted by the relief that my hot flash limped off to gather itself for another time.

Once we got released from the freezer, Supervisor Rabon headed immediately for his office. Maybe he went to reread the radio instruction manual. Maybe he went to rest his eyes. What he didn't do was walk around the cafeteria with Cindy and me, looking at the damage.

I saw Ernest escorted out of the cafeteria with a group of our inmate workers, headed back to their cells. Cindy turned to me and said, "After an incident like this, they always gather the inmates together for a count. Just to be sure that no one wandered away during the fights."

She and I sat at a table with a tumbler of tea, trying to wash away the taste of chemicals in the air. At first I felt an energy rush, but then I felt really tired. Shortly Cindy and I were joined at our table by the other staff on our shift. Some of them apologized for leaving us behind.

"Gosh, we thought you two were right behind us," the assistant supervisor said with fake surprise. Cindy and I shared a synchronized eye roll and small smiles, since we'd both seen him leading the rush out of the building. He definitely had not waited around to account for everyone. His idea of leadership seemed to be "get in front of the pack and don't look back" Oh, well.

We started then as a group to clean up. We wiped up the spilled remains of breakfast, sweeping grits and eggs into the trash. Since all prison furniture is bolted to the floor to keep it from being used as weapons or to build barricades, we only had to wipe it down during our clean up. We also hauled out from a back closet a big fan to blow the smell of the gas outside.

As we worked, I remarked, "You guys seem to have done this a time or two."

One of the workers said, "Yeah, it's been happening more frequently in the last month or so. But it doesn't look like much damage was done." He grinned at me, "So I guess now you're officially part of the group. You came through okay."

I didn't realize that this was the initiation process the other staff had been waiting for, but I was glad I passed.

The rest of the day we spent writing reports of what we knew about the riot. Since I didn't know much of anything, my reports were simple. Then we prepared bag meals to be delivered to the inmates' cells since the warden directed a lock-down of the whole prison. Even Ernest and the other inmate workers were kept in their cells, not allowed to come back to help us.

After a few hours, my adrenaline had drained as quickly as broth through a colander. By quitting time, all I cared about was getting home and into the bathtub. Sharon had given me some foaming bath soap that I'd set aside for a bad day. Hiding in a meat freezer during a riot clearly fit that definition.

The phone rang as I opened the front door of my trailer.

"Mom," yelled Sharon, "are you all right? I've called the prison switchboard all day, but they refused to forward outside calls. I've been so worried since I heard about the riot."

"I am fine, honey, just really tired. In fact, remember that bottle of Jean Nate Lemon Wash you gave me? I've been looking forward all day to using that tonight."

"Oh, Mom, don't make me cry. That was two Christmases ago. I can't believe you saved it all this time. Anyway, tell me really, were you hurt? Do I need to take you to be checked?'

"Honestly, I'm good. I didn't fall. I didn't get hit. It was quite an experience, but here I am, home again." I didn't mention the tear gas stinging my eyes or the panic that started to build in the freezer. The fewer details Sharon knew, the less fussing she could do. "How did you hear about it?"

"Well, it was really ridiculous. An inmate called one of our attorneys on a contraband cell phone. He wanted to sue the prison for violating his rights. A prison religious program he wanted to attend got canceled due to the lockdown, so that's when we turned on the news. I've been calling you every hour since then."

"I'm sorry you worried so much. What did the attorney tell the inmate?" I asked, trying to postpone the part of our conversation that was coming.

"He told the inmate they had bad reception and hung up on him." We laughed together, and then, of course, she said, "Mom, maybe this is a sign you should quit your job and use my Visa card for your surgery."

"Sharon, I'm proud I made it through okay today without panicking. I like how that feels. Thanks again for your offer, but all I need now is to get into the tub."

"Mom, I love you, but I wish you weren't so stubborn. Even if that job is fine for you, it's bad for *my* blood pressure." We laughed a little again, then she said, "I'll let you go. I'll order a pizza for you now, so it'll come just as you get out of the tub. Which do you prefer, hamburger or pepperoni? Not that either of them is good for you. In fact, maybe tonight's the time to take the step to join us healthy eaters and have a veggie with the works."

"Hamburger would be great. I'm sure your Daddy is still tumbling in his grave with you being a vegetarian. There's nothing that man loved more than a rack of ribs, unless it was a sirloin steak on his birthday."

"Well, I'm sure you gave Daddy a few tumbles today as well. But you're not playing fair. You know I cry just thinking of him. So now you've got me with tears both for him and for you. My eyes will be all red tomorrow."

"Thanks for the pizza, it's just what I wanted. I'll call you soon."

After we hung up, I rushed for the tub. When I got out, there was a voice message from Wilma, calling on her break. I called her back and left a message that I'd holler at her later in the week. Then the pizza came, and I laid back in Tom's recliner, wrapped in my pink flannel robe.

When "News at Eleven" came on, my prison was the lead story. And sure enough, Ernest had been right. They did call it a disturbance.

Six

Back at work the next morning, the cafeteria still smelled of the gas bombs used by the riot squad. Over by the ovens, Ernest stirred the big pot of rice for the lunch menu.

"It's good to see you, Ernest. I'm afraid to ask what's new."

He looked at me sideways, and said, "Did you hear that Jamal got shanked last night?"

My voice slipped to a whisper, filled with cracking, as I leaned toward him. "Shanked? What do you mean? That only happens on television."

Ernest talked so calm he sounded like a CNN reporter. "A sergeant found him late last night by the loading dock. He some kind of way got out of his dorm and came back over here after you all closed up. When they couldn't find him for count time, they checked around and some officer spotted him on the ground."

He put the lid back on the rice and added, "Good thing they found him when they did. The shank was still in him, right close to his kidney. The guys who heard the staff talk about it said there was blood everywhere." Then he looked at me.

And I stared back at him. We both seemed to be trying to understand why such a thing had happened. I remembered what Sergeant Murphy talked about at our interview meeting, about people getting hurt sometimes accidentally, sometimes on purpose. I thought then his warning was just preachy and over-dramatic, trying to make us be careful. Now I knew he was right.

"Why would someone try to kill him?" I asked Ernest, still whispering. Jamal hadn't been very friendly, and he was about as helpful in the kitchen as a one-legged man at a butt-kicking contest. But if bad manners got a person killed in prison, then we all needed to be careful. Which, thinking about it, was exactly what they taught in our orientation. They warned about staff caught in the middle of a turf battle, or even caught between one puffed up inmate insulting another. In fact, Sergeant Murphy's description of his injury was almost exactly that scenario. Oh, my.

"Ernest, help me understand this. Is this place so dangerous that it's normal for someone to be just randomly stabbed?"

He fiddled with the flame under the rice pot. "Well, it probably wasn't random. It might could be the riot was a diversion."

"A diversion for what?"

He sighed like he was saying something obvious. "So some contraband could be moved from some place here in the cafeteria out to the back dock. Remember when the disturbance kicked off? All the uniforms rushed out of here to the yard to deal with them guys. That could have been when the stuff got moved."

The more Ernest got into describing the possibility to me, the more he got into it. "Most likely Jamal came back to pick it up, but another inmate had the same idea. With that loud mess during the riot and inmates running around, that contraband bundle could easy be stashed in a good pick- up place during the commotion. Kind of like UPS leaving a package behind a porch chair to be got later."

What an old-fashioned word he used, *commotion*. A bunch of puppies cause a commotion at their supper bowl. Then I remembered at Sears during Christmas shopping last year, a man got injured when the crowd stepped on him during the rush to the electronics department. The newspaper called that a commotion. So maybe commotion fit this riot just right. If you want to hide the hand that throws the rock, or in this case the shank, then you sure enough would benefit from a commotion.

"Ernest, were you still on the street when that George Clooney movie came out about stealing money from a Las Vegas casino? That movie had the same idea. Every little action, like the electric power clicking off and on, was all part of a plan to create a commotion while their gang stole money. The movie is like a training video for what happened here yesterday. So, tell me everything you know about Jamal. The more I know about what's going on, the safer I'll feel."

"No, ma'am, I didn't see that movie. But I sure do like George Clooney. I mean, like, I really like him."

"Ernest, I am definitely not interested in how much you like him. I just used the movie as an example. You are smiling about him like you found oysters in the gumbo. Come on; be serious. Tell me more about Jamal."

"Well, ma'am, I don't mind passing stuff on to you. But the way it works in prison, the receiver of the information usually offers a little bonus, you know, like at a fancy restaurant, a person that helps out a customer gets a tip."

I understood that Ernest and I were not friends, but I was disappointed that he didn't see himself giving information in the same way I did. I thought it would be just to be helpful. He saw it as a way to cushion his life. The more I learned about this prison business, the more I realized how naïve I was. But I had no intention of reimbursing Ernest for information. They told us in training that we would be fired if we did such a thing. I also had no interest in putting Ernest in danger to share stuff with me. I didn't want other inmates to think they needed to hurt him because he might tell what he knew.

"Never mind, Ernest. Please don't tell me anymore about Jamal. I understand this isn't the street where we're talking about some neighbor who's stealing cable from someone else's line. I shouldn't have asked. This could be dangerous for you, and that was not my intention. Now, let's get lunch pulled together."

Ernest just nodded, as if he understood. I had no idea if he was relieved or disappointed, but I was definitely relieved that I had backed away from what could have been a big mistake.

Just as Ernest turned away to get tomato slices out of the fridge, Supervisor Rabon waddled up to me and said in a loud voice, "Mrs. Kelly, you're supposed to go up front right away."

I sniffed the air around him, pretty sure I again smelled rum. I didn't think it was his after-shave, and there was no fruit cake on the menu. Too bad we were slam out of paper umbrellas for strawberry daiquiris.

"Good morning, Mr. Rabon. I don't know what you mean by 'up front.' Where's that?"

Ernest scooted over to the ovens to make room for my boss to slide in closer to me with another waddle. But Ernest was still close enough to hear our conversation. It crossed my mind that while maybe Ernest didn't want to share information, he sure was nosy about receiving it.

Supervisor Rabon pushed his glasses up and answered. "The investigator wants to see you in the administration building. What have you been doing to get in trouble?"

This felt like being called to the principal's office, except many times worse. And, of course, Boss Rabon hadn't delivered the message quietly. Oh, no, he broadcasted it to every inmate in the mess hall with his high, screechy voice.

I took off my apron and hurried out of the cafeteria, across the wide prison yard toward the big brick building which held the staff offices. As I rushed, I stepped over the trash from the riot. Glass from broken windows littered the yard, along with soggy paper cups that the SWAT team used to fill with water to wash the sting of the gas from their eyes. There were also a few pools of vomit. Our trainer warned us that the chemical munitions could make us throw up. In the distance, I saw an officer with an inmate work crew sweeping up the glass and paper. They weren't moving too fast. Most likely they'd wait for rain to wash away the vomit.

The investigator's office at the end of the long hallway was right close to the conference room where Sergeant Murphy had talked to us on hiring day. The investigator opened his door after my first knock, as if he had been waiting for me.

"Good morning, I'm Investigator Joe Brown. You must be Mrs. Martha Kelly. Please have a seat."

He waved me into his small office. His desk had piles of neatly stacked folders. Radios in their chargers lined the top of the file cabinet. But he had no family photos or calendars of cute dogs to decorate the walls.

He got right to the point. "Mrs. Kelly, you probably already heard that an inmate named Jamal was found injured last night on the back dock of the cafeteria." He said this like a statement and a question combined. I nodded my head.

"Yes, I heard about it this morning from one of our inmate workers."

Investigator Brown went on. "When we went searched through the inmate's belongings after his assault, we found some papers hidden in his Bible." He stared at me and I stared back, except his face looked like he was getting his fishing gear organized, and I was the bait.

"Mrs. Kelly, can you think of any reason why the inmate had your social security number and birth date in his possession?"

All my chins trembled as I shook my head, trying to understand what he just said. A hot flash started its familiar climb upward. "No, that's impossible. There must be a big mistake." I jabbered too fast, sounding foolish.

"That inmate just started working in the mess hall a few weeks ago. Not long after I started work there, also. He didn't do much, mostly just washed pots and pans." I fanned my face with one hand while I dug with the other in my uniform pocket for a tissue.

"Did you and he get a chance to get to know each other well?" He asked the question in a flat voice as if he was bored.

"What are you accusing me of?" My voice shook, and a hot flash gained a foothold as my blood pressure rose. "I'm a victim here. He must have stolen those numbers. You know, identity theft."

Sharon had warned me about identity theft, but not related to my job. Instead, she disapproved of my orders to QVC, the shopping channel. Giving up that hobby would have been hard, since my favorite relaxation was to lay back in Tom's recliner with an ice pack on my knee and the phone in my lap.

When I mentioned identity theft, Investigator Brown nodded, leaned forward across his desk, and gestured for me to sit back in my chair. "Yes, ma'am, identity theft is certainly a possibility. But we have to check everything out. Sometimes in these situations an inmate pays staff to carry in contraband, so we have to ask questions."

He paused like he was about to make a big point. Like a prosecutor on the True TV Court Channel pauses right before he clinches a case. "You haven't been with the prison very long. I understand you may have financial problems."

"What? Good grief. This is ridiculous. No, it is not correct that I have money problems. I mean, I do in a way, but not like you mean. I have medical problems, not money problems. That's why I work here, for the medical insurance." The personnel office must have flagged my record, or maybe Boss Rabon told Investigator Brown that I had problems. Good grief, people make me tired. "Listen, Investigator Brown, I feel like I'm in a bad movie."

At this, he smiled a little and repeated his piece about "just looking into the situation" and "not jumping to conclusions" and "I shouldn't be worried." I wondered about his sincerity, or maybe he just didn't want to do the paperwork after he caused me to have a stroke in his office. I couldn't think of any more questions to ask, and I felt the threat of angry tears, which I didn't want to show. So when he stood to open the door to leave, I just nodded as if I believed his smooth words. As I passed him through the doorway, I raised one of my chins and said, "Just wait until my daughter hears about this. She's a lawyer."

He actually chuckled as he stood there. "You must be very proud of her."

As I walked back to the cafeteria after the interview, I felt embarrassed that my reputation had been questioned. I felt like a Pyrex casserole dish washed in cold water. Not dirty, just not clean. I couldn't believe that muddle headed moron, Mr. Investigator Brown, could be so ignorant to think I'd be involved with Jamal. Or to even think of accusing me of breaking any rules. I love following rules. I always use my turn signals, even in parking lots. I was also mad as the devil that this Jamal involved me in whatever he was doing.

Just my luck to cross paths with a crooked inmate.

Ernest looked up from cleaning the iced tea machine when I came through the cafeteria door.

"Welcome back, ma'am. We already heard about your interview with the investigator."

"How did you know who I saw?"

"Well, first of all, we heard Rabon tell you to go to his office. But, besides, you know how hard it is to keep secrets in prison. The guy who cleans the staff break room saw you come out of his office. He sent word with the runner who came here to get coffee for the warden's office. Everyone's wondering why you work here if your daughter's a lawyer. They can't figure out why she won't give you any money."

I remembered from training class, the instructors told us that inmates knew more about the inner workings of the prison than most staff people. And he also said they know lots more about staff than they should.

"Ernest, that is rude. My family life is private. I suppose that snoopy inmate heard me mention my daughter when I was in the hallway. So I won't do that ever again. Besides, that investigator told me that if I talk about our conversation, I can be fired for interfering with an investigation." I looked at the big plastic tumbler of tea in his hand. "How can you drink tea without sugar in it?"

He smiled and said, "Ma'am, it's a good thing sugar is not allowed in the prison. If we served sugar tea, every inmate on this yard would cook it down to make buck. And if everyone in my cell block was drunk, I'd have to hide under my bunk." He grinned even more.

In training, they told us the recipe for prison alcohol, called buck. Basically the only ingredient needed was something that could ferment, with heat added to it, and time to let it cook. Anything with sugar and yeast in it worked best, like a cinnamon roll or fruit. Since fruit was so tightly controlled, inmates used catsup or cake frosting or jelly and put the mixture close to a heat source. The heat didn't have to be direct. If the mixture was wrapped in a trash bag and snuggled against a hot water heater or even a fluorescent light, eventually it would give off gas, then produce a terrible tasting liquid. Even though it tasted terrible and smelled worse, it did the job of getting inmates drunk.

Our trainer said, "Some officers have found so much of it, their noses can smell it before their eyes can see it."

I laughed at Ernest's worry about drunk inmates in his dorm. Given his description, I bet they really could tear up the place. "I know what you mean about home brew. My husband liked to make it. And he didn't even have to limit his recipe to what he could steal. He just cooked it up and sealed it in old bottles."

I didn't go on to share with Ernest that I never understood why it was fun for Tom to make it. For me, it made more sense to grab his Pabst six-pack at the store rather than mess up my kitchen.

I interrupted my memory when I realized I had given Ernest more information about my family, just after I'd been so upset that the prison knew about my daughter, the attorney. I found it hard to watch my words in casual settings. And this definitely wasn't a casual setting.

With that, I remembered my problem with Jamal. "Ernest, I know you don't want to talk about Jamal, and I understand why. But just tell me this, why would an inmate want to have an employee's numbers. I don't get what he could do with them."

"With all respect, ma'am, I thought you weren't supposed to talk about this, and excuse me again, especially to an inmate."

"Ernest, I was born at night, but it wasn't last night. If I don't look out for myself, there's no good that can come from this all. Trusting that investigator to watch out for my interests is like a crippled person leaning on a broke stick. I need to find out for myself what's going on."

He glanced around before answering. When he started to talk, he sounded proud to be educating me about the world he lived in. "Okay, here's what I've heard. It wasn't just your numbers that Jamal stole. Supposedly he had the 411 on so many staff he practically had a phone book. How he got the numbers isn't broadcast yet, but it sure wasn't just you he planned to use."

Ernest looked around again and then went on. "I heard he came back this way to meet someone on the loading dock to buy the package. I don't know yet if he was meeting another inmate or an officer or a food service person."

I thought about Ernest's information, but had no ideas about how to find out who Jamal met on the dock. I said to Ernest, "I thought being locked down meant staying in place in the dorm.

How could he get out of there and all the way over here to the dock?"

Ernest grinned. "Money opens many doors."

"I swear, Ernest, my head aches too much to understand how all these rules don't always stay rules. Stir those beans. We need to get this food on the serving line." He started to move away. "And Ernest, thanks for telling me some things. I know there's no gain in it for you, but you are helping me and I appreciate it." He nodded and looked embarrassed, but didn't smile. Then he went off to finish up the lunch prep.

When I got home that night, I wanted to call Wilma to tell her about my interview with Investigator Brown. But I knew she'd get all excited and even though she'd swear to keep it quiet, she'd sell the devil's own secrets for one of her mother-in-law's fried apple fritters. Then Delores would tell her quilting group. I could hear it now. "Please put on your worry list this week Mrs. Martha Kelly who works with my Wilma. Mrs. Kelly finds herself in some trouble at work." By the time the worry list turned into a prayer chain and circulated around town, Sharon would hear from her bank teller, "Just so you know, I'm keeping your mother in my prayers." Sharon would chew her lip bloody, resisting the urge to ask the teller why her own mother needed prayers. After she bit her lip, she'd call me, and the acres of sink holes would stretch between us, with no bright yellow daisies in sight.

So instead of chatting with Wilma, trying to figure out with her how to help myself, I decided to stay off the phone. I got in my recliner, ate chicken wings, and watched qualifying for the weekend's NASCAR race. Jeff Gordon did only fair with his racing time, but he absolutely won the trophy for patience. At a press conference, he got asked so many questions about his possible retirement that he quoted his grandma by saying, "I just want to go until I can't go no more."

I laughed so hard, I got hot sauce on my Carolina sweatshirt and had to get up from the recliner for the stain remover. Like Jeff's granny, whatever keeps me going is worth the struggle. For my dream of new knees, I could put up with steaming rice and limping to the double ovens for more trays of biscuits. I could even put up with a grilling by Investigator Brown as I sweated under the hot glare of his office lights. I could defend the honor of my mostly honest Irish peasant ancestors against Joe Brown's hints that I maybe conspired with Jamal to bring in contraband.

For a school project a lot of years ago, Sharon researched our family tree. Most of my ancestors were potato farmers who ran out of potatoes in the famine. But several of the rest were chicken thieves who came to America to avoid jail. Maybe they did cut some corners to get here, but they knew how to take care of themselves. That lesson ran deep in my family.

As I dumped the leftover bones in the kitchen trash and slammed the lid, I thought, *Watch out, Jamal, and you too, Joe Brown. My plan is to give God a break and help my own self a little. Prayer is appreciated, but a closed mouth don't get fed.*

Seven

A couple of days later, I had a group of inmates around me while I watched the cleaning of the steel table and chair units bolted to the floor. Since we used bleach to scrub them, this project involved a lot of supervision.

The previous week, my co-worker, Cindy, explained the complexity of bleach in prison. She saw me pouring it out for the inmates, giving generous portions to scrub and rinse each table, and came over to whisper to me.

"Mrs. Kelly, I don't mean to mind your business, but I figure Supervisor Rabon hasn't had time to explain about the procedure for bleach."

We both half smiled at her polite way of saying that Supervisor Rabon hadn't provided much supervising at all. Together, she and I pretended to do a modified eye roll and then shared a laugh. "In prison, bleach is like liquid gold. Inmates drink it to beat urine surveillance tests."

I looked at her like she was nuts. "That's disgusting. Doesn't it mess up their livers?"

"Yeah, it definitely does," she answered. "But some inmates want to get high no matter what the risk. Kind of like they did on the street."

We both shrugged. Silently, I figured that if an inmate's goal was to spend his sentence in a blurry daze, having his skin turn yellow was only a cosmetic inconvenience.

Cindy explained that because of its value, some of the inmate workers volunteer to clean, just so they have access to it, with the goal of bringing it back to a cell block to sell. Cindy said, "Mrs. Kelly, you would be surprised at what gets stolen around here. The easiest thing to resell is food, so that's why inmates get shook down when they leave after their shift. But the best money for them is the bleach, since it's so hard to get."

She laughed again, "I guarantee you that if an inmate volunteers to scrub the tile over in a corner and wants to borrow the bleach bottle for a minute, he does not care about a sparkling floor. When he gives that bottle back to you, half will be siphoned off and replaced by water."

"Thanks, Cindy, I appreciate you letting me know. I had no idea that was something to watch." She and I both left unsaid that a good supervisor would have this issue high on his teaching list for new hires.

So having been schooled by Cindy the previous week, I kept the gallon jug of bleach in my hand. When an inmate needed more, I dribbled it onto his scrubbing sponge. In this amusing chess match to capture Queen Clorox, I was determined to win.

Busy doing this, I didn't notice my smarmy supervisor leave his sacred office to head my way until the inmates around me got quiet. They knew some fun was coming. When he got close to me, his smile was not the 'How you doing? It's good to see you working so hard' variety. Instead, it was the type of smile that said, 'Ho, ho, ho, how happy I am to give you a bad day.'

"Mrs. Kelly, again you are wanted up front. Can we assume from their interest in you that you won't be working for us much longer?"

He pitched his lilting accent so perfectly that all the inmates standing around heard my business. It sounded as if he was a butler in a Tudor mansion, and I was a poor Irish peasant washerwoman. In romance books, there's always a smart-ass butler. And the cover of the books shows a damsel in distress, her triple Ds not able to be held in by her peasant blouse.

"Supervisor Rabon, what a pleasure to see you. If you'll watch these inmates, I'll go see the investigator. He probably just needs another interview to finish his reports."

One of the inmates toward the back of the group around us, gave his play by play, "In this round, we have Rabon zero, Kelly in the lead with a two." The rest of the inmates laughed, and Supervisor Poor Loser Rabon headed back to his office.

As I walked out of the building, I had bad thoughts. My boss rarely moved out of his office, and now twice, in one week, he actually put his delicate feet in the dining room with the intent to either embarrass me or intimidate me, I didn't know what motive he had.

I played in my mind short videos of revenge. I envisioned him chewing Viagra with his feet on his desk, enjoying too much his view from the wall of windows, his eyes locked on inmates working, inmates sweating, inmates lifting their shirts to wipe their brows. Imaginary revenge was sweet, and safer than letting my sharp tongue put my job more at risk than it already was.

But as fun as it was to see Rabon as a problem, I also needed to think about Investigator Brown. His public messages to me were a bigger problem than a bothersome boss. If there was an inmate left in this prison who didn't know I was under investigation, it was because the poor soul was stuck in an isolation cell.

It was also interesting that although Supervisor Slimola Rabon was curious about my meetings, no other employee mentioned it to me.

I knew one thing for certain, soon my medical benefits needed to be extended to cover high blood pressure.

This time, when the Investigator opened his office door for me, I didn't quietly take the chair he offered. Instead, I leaned over his desk and shook a finger at him. "You need to tell me why you called me back again. The first time, I understood. But now, twice times, you're making me look like I have the Mark of the Lunatic on my forehead."

He sat down and propped a foot on an opened drawer. "Excuse me? I think you mean the Mark of Lucifer. But even that is a stretch if you are making a biblical reference." He grinned. "And good morning to you, too, Mrs. Kelly. Please have a seat. Your phrase 'twice times' sure makes you sound like you are a Shakespearean scholar."

I gave him a dirty look, but I did sit down. "Whatever. I don't really know the Bible very well. My point is, you're making everyone think I'm dirty."

"Great. I'm doing business with the only middle-aged woman in the South who never went to Vacation Bible School when she was a kid. What kind of parents did you have, anyway?"

Since he had the decency to smile when he said this, I didn't take too much offense and settled into my chair with a huff.

As I began to talk about my life, I forgot I was talking to a prison investigator. This Joe Brown had a way of listening as if he was really trying to follow my story.

"My parents were truck farmers. Summer was their busiest time. They needed me in the garden picking tomatoes. On weekends, we had us a stand out by the road to sell what we grew. My favorite thing was arranging my mama's zinnias in tin cans. They sold really well. My daddy said I lit up our little store 'like Shirley Temple of the Swamp People.' I had wonderful parents."

"Do you still grow that plot out that way?" he asked as if he was interested.

"No, we didn't own the land. After the hurricane came through in '57 and all the pine trees fell, the county figured they might as well put a highway on it after the wood harvesters cleared the acreage. I tell you this, though, if my folks had owned it, they would have had quite a payday."

I suddenly realized I'd been chatting away as if this Internal Affairs Investigator was really Marilyn, the girl who cuts my hair. I felt dumb to feel so relaxed. I needed to stay on my guard.

"But we need to talk about my situation with Jamal, not about my family. I am really worried about him having my personal numbers."

He got his serious look again and stared directly at me. "You are right to be worried. But if you are a victim, and by the way, I believe you are, you might want to help find out what's going on. For instance, who works in the cafeteria that maybe helped Jamal get access to staff information?"

It took me a minute to realize what he just said. "So you don't think he had my numbers to send money to me for helping him with contraband?"

"No, ma'am. I think your numbers were taken along with several other employees for some side project Jamal had in mind. Maybe he was going to sell the numbers to some inmate that files fake tax returns, or maybe he had a contact out in the world who was going to use your numbers for a credit card scam. But, no, I don't think you committed any crime."

I felt relieved to hear him clear me, but shocked at hearing him name crimes that I'd only heard about on the evening news, like when Anderson Cooper gets all serious on CNN and talks about credit card scams and fake tax returns. It felt strange to have big world problems associated with me.

Then the second piece of Joe Brown's message registered with me. "What do you mean, 'help you figure out what's going on'? Does that mean you want me to be a snitch person? Oh, no, I don't want to do that. I'd never get a decent night's sleep, worried that I'd rat out some poor person who turns out to be innocent." Just thinking of this idea started a hot flash that soon blossomed in full glory.

As I dug for my tissue, Investigator Brown went on. "You have definitely been watching too much television. No one says 'rat out' anymore. Let's put it this way. If you are a good citizen, you certainly don't want bad staff working around you. Any more than if you thought your neighbors next door had a meth lab in their kitchen, you would want to notify the authorities." I had to give it to him, the man did sound like a voice of reason.

"But how can I tell who's bad? It's not like they wear a sign saying, 'don't trust me'".

Then he looked really serious. "No, they don't. But in prison, inmates like to talk. Lots of time, they are just recycling rumors they've heard, and they tell a staff person just so they feel important. But sometimes they tell a rumor to see how a staffer responds. For instance, if they mention someone being dirty, and the staff person doesn't act surprised, then that could mean their rumor is substantiated. And sometimes, although this is rare, an inmate tells a staff person some news that is important, simply because he cares about what's going on in his cellblock. Just like you don't want your neighborhood inconvenienced by a deadly fire in the meth kitchen next door, some inmates don't want dirty employees in their area because it draws fights in which they could get injured, or maybe loss of privileges when their dorm gets locked down. Inmates can be as invested in their community as you are in yours."

"So you just want me to listen to what inmates have to say?"

"Yes, listen, but also encourage them to talk. Most times we don't want staff to encourage inmates to gossip with them, but occasionally it comes in handy to have a source that inmates feel comfortable enough to talk to. Just be your normal country queen self, listen to what's said, and let me know what you hear."

I gave him a dirty look at the 'country queen' remark. "What if an inmate wanted to hire me? Like suggest that I help him bring in some of this contraband? What would I do then?

"Well, in some ways that would be a huge help for me, since that would direct us to a specific target who had the resources to pay for the package. But you need to be really, really careful if that were to come up. These inmates are criminals. I know that can be easy to forget when they work alongside you every day and are nice and pleasant. But decisions about who to trust need to be left up to me. If an inmate suggests such a thing to you, you can maybe not say 'no' right away, just to keep him talking, but you need to get with me before you go very far. And you absolutely cannot agree to do anything illegal, since you can end up being charged for it. That would be a lonely limb to be out on all by yourself. That is not at all what I am wanting you to do. Do you understand the difference?"

"So I listen and encourage, but not commit? "

"That's it, no more."

Then we talked some more, mostly about me being careful. On my way back to the cafeteria, I didn't know whether to be flattered or insulted by his assumption that I could help, but it sure added spice to cooking that darn rice every day.

No sooner than I had returned to the dining room, I heard, "So, yeah, I did say, 'Hell, man, I'll mess you up.'" Malcolm, another new inmate worker hired at the same time as Jamal, shouted this across the steam table to an inmate standing in the lunch line. By the time I got over to that area, the other inmate had moved away into the crowd.

"Malcolm, you need to watch how you talk in the cafeteria. You shouldn't be shouting or cussing when you're working."

Malcolm seemed a little surprised that I told him this, instead of pretending that I hadn't heard. But then he said, "Well, Mrs.

Kelly, it's like this. I paid that dirty sergeant, what's his name, Wilson, two hundred dollars to bring in some stuff, and he still hasn't delivered. Then this morning, he came in here when I'm chillin' with my breakfast and rags me about my damn shirt not being tucked in. Like this is some spit-shine Parris Island. I'll show him some Harvard Business school if he don't deliver the product. Hell, he could end up wearing a shank in his neck. Sheesh, why he want to mess with me so early in the mornin'?"

I stepped back from the big spoon he waved and said, "Just because you're mad at him, doesn't mean you can make up lies about him. And actually, you're putting yourself in trouble by telling me you paid him. And don't get so excited, you're spitting in the rice." While I talked with Malcolm, Ernest came over to us, wiping the clean counter with a rag. I turned to him and said, "Ernest, go get a pan of red jello for the line while Malcolm here calms down."

Ernest walked away slowly, glancing back over his shoulder once. It wasn't clear if he wanted to stay close for my protection, or if he wanted to stay close so he could listen to our conversation.

Once Ernest was out of the way, I leaned toward Malcolm. "It makes me curious about you calling Sergeant Wilson dirty. If you and he are in cahoots together, why would he give you a hard time about your shirt? It just sounds like he was doing his job."

"Cahoots? What that mean? Sounds like you've been watching those ole timey westerns on TV. Nobody says that anymore." Malcolm smiled wide, like I was his favorite auntie.

The prison system paid for eyeglasses with dorkie frames for inmates, but for missing teeth, there were no replacements for missing teeth. So Malcolm's shower of spit was from poor hygiene, not poor manners. Whatever the cause, I protected the rice pot with a clean dishcloth as he continued to fuss. "That sergeant was showboatin' for his captain, trying to be all hard core. But it just an act. Next time he's on me, I might just dime him, and get my ticket out of here."

I tried to give Malcolm a hard look, which lost some punch due to my steamed up glasses and frizzy hair. "I tell you what,

Malcolm, if you can prove what you're claiming, I might could help you get a transfer out of here." *Oh, my, I hoped this was what Investigator Brown had in mind for me to do.*

Malcolm looked around and then straight at me. He whispered, "I heard some stuff about you." I must have looked puzzled, because he went on. "You know, after Jamal got stuck. I heard they pulled you up front with the Investigator. So maybe you got a little juice. If you get me the two hundred back and a transfer out, I could sure enough give you a dirty sergeant. Might even throw in some other good stuff if you're quick enough about it."

I squinted my eyes to look serious and wiped the steam drops alongside my nose. "Well, you can sure enough forget about getting your money back. This is not J.C.Penney's. But if you get me some proof, something might could happen. Now hush up and stir those green beans. Ernest is coming back this way."

After lunch, when the office was empty, I called the Investigator. "I didn't think I'd be contacting you so soon, but here's what happened." I told him about Malcolm, and gave him his inmate number. "I told him to bring me some proof about Sergeant Wilson, but I wanted you to know right away." I kept my voice calm while I reported the incident, but I had to ask, "Did I do the right thing?"

"You did fine. I didn't expect to get a lead so quickly, but that's great. And no, I do not want you to be the receiver of any proof. That kind of follow up is where the danger can develop. My office will take care of dealing with Malcolm." He ended his call, "Thanks. You did good."

On the way home from work that afternoon, I drove by Wilma's house. If she was home, I could ask her about staff on her shift and if she had suspicions about any of them. I definitely did not plan to tell her about my interviews with the investigator or about my stolen numbers. I didn't want her to know my situation, but I was curious if she had heard any rumors. Of course, she drove outside the perimeter fence line all night, watching for throw overs, so she didn't have much direct contact with inmates. Not like I did, rubbing shoulders all day in my hot, sticky mess hall.

When I went by her trailer, her car was gone, so I figured she had the kids over to Delores's house. I left a note on her screen door to say I had dropped by and would holler at her later. Then I headed home. As I drove, I realized that Investigator Brown would probably not have approved of me asking Wilma about rumors. It was a delicate balance he was asking of me. He wanted me to listen for rumors and tips, like with Malcolm, but he didn't want me out soliciting for them. For a nosy person like myself, those were boundaries that might have some gaps in them.

In the car, I listened to the end of Garth Brooks' "Thunder Road" and thought more about my day. The drama in that song was about a troubled marriage, which of course didn't fit my circumstances. But the heavy guitar and drums made me think of a person alone on a highway, in the middle of a storm. I felt like that now, but was surprised that I didn't feel too afraid. I felt confused and nervous to be trusted to help, but I didn't feel the 'hide under the bed' type of fear. When I took this prison job, I never thought I'd be dealing with an issue more complicated than scrambling eggs and not being embarrassed by the hobbles of my age. Instead, I felt connected to complicated problems like contraband, an issue which, before this job, I probably wouldn't have spent two seconds reading about in the local paper.

I wouldn't have had the sense to think about the people behind this problem, which stretched into our community. And I definitely wouldn't have seen myself as trying to help with the solution.

I smiled, remembering that both the investigator and Malcolm accused me of watching too many old movies. Well, maybe I do.

When I pulled into my driveway, I was happy to see the daylilies still blooming, even though we hadn't had enough rain. It was good to be home. My feet ached and my hair was salty from sweat. I felt tired, kind of like Jessica Fletcher on "Murder She Wrote." Of course, on the end of her show, ole Jessie went home to her fancy house overlooking the harbor, but I went home to my possum problem. Still, my daylilies were beautiful, and I had a meatloaf in my crock pot, waiting to be joined by some mac and cheese.

Aside from these differences, Jessica and I were both snoop sisters under the skin. Maybe this Christmas, instead of Sharon giving me a sequined shirt saying "Will Work for Food," I'll get one with "Will Snitch for Healthcare." If Malcolm wanted to trade for information, I did right to pass him on to the Investigator.

Getting involved with Internal Affairs had sure put a different spin on prison work. *This deal was for real*, I thought. Outside my front door, I fumbled with my keys and admired the potted marigolds on the cement stoop of my little porch. My mind flashed to the corner on the back dock where Jamal was stabbed. The bleach didn't get out the dark spot on the cement floor.

Eight

"First Responders, alpha unit; second responders, stand by. Clear the yard, the yard is now locked down."

As my shift started, this announcement blared over the radio. It was like the day of the riot all over again. Movement whirled in the dining room as inmates rushed to the windows to view the action.

Even though the problem started in another area, we still snatched up the cooking utensils, including the knives which were attached to long chain lanyards welded to padlocks on the prep tables.

Cindy rushed passed me. "I've got the knives from the dicing tables secured already, but my inventory shows there is still a darn spatula and a pair of tongs out in use. If you see them, let me know. We don't want to make it too easy for these fellas to stick each other." She paused and added, "Or worse, stick us."

If whatever problem existed in the alpha unit spilled over to our kitchen, we sure didn't want to have weapons ready for the inmates to grab. Removing the knives would at least force them to be creative in what they used. As I checked the grill area, I snatched a spatula from an inmate, "Hey, Miss K., I might be needing that." I gave him a dirty look and moved on. Nearby I saw a pot of boiling water, with tongs next to it to cook hot dogs, so I picked them up too.

"Cindy, I've got the tongs and the spatula, and I'm emptying this pot of water now." She gave me a thumbs up from across the room, and I felt proud that I had begun to be seen as a member of the team, not just a newbie who knew nothing. On my own, I remembered that boiling water was a weapon, too.

"Ernest, help me carry this pot to dump it in the sink. I don't want anybody throwing it." Ernest grabbed his end, and I waddled with the other side. Just as we splashed it in the sink, I saw our staff headed to the office.

As I turned to follow them, two security officers yelled at Ernest to join a group of inmates being moved away from the windows and the cooking area. "Move it. You all sit at these tables and do not move. You don't need to know what's going on outside. This ain't a Panthers' game where you got to keep score."

A captain came through to be sure the inmates had been secured in one area. He shouted to us staff, "I'm headed for the alpha unit to see if they've got it contained. For now, you staff can stay in the office. If it looks like the fight is getting bigger, we'll move you to the freezer. Or up front if we have enough time." He shook his head. "It's been a long time since we've had so many gang fights. All these drugs coming in have got these inmates fighting like dogs over scraps. We better find out how these throw overs are making it in or this whole place is going to blow someday soon."

He hurried out, his handcuffs banging against the gas canisters looped on his security belt.

The office that we were crowded into was more comfortable than the freezer for waiting out the emergency, but the locked door looked too flimsy. We staff people didn't talk much to each other as we waited. I whispered to Cindy, "How long does it usually take for them to take control?" She shrugged, but didn't say anything.

Supervisor Rabon stayed in his desk chair, frequently calling the control room for updates. His creased brow sweated with the importance of being the guy in charge, handling with ease the complexity of the two-button phone console. My expectation was that in a real crisis, like when this plywood door got busted in by inmates, he would sit with ivy growing up his leg.

He claimed to have received his food service experience in the military. I preferred to have a boss whose military time was served as a jungle commando, rather than the guy beating eggs and frying bacon. But people come as they are. And what I got was a pale clammy guy sweating out his Bud-lite six-pack from last night. It was probably the cousin of the previous six packs, which stretched the buttons on his white work tunic. His pink face showed that he too worked for medical benefits. High blood pressure medicine was expensive.

Within a short while, we heard a radio announcement.

"Central control, alpha unit is now secured. Transport of injured inmates is needed."

Soon, security staff arrived to escort our inmate workers back to their cells. As he gathered up the inmates, a sergeant said to us, "Looks like the fun goes on. We got four inmates stabbed over in alpha, so the whole place is now locked down." He shook his head like the captain had. "We got to get a handle on this contraband. That's what's causing all these gang fights."

He snatched up a glass of tea and said in a low voice. "It looks like the officer in alpha got his jaw broke trying to break up the fight." He drained the glass and muttered, "He should have let them slice each other up." With that, he rushed our inmates through the outside door, heading them to their cells.

Our training sergeant taught us that gang fights are like watching The Wave at an Atlanta Braves game. Each cell block wants to earn their stripes as good gang members. So if they had access to each other after a fight, there would be a series of skirmishes throughout the yard. Since today's fight had several inmates stabbed, everyone needed time in their cells to chill out.

A lockdown also gave inmates with short sentences time to remember their own self-interest. As our trainer explained, "For most inmates, their self-interest is simple. They remember they don't have a dog in some gang-related prison fight. They mostly just want to go home to their street corner."

The lockdown also gave staff time to sort out which inmates were involved in the fight. This meant a cell-to-cell search by security to look for fresh wounds, or to look for inmate uniforms with splotches of blood. Some inmates wouldn't report a wound, wanting to stay in the population so they could get revenge. If they were identified as assaulted, they would end up in isolation for a while. So it was important for the officers to know just who got stuck, as well as who did the sticking. Inmates who watched CSI on television tried to get the blood out of their uniforms by a quick rinse in their wash basin, but staff watched the same CSI shows.

With no hot meals to prepare and no inmate workers allowed

back yet, the kitchen staff made peanut butter sandwiches for the lockdown bag meals.

As Cindy and I stood together on the assembly line, I wondered why Supervisor Royal Ass Rabon wasn't helping us. "Is Supervisor Rabon going to join us in putting these bags together?" I asked Cindy in a cleaned-up version of what I really thought.

She laughed, "You've got to be kidding." She opened another loaf of Sunbeam bread and slid it further down the line.

We settled into a relaxed pace. I remembered how many years ago when I made bag meals for Sharon's lunch. I always drew a happy face in the peanut butter. But with these sandwiches, we just had the rhythm of swish on the spread, slap the bread together, and put a carrot stick alongside for the FDA required veggie quota. God forbid the carrot be left out of a lockdown bag. Such negligence would feel like a winning lottery ticket for some lucky inmate. He would spend the rest of the week drafting his lawsuit for not having his nutritional requirements met. He wouldn't win, but it would keep his hopes alive for a while, waiting for a big dollar settlement for his 'pain and suffering.'

Just as we finished the sandwiches, we got new instructions from Supervisor Rabon, who shouted from the door of his office.

"Change of plans, the lockdown is not going to extend all day. We'll use these bags for lunch, then we'll get some of our inmate workers back to help with dinner. But we're keeping it simple, just beans and hot dogs." He added, "Use the hot dogs that got dumped in the sink that we were fixing for lunch. Just rinse them off before we boil them again."

As a taxpayer, I appreciated his thriftiness. As a cook, this was a big leap from the three-second rule.

A short time later, Ernest and some of the other inmate workers came back into the cafeteria. Ernest came up beside me at the sink, tying his apron.

He didn't say hello, just mumbled to me, "That guy you was talking to, Malcolm, he's one of them that got shanked." He then looked up at me and frowned. "Ma'am, this is now two for two. Seems like the inmates you spend time with end up hurt."

At first, I thought Ernest meant he blamed me for their assaults. But then he added, "Ma'am, you need to be more careful who you be speaking to. Both Jamal and Malcolm were in gangs. It don't seem like you believe yet that these gangs are serious business."

I know I look like somebody's mother, but I never expected to be the source of semi-sibling rivalry between two convicts. Good grief.

"Ernest, we just worked the line together. Don't you be making something out that's not there. Besides, you don't seem very sad that Malcolm got hurt."

"Why should I care?" he said a little louder. "The Bloods paid for the drugs to come in, but the Crips stole the package when it arrived. Malcolm was a Blood, so he got to go after his product. It's only business. But he's not hurt so bad. The hospital just stapled up his head, and now he's back."

I checked the hot dogs for their re-boiling. "Well, I hope he doesn't come back to work. We don't need that mess carried over into our kitchen."

"Don't worry about that." Ernest lifted a couple of hot dogs that were hidden under a dish rag. "He'll stay in isolation for a while. The investigator will try to figure out if there's going to be more payback over the package that was stole." Ernest lined up the revived wieners into groups of two dozen, ready for cooking closer to time for dinner. He shook his head like a preacher worried about the sins of his flock. "You know, even for this place, it's getting a little too wild."

"I'm glad you're not involved in all this gang stuff. Now that we got the dogs ready to cook, why don't you slice some onions to put in the beans? That'll spice them up a little bit. But don't you add any salt, just pepper. Everyone around here has high blood pressure. They don't need more salt in their diet. I'll be back in a little while."

Supervisor Ralphie Rabon needed to let me out of the kitchen again to see Investigator Brown. It was important to let him know that the Malcolm I called him about earlier was the same Malcolm who got injured. He probably didn't know that stolen drugs were the reason for the gang fight. He also probably didn't know that Malcolm was paying a sergeant to bring in the drugs. Of course, the news would be about as welcome as a turd in a punch bowl.

Also, even though I downplayed Ernest's accusation that inmates who talked to me were some of the ones getting stabbed, I took a sort of twisted pride that both Malcolm and Jamal had been sources for me. It meant I was getting good information to pass along. Of course, I didn't imagine either of them ending up injured. Still, I was doing good, talking to the right bad people.

Nine

"*S*o*, what you got, little lady?*"

"*More than you think, Mr. Big Guy Investigator.*"

"*Oh, so this is about the horizontal mambo-mambo?*"

With a jerk, I sat up in bed. I gulped a breath to scream, and instead came out of my dream. As soon as I realized there were no real voices, I felt terribly sad from missing Tom. With me so involved at work, I felt nervous without his reassurance.

The day before, I tried to see the investigator to share my information about Jamal and Malcolm, but he was not in the prison. I left a message for him to call me right away. Shortly after, he called back on the cafeteria phone.

Supervisor Cauliflower-Ear Rabon yelled out to me from his office doorway. "Mrs. Kelly, Internal Affairs is calling you again." Inmates smiled sarcastically as I went by them toward the office. "Juicy-juice" one smacked his lips as I hurried past, something dumb inmates said about staff with some kind of influence. In fact, most of what I felt was confused. *It's hard to see a rainbow when you're sitting in a storm.*

When I took the phone from Rabon, he mumbled, "I have never had an employee who stayed in so much trouble." I gave him a dirty look, and reached for the phone.

I felt very flustered, knowing that I couldn't really talk to the investigator with others around. But I didn't know how else to make contact, and he did need my information. So I pretended to be Jessica Fletcher, all prim and professional. "This is Mrs. Kelly, may I help you?"

Supervisor Tricky Rabon's ear grew out from his head like a big satellite dish, trying to listen in. Then Cindy came in the office and stumbled against a chair, dropping files all over the floor. She picked them up one by one.

"I take it the office is full of people."

"Yes, sir, Investigator Brown. I'm sorry I haven't got that last report to you yet. I was wondering if I could have just a little more time."

Groveling and subservience don't come natural to me, but I'd seen it done by experts. In fact, one such expert stood at my elbow, Supervisor Supreme Rabon himself, who carried his chap stick in his tunic pocket in case his own boss from central office dropped in for an inspection. From Rabon's perspective, that boss had no soft spot left to kiss, only hair and a crack.

Investigator Brown chuckled and I worried the others heard him. "Mrs. Kelly, I need that report at 9AM tomorrow morning," he said loudly enough for everyone in the office to hear. Then he lowered his voice to a whisper, "I know it's your day off tomorrow. Meet me at the Cracker Barrel instead of my office."

Oh, my. Did I hear that right? "Yes, sir, I can do that."

After I hung up and walked toward the office door, I about stepped on Cindy who was still picking up papers. Rabon called after me, "Mrs. Kelly, your frequent contacts with Internal Affairs concern me about the security of your job. I hear the bowling alley needs a fry cook. Maybe you can get an interview on your day off tomorrow." A couple of inmates watching the fun laughed.

Unfortunately my day of stressful calls was not finished. On the way home, I practiced how to tell Sharon about my appointment with the investigator. Meeting in public, there was no way to keep it from her. Just like when I worried before about Wilma and Delores and the imaginary bank teller on an inevitable prayer chain, I knew I'd have the whole town as possible snitches to Sharon about my Cracker Barrel meeting.

I could hear the call from her. "Mom, I heard from several people that you had coffee with some man. Was he selling you a new vacuum? Or maybe storm windows? Or is there something you forgot to tell me...your only child?"

As soon as I got home, even before I changed out of my uniform or kicked off my work shoes, I dropped in the recliner and called Sharon.

"Hi, hon, just wanted to let you know that tomorrow morning I'm having a meeting with an investigator from work. I need to pass on some information that inmates shared with me."

"That's good, Mom. You need to be sure that he knows everything you hear. That will help investigations."

Now it got tricky. I skipped over the part about Jamal having my numbers, and just agreed with her about sharing information. "Yes, you're right. In fact, it's one of the job requirements that we have to report anything we hear, even if it's just rumors. Our trainer said it's not an option to keep stuff to ourselves. If we don't report it, we could be fired."

"Sure, I understand that. How did you get introduced to this investigator? Did he interview all the kitchen staff, or just you?"

That's my girl. She is so smart, zooming right to the trickiest piece. So then I told her about Jamal and my numbers. She got very quiet, then said, "I understand that identity theft is a problem in prisons. And I'm relieved the Internal Affairs office understands that you were victimized. I just don't get why the investigator is still focused on you, since you already gave him a report and he interviewed you." Now that she had gotten started, we were headed for some serious sink holes. "And I really don't understand why inmates seem to stand in line to tell you incriminating information. Mom, I think you've left out some pieces here."

Her voice was still calm, but a little testy. And I hadn't yet told her the final complication of tomorrow's meeting. "Oh, Sharon, don't worry. I absolutely plan to tell the investigator whatever information inmates give me. In fact, tomorrow's meeting is going to be at the Cracker Barrel, so we'll have plenty of time and not be interrupted by his office phone ringing."

Even to me, the explanation sounded lame. I wanted Sharon to think I only relayed information. I didn't want her to know I also tried to develop information, the phrase used on CSI last week.

Truth be told, except for my conflict with Sharon, I liked the notion that my new job description was like that old song, "Put me in, Coach, I'm ready to play."

Sharon interrupted my thought. "Mom, I have to rush to a meeting. But I am not really comfortable with what you describe. I need to think about it. Let's talk some more tomorrow."

After Sharon hung up, I sat for a while in the recliner. At first I felt bad about leaving her out of the details of the contraband problem. But I got past the guilt by reminding myself that since I was the parent, I got to choose how much to share. Then I started remembering the fun times Tom and I had at the Cracker Barrel. He always ordered pancakes. I thought I'd order those tomorrow to make me feel closer to him, like he was in the booth with us. I laughed at the notion of seeing Chris, the manager who was Sharon's old classmate. I was sure he'd be curious at me having breakfast with someone he didn't know.

Feeling better, I wondered what to wear to our meeting. I decided on the nice blue pants with matching sweater that Sharon gave me for my birthday. It looked good, kind of casual and kind of classy. I'd look like one of the ladies in Oprah's audience. It would be a hoot to wear really high heels like Oprah herself, but I'd probably walk like I was stepping over alligator backs in the swamp.

With my wardrobe decided, I heated some soup and went to bed early, only to wake up from that dumb mambo dream. It must have been the soup.

As I headed toward the bypass for my meeting with Investigator Brown, Sharon called my cell phone. "Mom, I'm running late. Can you meet me in the Cracker Barrel parking lot?"

"What? Sharon, what do you mean, meet you?"

"All last night I thought about your meeting. I decided I'm just not comfortable with you being interviewed by an Internal Affairs investigator without your attorney present. So if you wait in the parking lot, we can go in together."

"Sharon, you are not my attorney, you are my daughter. I mean, you are an attorney, but I don't need one right now. Everything is fine. If there's a problem later, like with the identity theft, then I'll be glad to have your help. But for now, it's all good. Now you go on to your job while I do my job. I'll call you later."

"Mom, you are making me crazy, sounding all hippy-dippy, loosey-goosey. Your job is to make biscuits and rice for prisoners. It is not to get involved in issues you are not experienced with. If Daddy knew what you were doing, he would pitch a fit. I will not have my own mother used to clean up a dirty prison. You could get hurt. I only let you go to work there so you could get medical benefits for your knee. Now wait for me, and I'll be right there."

Well, now.

"Let me work there? Now you listen to me, Sharon Kelly. Your Daddy and I are proud of you for getting your law degree at State, but you're still our little girl, and I don't like your tone. You are not to boss me around, young lady. I get to choose what I do and where I work, and you need to relax. You have your hands full with your new job, and I can take care of my new job."

Sharon sighed and spoke softly, sounding like she knew she'd overstepped herself.

"Mom, please listen to me."

"Hon, I was remembering this morning how much your Dad liked those strawberry pancakes at the Cracker Barrel. It was so much fun when we all went together. By the way, guess what I'm wearing this morning? That blue outfit you gave me. Did you get that at Penney's?"

I had almost muddied my way through the sink holes with Sharon, and the daisies were within reach.

"No, Mom, Belk's."

"Oh, my goodness, that's why I look so good. I didn't know Belk's carried plus sizes. You do know how to take care of your ole mama."

The yellow daisies were beautiful, but there was one more sink hole to wade through. "By the way, what did you mean about my prison being dirty? How come you never told me about that?"

"I never thought it would matter. The place is known to be an open contraband market for drugs and cell phones. The only way that could happen is to have dirty staff." She paused, then went on, "Mom, you know I am proud of you, but in contraband deals, there's a lot of money involved, and people get hurt. I worry that you are too trusting. And when it comes to money, people can get nasty."

"You know, you sound like Ernest."

"Is he one of your co-workers?"

"No, not exactly." A half-truth is only a half-lie. "Now don't you worry. I'll holler for you if things don't seem right. Then I'll get the benefit of that tuition money. Remember when we came to your graduation? Your Daddy changed his tie twice and scrubbed his hands so much he was clean as a dog's tooth. He said that Carolina clay might have paid for some tuition, but it didn't belong at your graduation. Did you know he talked about putting that tie away so he could wear it at your wedding some day? It only seemed right to bury him in it. But don't get me started crying. I about missed the turn off."

I do love me some fresh yellow daisies.

"Mom, don't start with the wedding stuff. I'm not even thinking that far ahead. Besides, there has to be a boyfriend first, and right now I'm only interested in work."

"All in good time. There's no hurry. Whenever and whoever is best for you. Dr. Phil had a show the other week about daughters who were lesbians who came out of the corner."

"You mean closet, not corner, and no, Mom, for me it will be a guy when it happens."

"Whatever. Why don't you come by tonight for dinner? We'll cook burgers out on the deck, and then watch the NASCAR race. Jeff Gordon is finally running good."

"You know I don't eat red meat, and I can't stand NASCAR. But yeah, I'll be over so you can fill me in on your meeting. And, Mom, be careful."

We hung up just as the yellow Cracker Barrel sign showed on the sign of the road. As I pulled into the parking lot, I wondered how much of Sharon's school tuition went toward learning that highly technical term, "hippy-dippy, loosey-goosey?"

Ten

Investigator Brown waited for me at a small booth toward the back of the restaurant. He stood when he saw me and waved me over.

"Hello. It's good to see you."

I gave him what I hoped was my Barbara Bush smile, one that showed I was a paid up member of the "Ladies Who Lunch Bunch".

"Yes, hello. How are you today?"

"Fine, thanks for meeting me on your day off, and also thanks for your willingness to help us. But before we get started, what can I get you from the menu?"

Now that I was here, this adventure didn't feel as fun as I imagined. Tom seemed so far away, not even pancakes could squeeze him beside me in the booth.

"Nothing, thanks, just coffee."

"You sure? They have great pancakes here."

"No, I never eat pancakes. Just coffee is fine." Pancakes belonged to Tom's memory, and the thought of eating them now soured my stomach.

The waitress came up to the booth to take our order. She was a young girl, probably still in high school. "Can I take your order?" She looked like she'd prefer to be anywhere else on a Saturday morning.

Investigator Brown ordered coffee for both of us, and a pancake combo for himself. "Anything else?" the waitress asked with great effort.

We both shook our head. When she left, he said to me, "Let me know if you change your mind. Maybe we can catch her awake later." I smiled politely at his pleasantry.

He leaned toward me. "Since we last talked, I understand you had a very interesting conversation with that inmate Malcolm before he was injured. I'm sorry I was out of the office yesterday, but getting together here works even better. Let me first say that the information you've given has been helpful.

Several of the inmates you've mentioned are the same ones my office has been tracking as well. Unfortunately, some of the staff names overlap, as well."

Him being so open helped me feel more comfortable. He made me feel like I was part of an inside group, like a Neighborhood Watch - not a snitch. The waitress brought over our coffee mugs and left a pot of coffee on the table. I picked up my mug. "It is surprising how inmates know things I wouldn't think they could know. I always thought a prison would be safe and boring. After all, there are so many rules on the job. But instead, it's loud and confusing. It's like peeking under the lid of a pot of bubbling spaghetti sauce. If the lid comes off, I feel like it will spill over and make a mess."

He smiled and nodded, then waited for the waitress to put his large plate of pancakes and sausage in front of him. "I like your idea of spaghetti sauce boiling over. For me, I've thought of prison problems as water sprinkled in a skillet of hot oil. But the end result is our same worry."

"Yes, you are right. That is my worry. At first I didn't care too much about what might be going on since I just worked there for the benefits. But now, I feel like I need to help."

I put my cup down and leaned across the table. "The last time I felt like this was when our local school board used the money in the playground equipment account to fly to Las Vegas for a so-called training conference. My, that was upsetting. It made me mad as all get out."

"So what did you do about that situation?" he asked, as if he was really curious.

"Oh, it was a crazy time. I wrote letters to the newspaper, and then the school board got stirred up, and there was a special election for a new board. My husband said I should run for one of the positions, but I was too shy. He called me a redneck, rabble-rousing tax payer."

"What does he say about this situation at the prison?"

I fiddled with my coffee spoon, then answered, "Well, he probably wouldn't think it was as fun as riling up the school board folks. In fact, he'd probably agree with my daughter that I should quit my job and find health benefits somewhere else. But he's gone now, and I have to decide things for myself."

"You say he's gone?"

I stopped fiddling and just answered softly. "Yes, you know, gone to the other side." My hand fluttered in the air as if showing Tom far up from the bypass. "He died about two years ago."

He twisted his coffee mug, and stumbled over his words. "I'm sorry, I didn't mean to pry. We'll go back to your problems at the prison. First though, I'm having another short stack. Sure I can't get you anything?"

"Well, okay, I guess I will have a stack of pecan pancakes with whipped cream on the side."

He waved our waitress over and told her what we wanted. When she was gone to put our order into the kitchen, I continued. "Let's back up a little. Truth be told, it's not, as you put it, my problem at the prison. It's really your problem now that I've made an official report. As I learn about more things, how would you like me to get the information to you?" When I said this to him, I sat up straighter in the booth, no longer leaning on the table.

He looked at me as if another person had joined us at the table. This new person was tall with no hot flashes, and her hair was smooth. In her blue suit, without flushed splotches on her neck, and without hair frizzing around her ears, she looked like she shopped at Belk's. He spoke slowly to this lovely lady.

"We need to be real clear about how this is going to work. Your information is useful, and I do welcome it, but the situation is really complicated and also dangerous. We have always had contraband problems at the prison, which is normal for a big place like ours. But the level of violence the last couple of weeks has escalated tremendously.

Several gangs are competing against each other to get the contraband in, so the amount of money involved is lots more than our normal market. You are a nice lady, but you need to not think that this is like your school board adventure. Your help is definitely appreciated, but we must be careful to not expose you to too much risk."

He stopped talking while our waitress brought our plates of food to us. Then he went on to say that one reason he suggested meeting at the Cracker Barrel rather than his office was so it looked social rather than business.

"The way I see your position in the kitchen is that you have two groups watching you. There are staff who are dirty, as well as inmates. Both groups are wondering if you are dirty, too. But there are inmates who think you are clean and that you can provide a direct route to me to make deals. And this is what has begun to happen. So, tell me the latest information you have about Malcolm."

I filled him in on what Ernest had told me about the stolen drugs, and how they related to Jamal's injury, and then Malcolm's. I also told him about each inmate's complaints about the staff who might be involved. He listened carefully as I spoke.

When I had given him all the information I had, I added, "What you said about inmates thinking I could help them make a deal with you is exactly what Malcolm was wanting when he talked about the dirty sergeant." I paused, but needed to ask, "I know Malcolm is a dirty inmate, but I was sorry to hear that he got injured before I could get his request to you. What happens to him now?"

"Actually, it's best if I don't give you a full answer, since there are some other people involved. But generally speaking, any time an inmate gets injured, like Jamal or Malcolm, I become their new best friend. After an assault, inmates are usually interested in trading any names they have in order to get transferred to a different prison, away from the problem they've gotten involved with." He smiled, "And I am always happy to be in the business of listening, so we are usually able to make a successful trade."

I smiled at his answer. "This contraband business is ridiculous. I never knew it was such a problem. Each day I'm confused about which team I'm on. It's like I've been drafted from my quiet position in right field, enjoying the clouds in the sky with no action to interrupt me, to suddenly becoming the catcher with too much action thudding toward me. That's how I felt after Ernest told me about Malcolm."

We laughed together, and he took a sip of his coffee. "My wife used to read mysteries where the heroine solved the problem in under two hundred pages. This gang thing is never that tidy."

"What authors does your wife like to read?"

He straightened his silverware across his empty plate before answering. "It's hard to know her current favorites since she ran off with her dermatologist three years ago. But I don't think you are listening to my warning about this business. Do you understand the risk in providing information?"

The waitress arrived to ask if we needed another pot of coffee, and since we didn't, she left the bill on the table. I checked the flavors of syrups available on the table for my last few mouthfuls of pancakes. As I read the labels, I asked, "Was she seeing the dermatologist for an itch?"

At that, he choked on his pancakes and spit in his coffee, and so it splashed on his tie. We laughed and enjoyed the rest of our breakfast, chatting about work and family - nothing else related to gangs or contraband or assaults. I finished my pancakes but resisted scraping the whipped cream container for the last little bit.

I started to gather my purse as he put money on the table for the bill. "So, before we go, let me just be sure that we are in agreement about your assistance in this situation." I nodded, understanding that he wanted to be orderly.

"If inmates approach you in the cafeteria about gang issues, or dirty staff, or rumors they have heard, you will only listen. You won't make any deals, or give any advice, or share anything you hear with other staff or other inmates." He waited for me to nod.

"When you hear anything that you think would be useful, you'll call me. And if I'm out, I'll get right back to you. I'm careful about checking for messages frequently." He looked right at me, "Is that how you understand our plan?"

I nodded and said, "It's a pleasure doing business with you."

He smiled and shook his head. As we headed for the exit, Chris, the manager, held the door for us, and said, "It's good to see you again, Mrs. Kelly." Chris's tie today was a glossy burgundy. He looked at Investigator Brown and back toward me and then said in a fake formal way, "Is this gentleman a colleague from your new job? I heard you took a job at the prison after all."

Investigator Brown held the door further open and said, "Hello, I'm Joe Brown, a friend of Mrs. Kelly's."

Then Chris got the toe of his shoe stuck under the door, but it didn't seem too awkward since he went on, "Hello, it's good to meet you."

With his shoe still stuck, he twisted back toward me, "I'm sure Sharon's concerned about your job. Did you tell her that I asked about her?"

I just smiled and waved as we walked on toward the parking lot, pretending to have not heard what he asked. But to myself, I resolved that by no means could I bring Sharon back with me to this Cracker Barrel. It would be my hope that she wouldn't be interested in Chris even if he did woo her, but I didn't want to run the chance that she might feel sorry for him.

Joe Brown and I were getting ready to get in our cars when Wilma and her kids came across the parking lot toward us.

"Mrs. Kelly, imagine running into you." Wilma wore a cute jean jacket with sparkly studs. It was only a little too snug around the chest. "I got your note that you stopped by the house, but just haven't had a chance to call."

She looked down at her daughter who had a tiara with pink sequins on her head. "We're celebrating Susie's birthday today, so this is a special treat to see you. Can you come back in to join us for another cup of coffee?"

Her daughter's twinkling tiara made me smile since it was clear that the glitter gene had not skipped a generation. When I checked out her son, I was glad to see no sequins on his camo t-shirt. With his dad in and out of jail, the poor little guy had enough to deal with.

"Thanks for the invite, but I've got a bunch of errands to run." I turned to Joe Brown and asked her, "Have you met Investigator Brown?"

Wilma smiled and pulled up a bra strap. "No, we haven't met. I'm just glad I haven't done anything wrong yet to be called to your office."

She giggled, and as she leaned in to give me a hug, whispered, "You look pretty snazzy for a little old lady. I can't wait for you to fill me in on your brunch date."

On the way home, I listened to the *My Fair Lady* song, "I Could Have Danced All Night." I swear, my morning at the Cracker Barrel felt like what I always envisioned a prom would be. Everybody was dressed up, and I ran into people unexpectedly. My high school had a prom, but Tom and I couldn't afford to go. He was getting as many hours as he could bagging groceries at the Piggly Wiggly, and I was washing dishes at a chicken place. I remembered that the only thing on the menu that wasn't fried at that place was the lemon pie. And that came frozen.

On prom night, Tom and I had a choice between watching *I Love Lucy* reruns or bouncing on the back seat springs of his rusty Chevy. It really wasn't a choice since the TV rabbit ears were too rusty to get good reception. Anyway, I've always been glad that Sharon didn't get planted that night. She would not like to be a distinguished attorney named Camaro.

So I sang along to *My Fair Lady*, faking the English accent, but enjoying the glow.

Later that evening, when Sharon came over, I filled her in on my meeting. She pursed her mouth in her agitated way, until I finished my remark about his ex-wife. Then she slid her eyes at me and asked, "You didn't really ask if she had an itch? Mom, you are *impossible*."

I laughed. "Oh, he was being all serious and scary. I wanted to enjoy my pancakes. But we did get our plans together on how I'll get information to him. Only his bosses at central office know that I'm one of his sources."

She put mustard on her veggie burger. "I checked him out at work."

I chewed my too big bite of a beef burger and stared at her.

"He has a good reputation as an investigator. The staff in my office said that his cases are well put together and he presents himself as an 'all business' type guy."

I was glad to hear that Joe Brown passed her screening test, but I felt a little strange. Then I realized that she screened him for my safety, just like I screened Chris for her happiness.

Soon after she carried our plates from the deck into the kitchen, she left to do some paperwork at her apartment. Maybe she just wanted to avoid watching the NASCAR race with me, but we still had a fun visit.

After she said goodbye, I stayed outside for a while, waiting for the pain killer to kick in on my knee. My Tom and I used to sit out here, him with his Pabst Blue Ribbon and me with a tumbler of sweet tea. We'd just sit and listen to the bug zapper sizzle whenever a big moth got too close. Sometimes we'd talk about our day, sometimes about Sharon, but mostly we'd just enjoy the night air.

I pulled my thoughts to the present, and to wondering if I should get Sharon a bug zapper for her little balcony. When I realized what I was thinking, it was clear my codeine was working. Sharon had no interest whatsoever in such a gadget. Moths might be on her endangered species list, or maybe she viewed moths as edible garnish for her veggie burger. I bet if I screened her friends, there would be a few foodies included. They would be healthy type eaters who would view my days as a fry cook as the equivalent of working in a third world sweat shop.

Smiling as I swung my feet off the table, the ice pack from my knee spilled on the deck, and at the same time, I heard a cough from a big shadow coming up the stairs from the backyard. A deep voice said, "Didn't mean to startle you, but I saw your light from the drive."

"Sweet Jesus, you're lucky I didn't have my shotgun out here. Don't you know better than to sneak up on me like that?"

Joe Brown leaned against the deck railing and said, "I didn't sneak up, and you sound like that writer lady on the TV show who thought she was so smart. What was her name?"

"You know, Jessica Fletcher. And she was smart. Although it wasn't hard to pick the bad guy when all the other characters were weekly regulars. It's not likely her bridge partner killed the scummy guy with the foreign accent." Of course I had to defend Jessie, she'd practically become my patron saint.

I changed the subject. "I'm surprised to see you. How did you know where I live?"

"If I was clever, I'd say that's what investigators do, find people. But actually I looked you up in the phone book. I wanted to show you some inmate photos, so when you name them in your reports, we'll be sure we're referring to the same guy."

"Good, that makes sense. Have a seat. Would you like something to drink?"

"That would be nice. What are you having?"

"There's tea in the kitchen, just let me get the pitcher."

As I started to get up, he bent over and said, "Here, let me pick up that spilled ice before you slip on it."

"Thanks, but I'm fine. I walk on slippery floors all day at work. At the end of my shift, I'm waddling like a duck just to keep my balance. Without Dr. Scholl's I'd be a workman's comp case."

With a smile he said, "Now that's a pretty picture, a duck with sore knees in orthopedic shoes."

"Kind of like the picture of an investigator with coffee spots on this tie and pancakes caught in his mustache. My daughter laughed when I told her about that."

"Oh jeez, she must think I'm a real doofus."

I headed for the screen door into the kitchen and asked, "Would you like lemon with your tea?"

Eleven

I had one more day off from work, some of which I spent in my recliner watching the QVC shopping network. The Special Value Offer I loved featured a silk flower arrangement with my choice of a ribbon accent in either blue toile or striped satin, tied around a china vase. I thought of shoppers across the country, their faces scrunched like mine, deciding on their preference. For me, toile won, hands down. It's always been my favorite pattern. Tom used to make me blush when he joked about the romantic activities of the milkmaids and shepherds as they roamed the toile landscape. He claimed to see the naughtiest scenarios in the patterns. Of course, choosing my favorite Special Value did not mean actually buying it. Not when the $29.99 bargain price also bought enough gas to get to work.

Besides my TV time, I thought a lot about the contraband problem. I understood inmates would try to bring in forbidden stuff. What I didn't understand was why staff got involved. Like me, they had a salary and benefits. I couldn't imagine any amount of money that made the risk of jeopardizing their safety worthwhile. Surely a whim purchase like the toile vase wouldn't tempt anyone to smuggle contraband. Of course, there were a lot of young officers who were single mothers. Hopefully, the dirty money at least got spent on diapers and baby formula. *Please, Lord, don't let me find out it bought fresh batteries for their vibrators.*

Now that I agreed to help with the problem, my view of work changed. I would be watching people around me with a third eye, trying to discover everyone involved. Of course, I assumed they would also stare at me with their third eye, wondering which side of the fence I had chosen.

When I got back to work the next day, my walk across the prison yard in the early morning provided many confusing images. Since not many inmates were out that early, I heard no profanities wafting around the corners of the gray cement buildings. The grassy areas sounded as quiet as a college campus.

But this peaceful scene had no bronze statues of nude heroes with velvet moss warming their private parts. Instead, the security lights cast a glow of sickly yellow on the prison dorms, like the color of the sky before a storm. With the glint of razor wire reflected off the muddy swamp marsh outside the fence, it was not the setting for a tranquil place of higher learning.

But it was true that learning did happen here. It was just that the learning was not the kind a parent chose for their child to master. No father wanted his son to learn how to get past the first rectal muscle in order to suitcase a bigger payload. No mother wanted her son to learn to sleep through the howls of a psychotic cellmate, or learn to make a shank out of anything.

As I waded through a tangle of feral cats on the cafeteria sidewalk, I realized I had already learned things about this prison world that had never before been in my thoughts. But now, using my biscuit-making skills in this world of weapons and corruption seemed as normal as using them at my neighborhood McDonald's.

Right before I reached the cafeteria door, I saw a big lump at the base of the nearby perimeter fence. "Oh, no," I murmured, "one of those gosh-darn cats killed a rabbit. I need to send Ernest out here to carry it to the trash."

As I walked across the grass to better examine it, a bright spotlight suddenly flashed toward me and the lump. The roving perimeter vehicle stopped on the other side of the fence, just as I walked forward on my side. When we met up near each other, I recognized the officer as Wilma.

"Hey, look what I found, Miss Kelly," she hollered. She shined her flashlight on the lump, and I saw that it was not a rabbit, or a cat, or a mound of fire ants. In the glare of her light lay a package which on a schoolyard would simply look like a football left behind by a kid when it got too dark to play. It glistened in the morning dew. Wilma and I looked at each other, knowing that inside the football was a treasure load of drugs or phones or cheap vodka. Someone threw it over the fence during the night, and it waited now for its owner to pick it up.

Wilma was so excited that she smiled despite her effort to keep a professional face. When an officer found contraband, supervisors saw it as a sign of good work. She whispered to me, "This is my first time finding one of these packages. They stress it over and over at shift briefings to be on the lookout, and now finally, here one is. This is a great way to wrap up my night shift."

"You did good," I smiled. "How did you see it from your truck?"

She stood up and stretched her back. "In training they taught us to look for what's not supposed to be here. So if there's any change in the landscape, we're supposed to get out of the vehicle and check it out."

Wilma looked sharp in her shiny boots. Her shirt was still crisp despite her hours riding around. It was clear that she was proud of her uniform.

She went on with her story. "When I first saw it, I almost didn't get out to check. It's been so boring, riding around in circles, I just wanted to wrap up the night and go home. But now, since I did the right thing, I could get a special call out at muster from my captain."

Right before she headed back to her vehicle to call it in to the control room, she said, "Oh, by the way, Miss K., remember that freaky librarian girl from orientation?"

I smiled and nodded. "Faith Miller? You shouldn't be so hard on her. She's just a little different. Why, did you see her in town?"

"No, not in town. I think I saw her a couple hours ago in a fancy black Mustang. When I drove by the front of the main building, she was pulling onto the road out of the parking lot. But it might not have been her. Librarians don't work the night shift."

"Maybe she was dropping off some paperwork at the front gate, trying to get her job started. Oh, well. Let me get into the kitchen to get the breakfast going. Congratulations, hon, you did good in finding this mess."

As we both turned away, she yelled back, "It sure was a surprise to see you with '*you know who*' at Cracker Barrel. I can't wait to hear about that new development."

We both waved and got back to work.

Inside the cafeteria, the breakfast feeding kept me busy. Cleaning up afterwards, I heard from the inmates that the contraband football was stuffed with drugs. They laughed about the cool camouflage tape wrapping around the package. It again surprised me that inmates knew details before even the staff knew the details. I laughed a little to myself that camouflage tape even existed. As I watched inmates throw buckets of egg shells and empty cartons into the trash compactor, I wondered if the wife of the contraband thrower saw the tape on QVC. Heck, it could have been right after the toile segment. I wondered how such a design decision got made. Maybe a bunch of people sat around their kitchen table, making lists about how to conceal illegal contraband, and a wife remembered the camo tape.

Based on the location of the throw over, the intended receiver was not clear. It would have been possible for a kitchen inmate worker to pick it up if it had been closer to the sidewalk, but getting close to the fence held a huge risk of punishment for an inmate. Maybe the thrower had tennis elbow and couldn't make the spiral distance throw he could in his high school football days. Maybe the camo tape slowed the package, made the design too heavy. Maybe the flapping, tangled end ruined its aero-push, like a car in the Darlington 500 slowed by its flapping fender.

The other possible scenario, a pick up by one of the staff cooks, couldn't be ruled out. If an employee wandered as casually as I had over to the fence to pick it up, there wouldn't be any suspicions. If he was successful in not being seen, a simple stash to hide it under an apron, then a quick walk into the cafeteria for breakdown and delivery, was all it would take.

When Joe Brown called me a little later, he thought the same thing. "Is anyone acting strange today in the cafeteria?' he asked on the office phone.

Since I had the office to myself right then, I talked freely.

"Given the range of strangeness of my colleagues, that question cannot be easily answered. Marilyn has spent most of the morning in the freezer with a new inmate worker. His prison name is Precious, so enough said. Since it's not likely they are romantically inclined, they may be doing each other's nails, or they may have set up an assembly line for the next package. Either scenario is equally believable, since no one who works here actually seems to do any work."

I continued my rant. "And my boss, Supervisor Supreme Rabon, has been busy this morning sliding around in his rolling desk chair, yelling, 'Work harder and faster, boys'. If he shared the rum and coke in his coffee mug with those inmates, they probably would be more help. But since he chose not to provide the motivation, they all just took notes for their lawsuit on being called 'boy'. Now he's on the back dock, getting some air, as he put it."

I started to run out of breath. "So in a briefer answer to your question, as far as I know, I'm like a mushroom. Kept in the dark and fed shit." It felt fun to speak so freely, something I couldn't do on the job normally.

He laughed and said, "I'll let you get back to frying bologna for lunch since it sounds like you're the only one actually feeding 1800 inmates. Hope your knee isn't bothering you too much."

A short time after our conversation, I heard loud voices over by the cafeteria bathroom, then I saw inmates scatter. By the time I got over to the area, a lieutenant was getting up off the floor. Cindy arrived from the other serving line at about the same time as me. We saw blood on his shirt.

For being such a weasel, when Supervisor Rabon rushed over to help us, he moved so fast he left wheelie skid marks from his office chair. Evidently the sight of blood motivated him.

We helped the LT move closer to the prep area which had a water faucet. "Be careful; don't let his nose blood get in the macaroni salad. We need to serve that for lunch," I cautioned.

The lieutenant whipped his head from side to side while Supervisor Rabon held a sink rag to the man's face.

"Well, I'm trying to help, but he won't hold still," Rabon whined. Then he asked again if we'd called for help, as if it had somehow slipped my mind. Good grief.

"Yes, the first responders lined up the inmates outside and a wheelchair for him is on the way. The responders are looking for banged up knuckles and bloody shirts to see who hit him." Then I turned to the lieutenant, "I swear, LT, you sure look as mad as a rooster. In fact, you look like you're ready to open a can of whoop-ass on somebody. Do you have any idea why it happened?"

He gave me a dirty look, stood up, grabbed his radio and went outside to where the staff was frisking the rows of inmates. Not only didn't he answer me, but he didn't thank any of us for helping him. I guess he had blood on his mind, and probably not just his own. I stood at the sink and watched through the window the shakedown of the inmates.

When the LT came up to the staff, they made an effort to move him away from the inmates, but he kept trying to walk toward them. When the wheelchair arrived, he was pretty much pushed into it by other officers and wheeled away.

I assumed the assault had something to do with the football package, but connecting the dots was not so obvious. The lieutenant usually got assigned to the yard clean-up crew. That crew does work close to the fence, since they are supervised. When he first came into the cafeteria, I thought he might be looking for a glass of tea to cool down from the yard work. But then I heard the shouts when he was hit. So, cliché number one: was he in the "wrong place at the wrong time", and a random inmate hit him for some non-contraband related reason? Or, cliché two: did he "see something he wasn't supposed to see" related to the contraband? Or, in my new mindset where everyone was dirty except for me, was he here for a pick-up, a payoff, or a payback? I wished for the good old days of random violence since this didn't seem random at all.

Later, all staff had to write our reports about what we'd seen. My eye-witness account was so short it was embarrassing. It sounded like one of those pathetic interviews on channel 3, with some toothless guy spitting into the microphone as they ask him, "What did you see?"

"I saw everything."

"Tell us about it."

"Some dude got popped, but that's all I saw."

One thing was clear. Our macaroni salad went back into the cooler since the whole prison was locked down again. So again, I got busy slicing carrot sticks and making peanut butter sandwiches. Hopefully Investigator Brown would fill me in on what he knew, or at least how much he wanted me to know.

Twelve

After the assault on the lieutenant, only a few cellblocks stayed locked down. As the yard captain explained it, "We got a solid ID on the inmate who hit the lieutenant. Now we need to figure out why he did it. But we'll leave that up to the investigator." So the plan was to allow most of the prisoners back on a normal feeding schedule.

We welcomed this news, since the lockdown bags barely met the health department requirements. And surprisingly, the bags cost more money to produce because of the paper products involved. If our kitchen went over budget, justification had to be provided through multiple reports, all of which the Supervisor of Fiscality Rabon designated us to prepare instead of him.

We were told that another reason to cut lockdown time was that inmates behaved better psychologically when they came out of their cells to the cafeteria each day. It drained off some irritability to walk to our building to see and be seen. It seemed to give the same social buzz that farmers used to feel on Saturdays when they'd come to the town square to visit and eat. And, yes, maybe enjoy some things they couldn't do down on the farm, like sip homebrew, trade some goods, and enjoy some romancing. Of course, inmates shouldn't do those type things, but I'd learned that in the prison world, 'should' was an elastic word.

Before the captain left the cafeteria after briefing us, he did say, "We just hope that whatever reason the LT got hit was an isolated incident. But we don't know that for sure. These gang fights are rough on my officers."

Our kitchen staff shuffled their feet and raised a few eyebrows, as if to say, 'it's not great for us either, not knowing when something is going to go off', but no one said this. Everyone understood that the uniform staff was on the front line of defense for us. Cindy did raise her hand to ask, "Is it just the amount of contraband coming in that have these gangs going at each other so much, or is something else going on?"

The captain told us straight, "To our best knowledge, it's the amount of money available on the yard to sponsor these packages. They're working through their contacts on the street to get it in, which is why we've got double perimeter rovers 24/7, driving outside the fence, to try to see the throw overs before the inmate spotters can get to them. Like you know, the gangs are a fact of life in prison. If we can just get some of the key players of the drug trading identified, things should settle down to a normal level of drama." We all smiled, pleased that the captain had been frank with us.

We felt tense during the supper meal, but it went well with no special problems. After the meal, I asked Ernest to stay over a little past his usual shift to scrub the mop buckets. Right before supper, I'd found the buckets snuggled up behind the ice machine, with the low heat of the motor throwing off enough warmth to brew the magic. They were full of a potential brew, including some canned fruit cocktail that was on the menu for tomorrow. The maraschino cherries bobbed cheerfully in the mess, kind of like a murky punch for a child's birthday party, prepared by a mother who had forgotten to read the recipe.

When I found it and dumped it down the drain, several of the inmates workers objected. "No, Miss Kelly, say it ain't so. We can't believe you found it." Another guy, who scours the roasting pans with efficient ferocity, even though it was a little frightening to watcb, said, "How we supposed to make it through these lockdowns without a little brew?" But I smiled as I dumped it, and said, "Sorry, fellas". I went back to getting supper on the line, and left the bucket cleaning for later.

Ernest scrunched his nose and complained, "Ma'am, that stuff still stinks." He had already helped the other inmates clean up from supper and was ready to finish his shift with this final project.

As he dumped the rinse water after the first scrubbing, he kind of smiled and said, "Whoever made this is sure blessing you out tonight. You really messed up his plans."

He wiped the buckets dry and went on, "I told you, though, a good batch of this gives enough kick to fly a man far away from these fences. And it ain't boring to be flying. It's just hard to get past the stink of it." He smiled. "Now, them ole timers had the best recipes. They could cook up a batch that tasted almost as smooth as what some guy in the street turned out in his basement."

I remembered Tom having fun making beer, but it didn't taste too good either. I told Ernest this, and he laughed out loud.

"No disrespect to your memory, ma'am, but on the streets, guys use regular bottles. In here, we got to use anything that hold liquid long enough for it to cook." He gave the mop buckets a kick, laughed again, and said, "Some time back, a couple of guys stashed their brew in trash bags and hid the bags up on top of the cafeteria ceiling tiles, up against the fluorescent lights."

He laughed so hard now I couldn't hardly understand him. "When it got cooked and gassy on a Sunday morning, the big black bags puffed up and split open, and the ceiling tiles came crashing down, all soggy and crumbly from the brew. The guys sitting underneath got all wet from it. They didn't know what to think. They'd just been eating bologna sandwiches, wishing for something good to happen, and bam, they're drenched in brew. It was just like the chaplain preached it that morning, good things happen with the power of prayer."

We laughed together about his story, and then he went off to put the buckets in the storage closet. I started to close up the office for the night. Most of the serving lights were dimmed, and the dining room was dark. All the rest of the staff had left since it was my turn to wrap up on our shift. I heard two officers laugh outside the exit door, waiting to escort Ernest back to his cell. It felt like the night closing of every café I ever worked at.

Ernest came back to the office door, and said, "Okay, ma'am, we're good for the morning." Then he looked over his shoulder and said with a lower voice, "Look, I just got to say this. You're a nice lady and a good boss. But it seems like you're playing with this contraband deal like a hobby or a puzzle to figure out. You're acting as stubborn as my grandmother."

I put down the inventory sheets I held and turned toward him. "I do appreciate your warnings, and I'm not meaning to be careless, but I have a duty to report what I know."

Then I added in a less preachy voice, "I've never heard you speak of your family. What was your grandmother's name?"

He looked at the officers outside in the twilight and mumbled, "Mildred. She was a school teacher her whole life. First she started in black schools, then was still teaching when the schools got mixed."

I nodded, "Yes, I remember those days. What a time it was. Was she strict?"

"Strict? I tell you, that lady, she did not play. She was tall, and stood as straight as a fence post. When she frowned at me over her eyeglasses, I felt like she knew all my secrets, even ones I hadn't thought of yet."

"Was she married?"

"Yeah, she and Pop Harold married way late in life. Pop shined shoes for a living. First on the trains, then he tried to make a go of it in airports until his arthritis got ahold of him. Every day that he worked, he wore a bow tie and white shirt under his long apron."

"How did they meet?"

"No one in the family knows exactly how he and Grandmother Mildred got together. My mom, Virginia, was their only child. Pop said my mom got good grades at first in school, but then in high school she hooked up with the guy who's supposedly my old man. Pop said she still might have made it all right, since she and me lived for a while with my grands. But then she started drinking pretty good, and there was a falling out, and one thing led to another. Sometimes even now I remember pieces from my time with them, like helping Pop trim up the yard in front of their house. I remember sleeping in a room off their kitchen, kind of like a porch. The sheets smelled clean, and it was quiet. No loud music or yelling over card games, like at my mom's."

I knew we weren't supposed to have personal conversations with inmates, but I also knew that Ernest needed to talk. I said to him real quiet, "It's too bad you couldn't stay with them longer. Why did you leave?"

He looked out the window and spoke as if I wasn't there. "I could have stayed, but see, Grandmother Mildred had done so many right things in her life, she thought the line between right and wrong was clear. 'Clear as day' is what she'd say. She didn't get that things can be more complicated than that. So after a while, it'd get irritating to hear that, and I'd slip back to my mom's. Mom's life was so confusing, I just felt more comfortable."

With that said, he nodded and looked embarrassed. "Well, is it all right if I leave now?" He asked as if I'd made him stay and speak of such private things.

"Sure," I played along to make him feel more at ease. "Thanks for your help. I'll see you in the morning."

I watched the officers escort him across the yard, being sure he went straight to his cellblock. I felt sad that prison fit Ernest so well. It had the rules and routines of his grandparents, and Lord knows, it had the confusion and noise and excitement that he found with his mom.

That night on the drive home, Bette Midler made me cry when she sang, "Wind Beneath My Wings." If Ernest had more wing support, he could have been a Navy Seal, with lots of both rules and excitement. Or he could have been an ambulance driver, keeping his rig spotless while he waited for a call. I could hear him with an accident victim, "Ma'am, just lay still. We're here to help you."

I didn't know what crime brought Ernest to prison, and I didn't want to find out. In prison, only staff in certain jobs knew an inmate's history. But I already knew that even if he got released tomorrow, he'd be back. It was 'clear as day,' as Grandmother Mildred said.

Thirteen

Looking back, we should have seen it coming. So many incidents happened in such a short time, with assaults on both staff and inmates. Of course, this prison was filled with violent inmates, but the addition of gangs and money created a volcano.

Just as Joe Brown said, just as Ernest said, and yes, just as Sharon said, this was a big problem.

I had not heard from Joe Brown since the day before. Ernest told me he heard that Malcolm, Jamal were both interviewed by Investigator Brown. I smiled inside when Ernest told me that, since Joe Brown had said he would be their best friend in order to get leads.

This morning's plan was that a small group of inmates would eat in the cafeteria, but most of the population would be fed lockdown bags in their cells. Security staff felt they needed more time to follow up on rumors and tips.

Supervisor Rabon gathered us staff for a morning briefing, something he had not done before. "Breakfast should be light since they're only sending inmates with job assignments, like the maintenance helpers, trash haulers, and our kitchen workers. Oh, and the plumbers' helpers are coming, too. Got to keep the toilets flowing in this place."

I laughed along with the other staff at his elegant phrasing. He went on, "The other inmates are staying locked up, the ones who might be involved in this gang stuff. Hopefully the security staff will soon have it sorted out, and we can return to normal feedings." He gave a tight smile, like a good bureaucrat delivering the company message. I liked him for being real for a change and laughed again along with the others.

He looked surprised to see us respond to him so easy. Then he added, "But you all know how things can go. So watch out for each other." With that, he went back into his office, and we headed to the floor to work the breakfast serving.

The fight started off as cursing between three inmates standing in line for grits. We called security, but before they arrived, the fight spread. It spread so quickly that the outnumbered security staff had to pull back their people. About five of us food service people rushed into the freezer, including Supervisor Rabon. We locked the door from the inside and stared at each other.

Supervisor Rabon told us, "I saw most of the staff head for the back dock, so they should be all right." I saw that Cindy grabbed one of the knives we had been using to slice cabbage for lunch. When she saw us looking at the knife, she said, "I don't think any of the other knives or utensils got pulled." She looked scared when she said this. Supervisor Rabon tried to raise central control on his radio to pass along the warning that the inmates could be armed.

Then we settled in for a long wait, like we'd had before when we sheltered in the freezer in the earlier disturbance. But soon, Supervisor Rabon heard on the radio, "Attention: All staff needs to evacuate the cafeteria due to fire. Repeat, cafeteria staff needs to evacuate."

I felt afraid. In the earlier riot, security stayed in control. Without their guidance, I felt lost. Supervisor Rabon wiped his sweaty brow with his apron, and cleared his throat. "Okay, here's what we need to do." We looked at him as if he was our rescuer. "Once we open the door, we all need to try to stay together, and head toward the back dock. If we get separated, and you don't think you can make it to the dock, find a hiding place."

He didn't give us a chance to nod our agreement, and it didn't feel appropriate to do the hands together in the middle thing like teams on the sports channel. Instead, he just opened the door, and we rushed into the chaos.

Cindy and a few other fast runners raced toward the back. I was able to stay with them for a few yards, but then I couldn't keep up. Supervisor Rabon didn't stay with them either, but hustled toward his office. Once I lost sight of him and the others, I froze, not sure which way to go.

Just in that brief delay, while I was looking around, the path to the dock was blocked with a barrier of cardboard boxes the inmates shoved in place. Some had wrapped the brown paper bags used for lockdown meals around long serving spoons, and set them on fire from the gas flames of the stoves. They used them as torches and set fire to the cardboard.

Since I no longer had the back dock as my goal, I lost my sense of direction. I half-turned to the left, then twisted right, not seeing any easy way out. Twisting around too fast made me feel dizzy. Then, across the dining room, I saw Joe Brown standing on top of one of the tables. He was also turning and looking and turning and looking. I called his name, but could hardly hear my voice myself. The smoke detectors were screaming, and the ceiling sprinkler system was raining down.

When he saw me finally, he jumped down from the table, ran toward me, and grabbed my shoulder. He looked like the Marlboro Man to the rescue. It is embarrassing to admit that when he grabbed me, my first thought was 'what a time for a romance.' It was just my luck to have a hormonal revival during a prison riot. But before we could speak or move toward the exit, a crowd of inmates pushed toward us.

In the crush of the scrambling inmates, I fell on the wet floor and lost sight of Joe. I felt clumsy and confused. I crawled under a serving counter nearby and tried to make myself small.

The noise grew louder. The steam kettles hissed, the smoke alarms howled, and inmates cursed and yelled. Many legs rushed by me. Inmates broke off mop handles to use as weapons. The discarded mop tops laid in puddles beside me, like decapitated Barbie dolls with greasy blond dreadlocks.

Then I saw Ernest standing over me. He leaned down to grab my arm to haul me up from my hiding place. At first glance, he appeared an unlikely savior. His shirt bulged with newspapers and towels and plastic serving trays, his stuffed version of a Kevlar vest. He had it packed so tight he moved like the Tin Man in Wizard of Oz. But, bless me Dorothy, I was glad to see him.

Together we backed toward the office and then saw Supervisor Rabon slam the door and head in our direction. Ernest half-carried me since my knees would no longer bend. It hurt like the devil, and definitely slowed us down. As he drug me, I looked around for Joe Brown, but could no longer see him through the smoke.

"Hey, Mr. Rabon, you got to take her," Ernest yelled. As Rabon moved closer to us, Ernest grabbed one of the wheeled serving carts and plopped me on top of it. Supervisor Rabon grabbed the handle of the cart from Ernest and yelled to me, "Hang on, Mrs. Kelly, we're in for a rough ride."

He pushed the cart with one hand, and in the other hand, he held a bundled apron. When the crowd wouldn't let us through, he swung the apron in an arc above his head. In the bundle were several padlocks and lanyard chains from the knife locks. As he cleared our path with his swinging weapon, he looked more like the Pillsbury Doughboy than Conan the Barbarian with numchucks, but as he pushed me forward, I saw light from the outside door.

As I turned to look back, I saw Joe Brown again standing on a table, trying to see through the smoke. When he saw me at the doorway to the outside yard, he smiled and nodded, then jumped down and headed back into the crowd of inmates, spraying the gas canister which was always on his belt.

In that last glance, I also saw Ernest standing at the service line with the handle of a toilet plunger raised above his head, ready to swing. Some pans filled with spice cake from the day's lunch menu lay spilled on the floor around him. Other pans stood ready for serving, with cream frosting still in smooth smears on top. It looked like Ernest was standing guard over the dessert, ready to break any arm reaching out of the riot confusion to grab for seconds of the cake.

Fourteen

Many hours later in my hospital room, Sharon spiffed me up for my first set of visitors. She stopped fussing at me long enough to spritz my hair to get rid of the tear gas smell. She also tried to control the drool at the corner of my mouth. But I so loved the magic of the pain killers, I waved her off. If I looked a little wild, well, it had been that kind of day.

Both of my knees were frozen into heavy casts and braces, scheduled for surgery. I couldn't feel them and kept peeking under the sheet to be sure they were still attached.

My visitors came in. They were pleasant but all business. I welcomed them because they were a bureaucrat's version of the lottery's front team and to my surprise, they delivered an unexpected gift.

"Are you sure?" I blubbered.

"Yes, ma'am, just sign here."

My knees now belonged to the government. The trifecta of medical benefits was now mine: free surgery, free hospital care, free time to recuperate, and salary while I was laid up. All of this was mine, way sooner than normal eligibility dates, and with no deductible out of my pocket.

"Did I already ask you if you're sure?" I blubbered again.

"Yes, ma'am, we're sure."

"Mom, I checked the forms. You need to sign them. Can you sit up a little?"

No one even cared that my knees had a history, that dreaded 'pre-existing condition.' As soon as my crooked, gimpy knees cracked on the cafeteria floor during the riot, they were born again, ready for fixing on the government dime.

Given this development, drooling seemed an appropriate social response.

I handed back their pen after signing and slurred, "Please tell me again about my job. Will it stay open for me?"

The lead Human Resources guy answered like he had said this more than once. "You will be assigned to a cafeteria in a different prison. It's not far from your home, just in a different area. You'll get the same salary."

"Don't they want me back at my prison?" Tears joined the drool in the growing pool under my chins. "I tried to keep up with the young workers. Did Supervisor Rabon refuse to let me come back?"

"Ma'am, you got a good recommendation from your supervisor. Who, by the way, is also taking some time off. But it's a policy that after an inmate related job injury, an employee spends some time away from where it happened. Sometimes it's not so good to go back to the same setting." I could see him resist the urge to look at his watch, being such a fine professional and all.

"You'll like your new prison. It's smaller, and the inmates have shorter sentences, mostly for drug crimes. They don't have the violent histories like at the max prison."

His assistant looked at Sharon and then me. "Are there any more questions?" This young man was definitely on a promotional fast track.

Their shoes squeaked on the linoleum floor as they left.

"Mom, do you want to wait a while before you see the Internal Affairs people?"

"No, hon, let's get all the business stuff out of the way." For feeling so relieved, I wasn't feeling so good. I wanted to be slouched in Tom's recliner instead of a hospital bed.

The second set of visitors looked much more serious than the earlier bunch.

After they introduced themselves, Sharon said, "Mom, these men would like to question you about the riot. And they also want to brief you on the investigation of the contraband problem." I looked at them, surprised to not see Joe Brown with them.

The guy in a gray suit nudged the lead talker in a black suit, and he said, "We're glad to see that you're all right."

Since the first group of visitors had just certified that I officially wasn't all right, it was clear that these government workers were communicating as well as normal.

The black suit guy went on to say, "We are assisting Investigator Brown with the investigation of the crimes that led to the riot."

The way he said 'assisting' made Sharon and me glance at each other. She stepped forward a little and introduced herself as my attorney. Then all the parties who came to this party ratcheted up their politeness levels. No loose lips here, except mine.

"Where is Investigator Brown?" I tried to sound casual, but Sharon tilted her head to look at me with a silent "Hmm?" My girl is so smart.

"Investigator Brown has been called out of town on other business. But before he left, he briefed us on recent updates of the gang and contraband investigation. He asked that we fill you in," he paused and added, "to the extent that we can. Some issues are not yet resolved, and of course, as Investigator Brown no doubt previously explained, we're never able to give full disclosure regarding investigations."

Sharon nodded at his fine turn of phrase, as one artist admires the work of another.

"The gang fights were prompted by the unusual volume of contraband coming in. We may not be able to charge anyone for the assaults of the two inmates, Jamal and Malcolm, since at this point we only have accusations and no solid proof. However, you will be hearing in the news media that a sergeant has been arrested for coordinating the contraband throw overs. We are continuing to interrogate him regarding his contacts in the community who, we believe, facilitated the packaging and delivery of the contraband."

I stared at him. I didn't know people talked like that in real life. He sounded just like a television actor. His navy and white striped tie was better quality than Chris's, but his twisty words made me dizzy.

"So Jamal was not lying about the sergeant?" My lines in this television script were not as fancy as Mr. Black-Suit's. "Do you know yet why Malcolm had my numbers?"

"No, ma'am, not for sure." Investigator Gray-Suit spoke more like Joe Brown, normal-like. "It looks like it was just an attempt by him to get a side project going. Lots of inmates steal staff identity numbers to sell to outside sources. From what we can tell, he hadn't gotten too far along and your numbers were not spread any further. But we have put you on our list for monitoring in case they get used later."

"I understand you can't tell me much about the dirty sergeant, but what about the lieutenant who got punched? Was he working with the sergeant?"

Black-suit silver-tongue said, "Ma'am, again we can't get into too many specifics. But generally speaking, at this point, it is our working hypothesis that the lieutenant saw activity that incriminated others and was assaulted as a form of intimidation."

Gray-suit added, "They didn't want him to report what he saw."

Although I didn't want to have rude thoughts, it didn't sound like much had come from all the pain and chaos. And as a taxpayer, it made me mad as the dickens to envision the damage done to my kitchen during the riot.

Maybe Gray-Suit Guy read my mind, because he said, "The problem with investigating crimes in prison is that all the inmates are suspects, and none can really be believed. We are lucky to get that dirty sergeant out of there, and hopefully he'll lead us to some people outside the fence." He paused as if to apologize, "It's not a very tidy business."

As he raised his hand to gesture his frustration, his gold wedding band glinted in the light from the window. Oh, well.

I thought about what he said and realized that Joe Brown had told me the same thing. Prison crime is very hard to investigate, even if all the staff were saints and not involved. Which most of them are not involved, just doing their job in a tough setting. But, by definition, criminals lie, and if they find bad staff to help with their crimes, and people in town to take part, we have what we had: injured people and wasted money.

"Before you leave, what about Ernest, the inmate worker who helped me? Is he all right?"

"Investigator Brown already briefed us on him, and he's been transferred out to another prison. Since he was seen by other inmates helping you, he may not have been safe to stay in place."

Saint Gray-Suit added, "We were able to get him reclassified to a different custody level due to his good behavior, so he'll have more freedom to move around."

I smiled inside at the notion of Ernest having fewer gates, not entirely sure that he would value that so much. But I was relieved that he was safe.

After the investigators left, Sharon kept her stern face on to remind me that she had been right about my job. She moved to the foot of the bed, so I had a full view of her disapproving frown.

"You know, Mom, it's all very well that your knees will be taken care of by workman's comp, but you heard the Human Resources people say that you'll be expected to go back to work when you're medically cleared. I want you to think about getting out of the prison business. Even though your next job will be at a different prison, it is still a risk. You need to think of doing something else."

I didn't need to tune in too carefully to hear her lecture since I had heard it too many times before. Granted, this time she was correct, but I would worry about that later. What I really wanted to worry about was why Joe Brown had not called. It wasn't that I expected flowers, since ours was a business relationship, but I sure didn't expect him to get out of seeing me by sending his bosses. I felt sad and confused.

Having to admit to your grown child that she may be correct about something is not near as hard as having to admit to her that she was right about two things. Good grief.

With her piece said, Sharon had to leave to get back to her job, which postponed any more talk about my misjudgments. I learned a long time ago to take my blessings in whatever fashion they might present.

No sooner than she left, Wilma poked her head around the door.

"Hey, Miss K.," she whispered, "I just wanted to pop in to check on you."

She was in uniform and headed for her night shift. "I've been so worried about you since I heard on the news about the riot in the cafeteria. I knew you worked today and would be caught up in it."

In her uniform, without any sequins, Wilma seemed like a more quiet person. We talked about what happened and gossiped about the dirty sergeant. Neither of us knew much about him, but that didn't stop our gossip.

When we finished with him, Wilma said, "So enough about that dirty dog. I haven't seen you since Cracker Barrel's parking lot." She waited a half second and added, "Fill me in on you and the investigator. And do not say you're 'just friends.'" She gave me a silly smile with pushed out lips, like a Pekingese puppy.

"Wilma, you make me laugh. But I can't even really say we're friends. I mean, I thought we were, but I haven't heard from him. So let's just say we were friendly, and had breakfast together."

Her giggle took me back to my high school days. "I'm sorry, Miss K., but I'm friendly with a lot of people that don't take me to breakfast. Come on, 'fess up."

"Oh, hush. We had a friendly breakfast to talk about some of the inmates who worked in the cafeteria. He had some of them under investigation and wanted to know what they were like at their job assignment. It was easier to talk away from the prison, so we met at Cracker Barrel. That's all there is to the story."

I felt a little buzzed from the pain pills, but there was no way I was giving Wilma any more than that.

"So, your turn. How are Delores and the kids?" It had been a while since I'd seen Wilma's mother-in-law, and I didn't want to ask about Ted.

"The kids are fine, doing kind of all right in school. Mama Dee is fine too but worried about Ted, as usual."

"What happened to Ted?"

"What happened is that he stopped asking her for money. You know how she always spoiled him, even though she knew he took advantage of her. Anyway, he hadn't asked her for any money for the jail canteen account, so when she visited this weekend, she asked if he needed any. Then he got all mouthy on her and said he was tired of begging and figured out another way to take care of hisself. So Dee doesn't know what that means since she's used to him nagging her. But she also knows how easy it is for him to find trouble."

Wilma paused to brush her sleeve over her officer badge, squinting at a little fuzz caught in its shine. "Personally, I don't care a bit what he does, but it wears heavy on her, being his mom."

I didn't believe for a second that, in her heart, Wilma had let Ted go, but I liked hearing her brave words. On his show the other day, Dr. Phil talked about, "Fake it until you make it." I thought that was what Wilma was trying to do.

I was starting to nod off, but out of politeness I asked, "Anything new around town? I've been so busy I feel out of touch."

"No, ma'am, not that I know about. I did see your space cadet librarian at the stoplight on Main Street the other day. And she was still driving that fancy black Mustang. Boy, if I could afford a car like that, I would bling it out even more. Maybe get fancy rims and drive by the jail to make Ted jealous."

"You and Faith Miller. Just because she's a librarian who drives a nice car and dresses kind of strange, you surely do trash talk her. I hardly even met her, but I feel like I should help defend her name. Lord knows what you say about me behind my back." I put on a fake pout, like she had.

Wilma laughed, "I think your Dr. Scholl's are real trendy, and your car is as old as mine, so I can't really trash on that." She stood to leave. "I've stayed too long, and you're half asleep. When you get out of the hospital, call me, and I'll drive you to your physical therapy appointments. Of course, I ain't got a Mustang, so you'll have to ride in my junker."

She reached out, touched my arm, and said no more, just hurried out the door.

After she left, I daydreamed about the flowers Joe Brown would think I'd like. He knew me well enough to eliminate calla lilies and Boston ferns, but I felt sad that he didn't know if I'd prefer red tulips or white shastas. I spent some time feeling disappointed, but then I smiled when I remembered Tom once gave me a cactus plant for Christmas. He was so puzzled when I wasn't thrilled with it. Too much water took care of that spindly thing. It hardly made it through New Year's. *And I didn't feel at all guilty.*

As I shifted in bed away from my damp pillow, soggy from tears and drool, I opened the hospital information packet. It had a big *Welcome* on the front. I found out that the television in my room got cable, and the dinner menu had lasagna. I squirmed my butt to a more comfortable position and added two things to my blessings list.

With television and lasagna, I was good to go.

Bruised Fruit

Wilma's Story

He has an asshole problem.
Hemorrhoids?
No, he is one.

One

"Hurry up and sign your paycheck. I want to be at the bank when it opens." Ted hollered to me from the kitchen table when I came in from my night shift.

On television, I'd heard some husbands say, "Good morning, honey. How was work? Can I get you some coffee?" before they talked about money.

But then, those husbands wear wife-beater tanks for fashion, not as a damn warning.

"Sure. I've got it in my purse. Are the kids awake?"

"No, they didn't want to get up. And I didn't have time to mess with them. I wanted some coffee before I had to get to the bank. Besides, if I'm late for work again, my old man will give me a bunch of shit."

In my television family, getting kids to school on time counted as a big deal. And there was no rush to deposit a paycheck before other checks bounced. And the words 'old man' and 'shit' were not in the same sentence.

"Ted, they need to be at school on time. It's important. When I started my night shift, you promised you'd get them up and fed by the time I got home."

I wanted to ask 'is that so hard, dumb ass?' or maybe 'can you just do one thing right, you stupid shit?' But I would be the dumb ass and the stupid shit to start that fight, so I left those words inside. They rested along with the others that rotted my teeth and soured my stomach. I had a whole stinking list of fighting words that sloshed around inside me.

Despite the family complications of me working full time, I loved my new job at the prison. My uniform made me look important, particularly my shiny boots. At the job I had before this, as a maid in a sleazy motel on the other side of the bypass, they didn't care what we wore to work. They only cared that I show up. In fact, if I'd worked buck naked, I'd have made better tips.

Ted's mom, Delores, gave me the idea to get the prison job. "Wilma, working for the state will give you a future," she said. She even bought me a new outfit for the job interview. I was so nervous that day, I almost turned around and left the parking lot. But my neighbor, Miss Kelly, was there to interview for a cafeteria job, so we went in together.

Delores's words gave me courage to try to better our family. Unfortunately, her magic didn't work with her son. Even though she and Ted's dad, Wilbur, were the nicest people in the world, it was a damn mystery why Ted didn't get those genes.

As I sat at the table and untied my boots, Ted tore the money part of the check from the deduction part. He slid it across to me to sign. "I don't know why you have so much shit taken out of your check. We could get ahead if you didn't waste money so bad."

When I signed and gave it back to him, I explained, "Ted, I told you before, the only thing extra they take out is the dentist insurance for the kids. We need that 'cause they inherited so many cavities." I did hold back a little secret from Ted; I also had twenty dollars pulled each check for savings. I knew it would never grow to one of those 401 accounts, but I loved having money put aside. For sure, Ted didn't need to know about that little stash.

He stuffed my check in his pants pocket, leaned across the table, and grabbed the front of my shirt. "Don't you be saying those cavities came from my side of the family." I didn't move, and I for sure didn't look him in the eye. "That shit is from your stupid mom."

He stared hard at me to be sure I got his point, then dropped his hand. He snatched up the plaid shirt I'd ironed for him the day before. "After work I've got to meet some guys, so you need to take the kids to mom's after you get them from school."

As he left, he slammed the front door of our trailer and hurried to his truck.

The slam of the door and the rev of his truck sounded sweet to me.

Two

I watched out the front window to be sure he was gone. I felt too tired to cry. As I stared at the driveway, I couldn't remember why I married him. But I'd made so many big mistakes in my life that our marriage was just a number on that long list. It didn't matter any more why I'd married him. What was getting harder to remember was why I stayed with him.

Since I'd started my job, I'd had ideas that were new to me. This was the first important job I ever had. Right on my job description, it said that I was responsible to keep inmates locked up so they wouldn't hurt our town. Me: It's my job to do that. The recruiter even told us that in a few years, if we didn't screw up, we could get promoted.

Of course, a promotion is too scary to think about, since before this job I've only ever been responsible for my kids, and for that, Ted's parents helped a lot. Still, the idea that I don't clean motel sinks for a living any more makes me happy. True enough, the prison job could be dangerous; like when Miss Kelly got her knees broke in a riot not too long ago. But like that ad for the Army says on television, 'no risk, no glory.' That's how I see this job,

At the graduation ceremony from the training academy, we took an oath. I can't remember all we swore to, but mostly it was about following rules and laws. What I do remember was raising my hand and feeling serious and certain, grateful to have this chance to do right. It felt similar to the voice I heard both times when my kids were born. The voice told me, "Wilma, don't screw these kids up." Just that simple, but it gave me a powerful desire to finally figure stuff out.

Maybe if Ted had come to my graduation, he would understand my job better. At the time, he was still locked up at the county jail on a DUI charge. But Delores came, and she even sat in the front row. She got teary and gave me a big hug. "I am so proud of you, Wilma. You make our family better."

After the ceremony, the kids and I went to her house for some cake she made. She wrote my name in blue across the chocolate frosting. "The blue is the color of your uniform shirt," she explained.

Wilbur, Ted's dad, also gave me a present. He's the manager of the Dollar Store here in town. He had put a rubber band around a store bag and handed it to me with a shy grin. Inside were six tins of black shoe polish. "You're going to need this," he said in his gruff way. I liked to have cried that this quiet man gave me something so personal.

Wilbur stepped up again when Ted got out of jail this last time. Because he lost his driving license with the DUI, Ted had also lost his job hauling chickens to the processing plant. The only work he could find was a job his probation officer offered to him, working at a car wash. "I ain't doing that," he told her. So Wilbur offered Ted a job in the stock room at the Dollar Store, unloading deliveries shipped from the warehouse. Ted gets paid in cash by Wilbur. My guess is that the money comes out of Wilbur's own pocket, not the store payroll.

I could have spent the morning staring out that window, listening to the crowd of voices in my head. Except Richie, my son, quietly came up next to me in his Superman pajamas. "Mama, is this a school day or a cartoon day?"

I leaned over to hug him. "I was just fixing to wake you. Since we're already late to school, I think we should get breakfast at McDonald's on our way. Hurry and wake your sister and let's go."

He smiled big and rushed off, then skidded to a stop in the hallway. "Will my teacher be mad at me for being late?"

"No, son, it'll be all right. I'll tell her we had car trouble. She can't be mad about that."

Three

A couple of days later, I got home from work to see my living room filled with cardboard boxes. They were stacked on my plaid couch, the kitchen table, and there were even a few on the stove top.

The kids weren't home since they spent the night at Ted's folks, who drove them to school. Coming from work, I looked forward to not having another fuss with Ted about them. I even thought I might fix him some breakfast, just to be nice. But with a house full of boxes, I forgot about my good mood. I didn't understand what I was seeing.

"Ted, what in the world is all this stuff?" He was bent over one of the boxes on the floor, resealing it shut.

"Don't even worry about it, Wilma. A guy's coming to pick it all up in a couple minutes." He didn't look up, just kept counting boxes and sealing ones that were loose.

"But what are they?"

"Wilma, it's not any of your business. If my guy wasn't running late, you wouldn't even know about it. So just shut up and go in the other room."

I bent down and looked at some boxes that had invoices taped on the front. One box had a list of twenty-four bags of chips; another listed twelve double rolls of toilet paper. Stacked over by the television were three cases of soda. All of the invoices listed the Dollar Store as the receiver.

"Why is the store's stuff here? Did your dad have a fire? Did he have extra shipments, or something?"

Ted stood up and slammed down the roll of tape in his hand. Before he could yell, someone knocked on the door.

Glaring at me, he rushed to open it. A tall man stood outside with a smaller guy behind him.

"Hey, man, sorry we're late."

Ted snapped at him, "If you can't be on time, I can find another buyer real easy."

"No, no, now that we know where you live, we'll be fine. "

As the men moved into the room, the taller one spoke to me. "Morning, ma'am." I just stood there, with a stupid look on my face.

Ted said, "All right, let's get this stuff loaded." No one spoke again as they carried the boxes and sodas out to their cargo van. I watched from the window as the tall guy handed a roll of cash to Ted. Slowly Ted counted it, then they shook hands, and the men drove away.

When Ted came back into the house, he used his nice voice. "I'm sorry, baby. I really didn't plan for you to know about this little extra business I have. But they ran late, so now you know." He lifted the coffee pot, "You want a cup?"

I shook my head at the coffee. I kind of understood what just went on, but I still hoped I misunderstood. I hoped Wilbur's store had a terrible emergency, and Ted was just helping out. "Ted, you say, 'now I know.' But what do I know?"

He splashed his mug of coffee into the sink and grabbed his truck keys from the counter. "You don't know shit, that's what you know. You need to just forget what you saw and don't even think of being Miss Goody Two Shoes, Miss Po-lice. You remember that I run this house, and I provide for my family the way I see fit. Your little prison guard money don't come close to paying our bills."

"You stole stuff from your dad's store." I said it in a low voice, too surprised to even be excited.

"See, I told you that you don't know shit. This is inventory that never made it onto the store floor, so no; I didn't steal it 'from the store' as you put it. The regional office allows for some extra orders, to make up for loss or damage. Since I run the stock room, this stuff technically never even made it into the building."

He leaned near me and raised his eyebrows. "Do you need anything else explained to you?"

I moved away. "Won't your dad's audit come up short?"

"I'm done answering your stupid questions. You have no idea how much shoplifting goes on at that place. You think the world is a tidy place, and now in your clown uniform, you want to make it even more tidy. Well, this is the real world. Customers steal shit from that store every day. It's part of the cost of doing business. So I'm out of here before you waste any more of my patience. He stepped closer to me and cracked his knuckles. "I'd hate to have to teach you a lesson." He turned around and stomped out the door, slamming it behind him.

I sat down to take off my boots. My clumsy fingers fumbled with the laces. Ted's stealing from Wilbur made me sick. I don't mean it made me feel sick; I mean it *really* made me sick. I pulled only one boot off before I flat out ran to the commode.

Four

For the rest of the week, Ted and I avoided each other. By the time I got home in the mornings, he was gone. The kids spent a lot of time at their grandparents' house. I picked them up from school in the afternoons and dropped them with Delores before my shift started in the evening.

But yesterday when Delores gathered them into her house from my car, she asked me, "Do you have a minute to come in for a visit?"

I didn't want to talk to her. I didn't want to look at her sweet face while I hid my dirty secret. She opened her screen door and made me feel worse. "I've got some of those coconut macaroons you like." The only person in my world who cared enough to know I loved macaroons now wanted me to chat with her. And maybe break her heart.

"Sure, Miss Dee, I always have time to kick my feet under your table. Particularly with a bribe like that." I smiled at her and followed inside.

She got the kids settled in front of the cartoon channel with peanut butter sandwiches and a juice carton each. Spread out on their grandma's couch, they looked safe and happy.

When Delores settled at the table across from me, her sweet face looked troubled. She was flushed and her eyes squinted, as if she had a headache. "Are you feeling all right, Delores? Have the kids been too much for you this week?"

She dug a tissue from her pocket and clenched it to her mouth. "Wilma, you are so busy with work and the kids, I hate to burden you. But I am so worried, if I don't talk to someone, I might just pop."

"Oh, Dee, what's wrong?" She definitely deserved someone better than me to share her burden, but I was the one she chose.

"I'm so worried about Wilbur. He has a problem with his job, and now his blood pressure has got too high. Of course, he won't go to his doctor. He just keeps taking more headache pills. And last night he couldn't sleep at all."

Please, Lord, there are lots of problems a store manager could have besides a thief for a son. Please let it be one of those other problems. "I'm so sorry, Wilbur is such a quiet guy, I never figured him to have blood pressure problems." I played with my macaroon. "What's the problem in his store?"

"Never once in all his years running that place has he ever had a shortage like he's got now. The regional auditors plan to come tomorrow to do a full inventory. His sales don't match his orders from the warehouse, and he doesn't know why." Delores sobbed into her tissue, glancing at the kids to be sure they couldn't see her. "If he loses his job because they think he's careless or too old, or whatever..." She didn't finish her thought, just went on. "I worry so, Wilma. The shame will kill him." Her sobs were so deep and quick that she sounded like she was choking.

I hadn't been lucky enough to see a lot of love in my life, but I knew I saw it now across the table. Delores was lovesick for her Wilbur.

I stood up and put my arms around her. "Come on, Dee; let's go out on the front steps." On the way, I put the plate of macaroons between the kids.

"Grandma and I will be right outside for a minute." They didn't look up from the television, but two little heads nodded as two short arms reached for the cookie plate.

Delores and I sat close together on the cement step. Delores took some deep breaths and looked out toward the late afternoon sun. Without looking toward me, she found my hand and squeezed. "I don't know what I'd do without you, Wilma."

I had already made my decision. It was the right thing to do. "Delores, please don't hate me when I tell you what I'm fixin' to tell you."

She patted my hand. "I already know. You're going to tell me not to worry so much. How could I hate you for giving me comfort?"

Our hands were together around the mushy tissue. "Delores, Ted stole from Wilbur. That's why Wilbur's inventory is short." I told her what I had seen and what Ted had told me. The sun still warmed us, and Delores still held my hand. But when I finished, she wasn't squeezing it any more. She simply held it.

"Delores, did you hear me? Ted stole some boxes and sold them to some guys. I only found out earlier this week."

After a moment I added, "I didn't know what to do about it."

"Wilbur should be feeling better in time to dig up that iris bed by the driveway. Those iris bulbs need to be divided."

I started to cry. "Delores, we need to talk about this. We can't pretend it didn't happen. Ted did a terrible wrong."

"We're not pretending. We're planning for what's ahead." She took a deep breath. "We've both had practice with Ted doing something terrible." She turned a little from the setting sun to look at me. "I expect we'll get more chances to have our hearts hurt by him."

I wiped my nose on my uniform sleeve. "What do we do next?"

She stood and pulled me up with her. She tried to put on her cheery face, but the twist in her chin told the truth. "Here's our plan. First, we give those kids some sweet prunes, so they don't get clogged up from all that peanut butter and coconut. Then, you go to work and stay safe from those criminals. And then, when Wilbur gets home, before I feed him supper, I will tell him what Ted did."

In my mind's eye, I saw Delores talking to Wilbur about Ted. I saw her arm around his shoulder as he sat at their kitchen table, a meat loaf in front of him, waiting to be sliced. I felt sad for them. And I was also ashamed at the comfort I felt now that grown-ups were in charge of the problem.

"What do you think Wilbur will do?"

"Of course, I've never been in the business world, but I expect Wilbur will use some of our savings money to make the numbers right for the auditors." She paused a heartbeat. "And then he'll need to fire Ted."

"Do you think he'll turn Ted into the police?"

"You're asking me to guess. But I'm inclined to think that families settle things themselves."

Five

The next afternoon, as I was fixing to pick up the kids from school, I got a text from Ted. "Meet me at Walmart's."

I didn't want to go. I wanted to keep avoiding him. I wanted to hide my eyes from the problem until the days in the future when Delores said, "Oh, you know the problem at the store? Well, Wilbur straightened it out. It was all a big mistake. And by the way," she'd say as she squirted whipped cream on my bowl of banana pudding, "Ted will be gone for a semester to the university. He's enrolled in several accounting classes." In my head, my voices had a wonderful story worked out. I enjoyed the comfort the story gave me.

When I got to Walmart, only a few cars were in the parking lot. I didn't see Ted's truck, so I parked close to the store and ran in to get hot dogs and apples for the kids' dinner. The speedy checkout lane was a little slow, so by the time I paid, I felt nervous. It was never a good idea to keep Ted waiting.

Outside the store, I saw a bunch of people gathered around my car. I started to run toward it, but I slowed down to keep from getting run over by a police car rushing into the lot with its blue lights flashing. The siren cut off when he stopped by my car.

"Put it down, sir." The officer stood by his cruiser while he watched Ted wind up for another swing. I walked closer and saw Ted shatter the windshield of my car. Pieces of glass from the side windows already lay on the ground around the car. Some glass sat on top of a McDonald's hamburger box, like sparkles glued on by grease.

"I said, put it down," the officer warned Ted again. But Ted lifted Richie's baseball bat over his shoulder, ready for another whack. He saw me on the fringe of the crowd, my hand to my mouth, my eyes on his.

When he spoke to me, his voice sounded reasonable and logical, like a simple explanation to a simple problem. "This one's for you." And he swung the bat into the quarter panel of my car.

Then it was done. He dropped the bat and turned toward the officer with his arms stretched out. "Cuff me up and get me out of here," he said, as if he was in charge.

Once the officer cuffed him and put him into the cruiser, the crowd drifted away. I went up the policeman. "Sir, just so you know, that's actually his own car. His own property. Even though I'm driving it, the title's in his name. And thanks for coming, but I didn't call you." I said this loud enough for Ted to hear. My voice sounded stupid, but I wanted this problem to go away.

The officer looked at my uniform and slowly shook his head. He didn't add a smirk, but he could have. "Doesn't matter, ma'am. He's charged with disturbing the peace and refusing to obey a directive. Doesn't matter who called 911."

"But the car is registered in his name. It's his property." I hated that I sounded like a cheap lawyer. I added in a lower voice, "Sir, he's already on probation. More charges will really mess him up."

"Look, ma'am, he's not charged with destruction of property, so it doesn't matter that the car is technically his." His voice was no longer as patient. But then he glanced again at my uniform and steered me away from his cruiser and Ted's ears. "Ma'am, because he's on probation, he'll probably get some time for this. Which may not be such a bad thing. It'll give you some time to think about what we'd be dealing with if you had been in the car when he went off." He looked hard at me, as if making sure I understood. Then he turned back to his vehicle and drove Ted away.

It wasn't until the patrol car turned out of the parking lot that I fully realized what the officer said to me. Maybe Ted didn't mean to hurt me physically this time; maybe messing up my car would have been enough for him. But he sure as hell said to me, 'this one's for you' as he hit my quarter panel. Those words scared me real bad. The punches Ted gave me before this were with his fist, not with a baseball bat.

I clutched the grocery bag to my chest, refusing to cry. My family had already provided enough entertainment for the Walmart shoppers. I didn't cry, at all, not even when the apples spilled out of the bag and bounced on the asphalt. One rolled toward the gutter.

Sour Cream

Mrs. Kelly's Story

Sometimes the best decisions are ones not made.

One

I had finished with my knee surgeries and rehab. And like Sharon asked, I did think about taking my biscuit making skills to McDonalds' instead of returning to prison work. After all, not only did cooking skills qualify me, but after two prison riots, I had the combat skills needed for Saturday night robberies under the Golden Arches.

But the prison system had paid for my treatment, so truth be told, I felt some obligation to return. They treated me well, and it felt right to stay loyal. Of course, I carried some definite negatives with me, like pain, fear, and betrayal, but there was no need to think about such things today. Today was a new day.

Today was my first day back at work, sweating in the steam of another prison cafeteria. But I   was no longer bruised and limping, so I was happy to be working again. Sharon said I'd changed since the riot, that I had lost my innocence, whatever that means. I thought it was just the lawyer in her, trying to get me a bigger settlement. In fact, my innocence had been missing for a while. My eyes were as open as any sixty-year-old widow lady's could be, framed as they were by crows' feet and turkey wattles. Experience was a comfortable friend with me. More of a friend than Investigator Joe Brown, who totally disappeared after that riot.

I thought we had a real friendship, maybe even, kind of, how shall I say this delicately? A *spark*. But after our brief contact during the chaos, I had heard nothing from him. Not a call, not a card, no flowers, nothing. It was like I served a useful purpose for him, gathering information, and that was all he wanted.

The Internal Affairs staff handled all of the follow up criminal charges on the inmates and the dirty sergeant. I only had to testify once in court. It was at that court hearing that I heard another investigator tell the judge, "The primary investigator, Joe Brown, has been temporarily reassigned out of state, so we will present the evidence of the case in his absence".

Only then did I stop expecting him to make a surprise Perry Mason appearance in the courtroom. The judge proceeded to find the sergeant guilty of trafficking drugs in a prison, but only gave him a light sentence since he had no prior criminal record. But of course, he didn't have a prior record; he had to have a clean record to get the prison job in the first place. My head was spinning from the crazy logic.

At the trial's lunch break, I walked by myself to a Mexican restaurant and ate tacos. I felt too sad to enjoy the day's pleasant weather - sad because of the outcome of the trial. Then I felt even more sad when I dribbled taco sauce on my good Hillary jacket. But when I got up to leave and realized that I was walking around town like a normal person with no knee pain, I had to admit that for me personally, the past months had been good. So freedom from pain, and my new confidence in my health, definitely had to be added to my blessings list. But given the court's ruling and the absence of Joe Brown, my list was shorter than I wished, even if I included the guacamole dip, which was really delicious.

A follow up article in the newspaper repeated what Gray Suit had said at the hospital, that prison crimes are particularly hard to solve. The paper made a big deal about the guilty verdict for the sergeant, but it didn't mention anyone in town being charged for arranging the actual throw over. It was as if all the drama and danger of those weeks were now filed away with lots of loose ends, and with the prison staff now distracted by the current dangers of the day.

I had filed it away in my memory file and I was ready to move on, except for the puzzle of Joe Brown. It bothered me that I had so misjudged our friendship. But, oh well, that was past, and there was no need for me to whine like the sputter of a country song.

My job in this different prison had just opened up. The former cook had his guard unit suddenly called up for Afghanistan, and the prison needed someone with experience supervising inmates, and well, that would be me. I had to smile at the notion that this old girl was now described with words like "supervise" and "experience". I felt proud that I wasn't just the "new lady" anymore.

This facility was actually an old prison farm, the kind in the movie *Cool Hand Luke*. It had housed inmates for more than a hundred years. In the older cell blocks, the cement floors had ridges and grooves from the decades of inmates dragging their shackles. Most of the place was now modernized and run more like a farm business than a secure prison. It was surrounded by acres of corn and row crops but also had a dairy and a hog lot. It provided dairy products for prisons all over the state. The central office allowed the cafeteria the flexibility to serve what was in season. It was a perfect farm-to-table kitchen, without the trendiness.

New drywall and metal roofs had scared out most of the ghosts from the past, but from where I stood on my first day, looking out from the cafeteria serving line, I saw hundreds of raggedy boots slumped at tables, and streaks of muddy footprints on the linoleum. Maybe this was a farming operation, but it was still definitely a prison.

Just like the lyrics say in Johnny Cash's song, "There ain't no such thing as a good chain gang." Maybe the inmates here had shorter sentences than at the max prison, but it was clear that while they were here, they were field hands or fed slop to the hogs or brought the cows in for milking. In the old days, it would have been called a work farm, and maybe in the real old days, it might have been called worse.

I saw an inmate worker who had been in the corner for at least thirty minutes, standing by his mop bucket. His work boots were shiny - a sign that they had not been actually used for work. The water in his bucket was dirty from last night's meal, which was also not a good sign of his work skills.

So I walked over to him and said in my nicest voice, "You need to empty that bucket. Then fill it with clean water and mop the floor. We're too busy to take a break right now."

He looked at me like I had spoke Swiss Mandarin. "What?"

he asked, his eyes squinty at the effort of speaking so early in the morning.

I moved closer to him and introduced myself. "Good morning. I am Mrs. Kelly, the new supervisor here. Since you already have the bucket, please fill it with clean water and mop the floor."

He looked surprised at my intrusion and said, "Well, actually, this isn't my bucket. I'm just minding it for a buddy. My job is carrots, not the floor."

So then I looked at him with my "why does everything have to be so difficult?" look, which isn't hard at all for me to produce at any time during the day. I asked him, "What's your name?"

"Joshua," he answered, with no expression.

It always made me sad to hear prisoner names that are "special," that sounded like some sweet mother had really high hopes for her new baby son. Names like Matthew, or Junior, or Jonathan, or Ezekiel, and yes, Joshua, these are special names. And Joe. Joe is a good name. *Hmm, didn't I know a Joe at one recent time?* Never mind, that busload of thoughts was too distracting.

"Well, Joshua, it's good to meet you. My way of doing things in the kitchen is that there are no specialists. Everyone will do carrots, and everyone does floors. So you need to get the clean water and get started."

He stared at me, and I stared back longer. Then he slowly dragged the bucket to the faucet, taking care to keep his shiny boots from getting splashed. If I was his ma, I'd be folding my arms to keep from popping him upside his head and while at the same time, chewing my lip to hold back tears, remembering the shiny hope I had at the time of his birth.

Supervising inmates was a lot like managing a crew of prima donnas. Some inmates, like Joshua simply didn't like to work. Some inmates, like Ernest at my old prison, were great workers, and took as much pride on the job as a member of the Chamber of Commerce. Those kind of inmate workers used work as a way to make their time go faster. Ernest's day would not be good if the rice turned out sticky or if the milk soured. And of course, there were inmates who came to work for their own reasons, like to make a deal, move contraband and steal food to resell, basically all the same moves that got them to prison in the first place.

As I watched Joshua's slow mopping, I looked out over the dining room. From my view, it was clear that these inmates had got their prison time due to drugs. There was one corner filled with young guys, most missing teeth from their meth use. Gumming their morning grits was a dental challenge. It would be even more of a sport if the budget provided some stringy bacon to up the degree of difficulty for chewing. Watching them eat gave me a flash forward to the nursing home of my nightmares. Since becoming a bureaucrat, calculating my pension was my new hobby. If I could stay with the prison system long enough, I'd have a nicer senility.

In another corner of the dining hall sat a bunch of guys dumb enough to sell marijuana on street corners near schools, a charge which carried serious prison time. Comparing levels of dumbness, the meth users, in addition to losing their teeth, also lost their minds. They were too dumb to even find a street corner. Lucky for them, the meth runner delivered to their rusted-out trailers, kind of like the convenience of the Avon Lady.

If the marijuana dealers had changed their business model and moved down a few blocks from schools to avoid the additional ten-year sentence, they would still be on the street on probation. Of course, their smart lawyers didn't suggest that to them since it would cut into their fees.

While I watched these two groups and wished for the entertainment value of a meth user asking a drug dealer to 'please pass the salt,' a young woman entered the cafeteria. It was that librarian, Faith Miller.

She wore a saggy brown sweater buttoned over a droopy beige skirt. She paused at the doorway and looked around with a half-smile, half-frown. She didn't look thrilled to be here, but she did not seem particularly frightened either. When she saw me, the smile became firmer, and she headed across the dining hall toward me. Midway across, she slipped on the greasy floor and fell on her skinny behind.

"Oh, my goodness," I muttered as I rushed toward her. Most inmates stayed in their seats, staring at the unexpected gift of her legs flashing. Only Joshua, the carrot specialist, got his shiny boots to her before I did.

"Thanks, Joshua, I'll help her up. You can stand over there," I told him as I bent to help her up. Her face was red, but she wasn't crying.

As she struggled to get up, I whispered, "Whatever you do, don't cry. Just smile and follow me." I leaned in close to her as we walked away from the serving line to the staff office in the back of the kitchen. As she entered, she tripped over a case of canned tuna by the door, and in the process, spilled papers from a tote she carried. I was glad she herself hadn't fallen again, and I hurried to scoop up what papers I found on the floor. I handed them and the small books back to her, and she stuffed them in her tote.

"Here, sit down in this chair and I'll get you some water. By the way, in case you don't remember from orientation, I'm Mrs. Kelly .We sat together at the orientation meeting. Of course that's been a while." She smiled and nodded.

"Are you okay from your fall? Maybe you should get checked out at the medical clinic."

"No, no, I'm fine. I'm just so embarrassed. I do remember meeting you. I'm Faith Miller. I finally got hired on as a librarian, and this is my first day on the job. I came over to the cafeteria for a cup of coffee." She looked out the office window at the cafeteria floor and asked, "What do you think the inmates will think about me falling?" She didn't sound particularly flustered, just curious.

"Oh, don't worry. It happened so fast, most of them didn't even notice." I lied, knowing for certain that most of the inmates surely did notice her fall, also knowing that they definitely admired the red thong she wore under her boring beige skirt.

Two

After Faith Miller's dramatic first day on the job, I was so tempted to call Wilma to fill her in on her favorite mystery girl, I had to 'bout slap my own hand. But I am really squeamish about passing on juicy gossip. I try to be a pretty good person, but Lord knows, I can be plenty bad. But with gossip, I'm afraid of voodoo karma, or bad juju beans, or whatever that is that will cause needles to be stuck in my spine. Of course, I have no problem being on the hearing end of gossip, able to suck my teeth even without my church hat on. Once I worked with a lady who baked pies in a café where I fried catfish. When I'd claim to not know new gossip, she'd say, "Girl, you're just no fun." But when she filled me in on the latest about the owner and his wife and his girlfriend, I was all ears.

So I resisted calling Wilma to fill her in about Faith, but I sure wished she would call me. Then I could slip in, "Oh, by the way, you'll never guess what happened to Faith." Then we could go at it. I know, it makes no sense, but it makes me feel holier than I have a right to feel.

Anyway, a few days had passed since Faith had been in the cafeteria, and I continued to puzzle over her. I wondered why an attractive young girl dressed like a nun just released from her convent.

Not that I am some fashionista, with my work uniform as flattering as an igloo. At my age, I unfortunately no longer sizzle or even steam, but still, I try not to wear a shroud.

Something didn't make sense about Faith.

Then, unexpectedly, she showed up again. She walked quickly up to the serving line with no drama. She smiled at me and said, "Hi, Mrs. Kelly, do you have any coffee left?" While she smiled, she looked out over the inmates in the kitchen, as if looking for someone. The inmates looked back at her, as if they hoped for her to fall again and brighten their day. I interrupted their trances and told them to get back to work. I looked for Joshua to tell him to keep mopping, but I didn't see him. I figured he must have found a new place to hide, so I'd leave my fuss with him until later and take a coffee break with Faith.

"Of course, I've always got the coffee pot on for staff. Let's go back into the office where it's not so noisy." The small office had a big window view of the inmate workers, so while I visited with her, I could keep my eye on the inmate workers who were still cleaning up from breakfast.

After she settled in with her coffee, I asked her, "So, Miss Miller, how's your first week going over in the library?" Today she had on a black version of her earlier brown ensemble, and I almost smiled, wondering what color lingerie she had on underneath.

She leaned forward and said, "Please call me Faith. The job's going all right. I actually came by to thank you for being so nice to me when I fell. You were such a comfort. You seem to be one of those people who knows just the right thing to say." She said this in a sweet, sugary voice, only a little above a whisper.

It felt good to hear such nice words, especially since I'm such a busybody, and rarely, in fact, do say the right thing. But she gave me the compliment as if she had memorized the words from a script she practiced in front of a mirror before she came to see me. I tried to quiet my harsh opinion, remembering that I'd been the new person on plenty of jobs and felt nervous about how I would be seen.

I smiled back, and assured her, "It's no big deal. Once you get used to inmates, you find that their behavior is far more startling than ours is. You never know what might happen on any day. That's why I like prison work. There's always something interesting going on. Is this your first time working in a prison?"

She leaned back in her chair, with her long black skirt catching the dust and flour from the floor. "Well, it's the first time I've actually worked *in* a prison, but as a child I used to travel around with my family to prisons all over the state. We had a singing ministry called the Angel Choir. My daddy drove the bus and my mama coached my two sisters and me in our harmony. At Christmas we had so many bookings, we weren't hardly off the road."

Faith fidgeted with her coffee cup, as if surprised that she had given this much information about herself.

"My goodness," I said, "I never knew they let children come in as volunteers. They must have changed the rules in recent years, since that's sure not allowed now. I imagine that must have been frightening for you little girls." I paused and added, "No disrespect intended towards your parents." In fact, I thought parents who exposed their little ones to prison life in such a way were plenty ignorant, but I didn't want to be rude to Faith.

She smiled an almost real smile and answered, "Yeah, it wasn't a very good idea. You would think that the prison chaplains would have better sense than to set up such shows. Or maybe they enjoyed it as much as the inmates, which is creepy. But whenever the inmates got enough money together for a love offering, the chaplains called on our daddy to provide the love." She giggled and said, "Oh, excuse me, that's how us sisters described it. The advertising pamphlet called it our 'family ministry for musical prayer.'"

At this point, I thought it was a good idea to change the topic to talk about the weather. I started to ask her what she thought about the rain that was expected for the weekend when she got up to pour herself another cup of coffee. As she poured, she kept her eyes on the inmates through the window. She spoke more about those family trips, and as she did, her voice had a sing-song tone to it, like she was telling a story and not really talking to me.

"Daddy drove the broke down bus and collected the money. Mama helped us three girls get ready to be blessed angels up on the chapel alter. Sweaty inmates stared at us as the spotlight shined through the tutus of our skirts. Our leotard tops fit so tight across the chest, I could hardly raise the tambourine as high as mama wanted. The inmates in the front rows smiled and clapped as we sang, but we didn't want to even think about the hands of the inmates in the dark back rows."

Faith stood still, with her back to me and her eyes still on the inmates. Most of me knew that she needed to stop talking about those family days, but part of me could see that she seemed to need to talk about them. I stayed quiet as she went on.

"When I turned twelve, I finally understood the whole deal. That year I wanted to wear a cardigan sweater over my costume, but mama said it ruined the effect of the costume. I lied to her and said the weather made me shiver. But it didn't work. "

Faith's voice started to rise. "Mama went off on an absolute rant. She screamed that since our bodies were temples of the Lord, we needed to be humble about such holy vessels. She even said since they were temples of the Lord, we should be proud to share our innocence with the downtrodden." As Faith finished her story, her voice rose to a crooning sound, like an evangelical guy on television. Then she got quiet. She seemed to realize that she had gotten lost in her memories.

"I just wish we could have sung in the neighborhood church down the road from us. But, so be it."

Well, I had nothing to say. Faith didn't speak either, but she had no tears. I felt like an audience member at a Dr. Phil show. I felt bad for her exposure. And I felt guilty for my earlier silly thoughts about her lingerie. It pricked my conscience that I had made light of her private life, even though I hadn't known it was so complicated.

What I didn't feel at all bad about was thinking of her parents as stupid asses. I stood and collected our coffee cups, rinsing them in the small office sink, wanting to be busy.

I turned to her and said, "Your schooling as a librarian puts you in a good field for jobs." I didn't want to be rude by changing the subject, but I really thought we needed to talk about something else, so it was either jobs, the economy, or the weather. And my earlier reference to weather hadn't worked so well.

"Yes, my sister Chastity pestered me to finish my degree. She kept at me to take the scholarship money I was offered and run out of town. Of course, by that time, Daddy had died from meanness, and it had been years since our baby sister Patience was able to go on stage with us. The cuts she liked to make on her arms didn't look good in the shine of the show lights. For a while, mama struggled to fix our costumes so her cuts wouldn't show, but sweet Patience could always find a new place to cut. She never tried my sweater trick. She already knew it wouldn't work."

I went over to Faith and laid a hand on her arm. "You have had a road to struggle, and I understand that. But I think we both better get back to work. Maybe tomorrow you'll come back for another cup of coffee. Then you can tell me more about your college studies. I've never really understood how librarians do what they do."

I babbled on about librarians because I knew Faith didn't need to stay in her head with her memories. In a prison, it's safer to stay focused on what's in front of you. If a staff person is distracted about worries outside of work, work can get dangerous.

Faith looked at her watch and said, "My goodness, Mrs. Kelly, why did you let me go on this way for so long? I need to get over to open the library. Thanks for being such a good listener."

She started to leave, but at the door, turned back. "Actually, I do have one quick question about work. You asked how I'm doing on the job. In fact, I do have a little problem. It's been hard learning all the rules and being responsible for so many locks and keys. What would happen if I lost a key?"

I gave her a sharp look. Keys are a very big deal in a prison. If you lost one, then an inmate could find it and have access to somewhere that he's not supposed to be. If you think you have lost one, you need to report it to security right away. Even if you find it later, the sooner they know there might be a problem, the quicker they can respond. I know the phone number if you want to call them now."

"Thanks, but let me double-check first. It could be on my other key ring. But if I don't have it, I'll call security, just like you said."

She smiled at me like I was the clerk at Belk's who gave her directions to the ladies' room. She thanked me again, and headed toward the cafeteria exit. As she left, I realized that while Faith told me too much about herself, I still didn't understand why she chose to work in a prison. Logically, I figured a prison would be the last place she'd want to work.

It looked like Wilma had been right. Faith Miller did have some "issues."

While Faith and I had talked, I felt embarrassed to see her skirt dirtied by the mess on the office floor. After she left, I grabbed the broom for a quick sweep before going back out on the floor to wrangle inmates. When I reached back into the corner under the counter, loose papers, dust, flour balls, and a bunch of mouse turds came out.

I checked to see if the papers needed to be filed or trashed, and saw that they were not cafeteria paperwork, but ones that spilled from Faith's tote during her first visit. I thought I had found them all when she tripped, but I knew from the happy face stickers that these belonged to her. When I'd seen the stickers that first day, I'd thought it was quaint that a prison librarian used such stickers. But now that I knew her story, any cute in quaint was long gone. I gathered the papers together to give to her the next time she came to the office for coffee, but then noticed a paragraph in her handwriting about the prison.

And, yes, I read it. So sue me.

The question about why she came to work in a prison was answered in one of the pages, which were not file papers, but pages from a loose-leaf diary. I figured if she can write trash, then I can read it.

This was the part that caught my eye. "I am really glad that I finally got the prison job. Not that it will be much of a job. I plan to spend all day every day sitting at my desk, reading my vampire stories. When an inmate asks for help, I'll point him to the legal reference shelf. That's it, that will be extent of my librarianism. Most of those inmates can't half-read anyway. But even with the low salary of the job, my side projects will pay well. In a few months, I'll have enough cash for a down payment on a new Mustang. The one I'm driving now is nice, but it doesn't have heated seats, and it's last year's model."

When I read that last sentence, I shook my head. To Wilma's eye, Faith's Mustang had been perfect when she'd seen it that one time at the prison, and then the other week downtown. But I guess Faith had fancier taste. One woman's pie ala mode was another woman's mushy cobbler.

I read on toward the last paragraph of her note. "I need to be careful about drawing attention to myself. The more invisible I am, the better the side projects will work. Of course, I don't know exactly what opportunities will develop, but whatever they are, I don't need to have my name out there for the staff to be talking about me. The only attention I want is from inmates with money. So, this job will fit me fine. I sure as hell know about prison life, and now I don't have to bang that dumb tambourine."

Good grief. I didn't understand what her plan was, but I knew that when a prison staff person talked about getting money from inmates, disaster followed. Faith talked so sweet, but it was just the devil trying to get out. But the devil's going to be the devil, so I knew I needed to do something before there was a big problem. At my old prison, I would have called Joe Brown and rushed the notes to him. But since he chose to not be around anymore, I didn't even sniffle when I reached for the phone to call security. But as I fumbled for the receiver, the loudspeaker blared.

"Roll call count. All inmates line up to be counted immediately. Count is to be done by name. All inmates must be accounted for." Then the speaker repeated the message.

Counts in prison were a very big deal, on the same level of importance as keys. We had to always keep track of the inmates assigned to our areas. Usually counts took place at regular intervals during the day, unless something unusual happened. To have a count right now, meant something unusual had happened.

My co-worker, Mel, who had stayed on the floor while I'd been in the office with Faith Miller, helped me with the count. We matched our roster names with those present, and did it again, and then again. With each recount, Inmate Shiny Boots Joshua did not show in line, nor could we find him in our area.

As I headed toward the office to call this into the control room, the yard lieutenant rushed into the dining room, flushed and breathing hard. I turned around and met him by the iced tea machine.

"Sorry to rush you, but have you finished your count yet?" As he asked, he leaned against the serving rail to catch his breath. I handed him a glass of tea.

"Yes, Lieutenant, we were just now calling it in. It looks like we are definitely down one inmate. I thought he might have gone off to sleep somewhere and missed the call for count, but he's not in our building. What's going on?"

Quickly he filled me in. "A farmer nearby was planting some acres not far from our fence. He thought he saw a young man dressed in a white jumpsuit come out of the tree line. He couldn't be sure it was an inmate, but he called the prison to see if we had anyone missing."

The lieutenant gulped his tea and reached for his radio to call his supervisor. We both knew that only inmates assigned to work in the cafeteria wore white work uniforms. That's why the lieutenant came to our area right away to check our count results.

When he keyed his radio to call in our count shortage, he only got the static crackle of bad reception. He told me in a rush before he went outside for better radio reception, "We've got the search team called to stake-out posts, and the tracking dogs have already possibly picked up a scent from the library gate, which wasn't locked. So now that we know it's your inmate who went missing, hopefully we can wrap this up pretty quickly."

Oh, dear. I was no Einstein, but Dallas, we had a problem. It looked like Little Miss Fancy Pants really messed up. Before the lieutenant could get out the door, I called him back.

"Wait up a minute, LT. I may have some more information for you."

I briefed him on what Faith Miller asked about the key problem and her note about using inmates for "special projects". The lieutenant grinned at the prospect of his promotion for gathering the background information and rushed off with the notes I gave him in his pocket to tell his chain of command.

Shortly, they pulled our inmates back to their living areas. Mel and I sat alone together in the kitchen. We felt a little embarrassed that our inmate had escaped, but we were relieved that it wasn't our error. After we had spent enough time worrying about it, we made a few sandwiches for the stakeout team. I felt sad not having my best inmate worker from my old job helping us through this emergency. I missed Ernest, and I missed that gosh-darn Joe Brown.

My go-to guys had done gone.

Outside the cafeteria windows, the rain made puddles in the marshy fields on the other side of the fence. Drips of dull silver fell from the fence's razor wire, like leftover holiday tinsel caught in suspended time.

The rain would make tracking hard for the dogs and miserable for the stake-outs. Mel and I put on another pot of coffee, and quitting time became evening as we sat, waiting.

Three

Mel drove the old white van usually used to carry milk from the dairy to the cafeteria. It didn't have the flashing lights of an armored SWAT vehicle, but it got us into the field to bring meal bags out to the stake-out officers. Mel and I didn't know each other well yet, but he seemed like a nice enough guy. He was maybe a little excitable, always sure the inmates would riot if the tea dispenser ran dry. From my experience, inmates certainly did riot, but more likely over money and drugs than iced tea.

We loaded the coffee urn into the van, along with the bags of ham and turkey sandwiches. It seemed sweet, in a vintage way, to provide such a service, like an old timey horse drawn produce peddler's wagon, making its slow route down country roads. The officers would appreciate the food since they'd been stuck for hours under the trees in the swamp. They had their own duffels with toilet paper and bug spray tucked in with their extra ammo, but they had well earned some fresh food.

Mel propped his shotgun in the back, and I had mine across my lap, broken open. It was escape policy that any employees in the search area were required to carry weapons. During training class, they had accuracy requirements for people not used to weapons. At home, my shotgun lived in my hall closet, so I enjoyed the class. It gave me a chance to practice shooting with the state's ammo.

We had a map of all the stake-out positions and had already gone to two of them. Our next stop brought us further into the swamp, on dirt roads lined by shallow ditches. Beyond the ditches, heavy brush and tangled vines blocked our view past a few yards, and, of course, kudzu draped like an umbrella over everything in its reach. With the swamp waters shallow, gators probably hid further inland, but since the ditches along the road still held water from the day's rainstorm, even with no gators, nature squealed and flitted and slithered with snakes and frogs and what all. The rain had the "what all" stirring, so beyond the van's headlights, we heard the noises of twilight above the squeal of the van's transmission.

We pulled up a little past a fork in the road to check our map, being careful to follow the procedure for dropping supplies. The most important thing was to be as quiet as possible, so if the escapee hid close by, we wouldn't give away the stake-out's position.

Mel spoke in a low voice. "You got the last delivery, Mrs. Kelly, so I'll take this one. Just let me stretch my legs first before I unload the food."

"Thanks, Mel. If you need more bug spray, there's some in the back." Of course I knew that "stretch my legs" was man code for needing to pee.

He took the ignition key with him as he swung his pudgy legs out of the van and moved further down the road. I used the sleeve of my uniform to clear fog from the window, and watched from the side mirror as Mel disappeared from sight when he rounded a bend.

Through the window I saw a big toad hop into the ditch on my side of the road, and then heard a muffled yell and a splash. At first, I thought the frog made the noise, but then I worried that maybe Mel had slipped into the ditch. So I got out to check on him, deciding to ignore the etiquette of seeing him struggle in the mud with his little thingy drawing gnats and no-see-ums. *What a vision*, I grinned. Because of the need for silence, I couldn't holler out to him. I took the shotgun with me, in case a water moccasin had startled Mel instead of a toad.

As I rounded the corner of the van, I saw Mel on the ground a few yards down the road by the bend. I also saw escapee Joshua, standing over him, leaning down for the key to the van which Mel had in his hand. The inmate turned and started toward the van as I chambered the shotgun.

The shock-a-lock sound made him pause. We stared at each other.

"You'd best throw those keys my way." My shaky voice did not sound at all like the one secret agent Angelina Jolie used right before she kick-boxed the enemy. But I stood tall and held the shotgun on him.

He smiled. "Mrs. Kelly, I don't want to hurt you. I just need the van. Put the gun down, and I'll drive away."

The voice he used sounded like what he probably used to wheedle his auntie and granny as he went through their purses, looking for their social security money. In fact, I'd heard the same voice from the insurance adjuster as he explained why, so unfortunately, my policy didn't cover the hail damage to my trailer's roof. And I'd heard the same twang from the guy who fixed my carburetor, which didn't stay fixed. All those voices just needed us little old ladies to be reasonable.

"You need to sit down in the road, and toss those keys to me." This time my voice was stronger.

"Come on, Mrs. Kelly, you know you're not going to shoot me. You're just a lady cook. You're not even part of security. You'd shoot your own foot off if you pulled that trigger."

"I've been shooting squirrels out of oak trees since I was a child. Now sit down and be quiet." I fired into the air to let the stake-out know our location, just as Joshua took a long step toward me. As I shifted my weight to fire toward him, the bloodhound-tracking dog rushed out of the woods, barking and smacking at Joshua's knees. Then the stakeout rushed past from behind me, and shoved Joshua down into the muzzle of the happy dog. With the stakeout officer, the dog handler, and the dog, our little bend in the road grew to a nice little crowd. Plus Mel, of course, still lying with one foot in the ditch.

"Mrs. Kelly, are you okay?" The officer skidded to a stop beside me. The dog handler looked up from gathering in the dog's leash and also spoke.

"You look like a swamp version of a frontier woman."

"I'm fine, but please check Mel. He maybe had a darn heart attack."

Noises erupted from the men's radios, and a siren blared in the distance.

The dog handler pulled a dog treat from his cargo pants for the dog who sat staring at Joshua on the ground, drooling with a big dog smile. "We picked up this guy's scent about a mile back and were gaining ground on him when I heard your voices and then the gunshot. We were just on the other side of the brush."

Together the men cuffed Joshua and laid him out in the road, not far from a fire ant hill. I stood close by, and Joshua gave me a dirty look. Any escape carries an automatic ten-year sentence, added to whatever time the inmate started with. No parole, no time off for successfully using his pretty voice to convince a judge of his specialness. The look Joshua gave me didn't show him thinking of his future flashing by. Instead, it showed his fear that his future would crawl by, very, very, slowly. Before I turned away, I mentioned to him, "You got your boots muddy."

By now, Mel was sitting up on his own and took a little water from the stakeout officer's canteen. But he couldn't talk yet.

I headed back to the van. As I went, I slipped a little in the mud and decided that the back fender was a fine place to rest. I didn't think I could make it as far as the front seat. My hands shook, and I felt clammy. On top of that, mud had splashed on the new work shoes I had just ordered from QVC. My other work shoes got trashed during the riot. This job was definitely hard on my footwear wardrobe.

For a few minutes, while the officers were busy with the inmate and talking on their radios, I rested on the fender. I tried to find my game face, but if I'd been near a mirror, I knew my game face would have the look of a constipated goat.

Soon, with the arrival of several state vehicles and an ambulance, our deserted road had a traffic jam. The ambulance crew jumped out with a stretcher for Mel, who seemed to be more alert. He gave me a weak smile and a little wave.

Then another car came roaring down the road with its blue lights flashing. As it tried to stop, it slid in the mud, swerving not far from me. Through its windshield, I tried to see what hot-shot drove too fast into our cluster of people. *If I had the energy*, I thought, *I'd like to bless him out.*

The driver jumped out of the car in an angry rush and hurried toward me. I saw that it was Joe Brown. And he was not smiling.

"Mrs. Kelly, we meet up again," he said in a very serious voice. He held out his hand for the shotgun I'd forgotten I still held. I tried to hand it to him, but my fingers didn't know how to get unwrapped from the stock. My brain and my hand had stopped their connection. Then Joe Brown calmly held the barrel until my fingers decided they could safely let go.

He passed it on to an officer nearby and said, "This will need to be processed as evidence."

Then he crouched down in front of me and asked, "Do you want the EMTs to check you out?"

"Oh, no, I'm fine, just a little winded," I answered, trying to sound casual, as if I'd walked too fast in the mall.

"I'm sure you are. But it wouldn't hurt to have your blood pressure checked."

"No, really, I'm fine. Can I leave now?" Even I could hear the shiver in my voice. Everything I needed was not here: a hot bath, my blue slippers, and a call to Sharon.

He offered his arm to pull me up from the van's fender, and said with a small smile, "It's good to see you again."

As I stood up, I slipped again, and he grabbed my shoulder. Just like he had during the riot. *Well, now, be still my heart.* Was I dizzy because my blood pressure was spiraling up and down, or because it felt good to lean against the previously missing Mr. Investigator Joe Brown his own self?

As he held on to me, he said, "Let's have you and Mel go on to the hospital in the ambulance. We'll worry about paperwork later."

With that, the EMTs put me on a gurney. I remembered the last time I'd ridden in an ambulance, after the riot. I just laid my head down and rested.

Good grief.

Four

The hospital only kept me long enough to get my blood pressure back to normal. Mel didn't need to be admitted either, which probably disappointed him. It kind of took some of the gravy off the story he'd be eating out on for the rest of his life.

The worst part of being at the hospital was calling Sharon to pick me up. One of the signs of getting old was worrying about your daughter being mad at your old foolish self, instead of the other way around. As a kid, Sharon didn't give Tom and I much reason to be upset. Unlike our status, where I provide her lots of opportunities to be unhappy with me.

But even though she disapproves of me a lot of the time, she never lets me down. Tonight, she'd just gotten home and dressed to go out with a new guy when I called from the emergency room.

"Mom, let me get this straight. You have been back at work for less than a week, and you are again in the hospital due to your job. I can't believe it. This has got to stop. I'll be right there to pick you up. We can talk about it on the drive back."

"Sharon, hon, it's okay. I'm not in the hospital exactly, just *at* the hospital. I can go home, but my car's still at the prison since I came here in an ambulance."

"Mom, I'm on my way."

She brought an afghan with her and tucked it around me. When I settled in her car, she turned the heat up high. On the drive home, I pretended to be too tired to do much talking. I did give her the story of the escape. She held my hand while she drove too fast, which felt so good I didn't even mention that she should keep both hands on the wheel. I kept my mouth shut, which proved I wasn't a total fool. The dangerous sink holes of our relationship dotted the landscape ahead of us, with no daisies in sight.

Sharon looked nice for her date. She wore a red top with gathers at the scooped out neckline. The ladies on QVC call it ruching. It's a new fashion trend, but probably not yet at Walmart. The ruching made her look busty, a good thing for her, but not so much for me in my plus sized styles. I smiled as she caught me looking at her, and I thought how nice it would be to have some grandkids. With just the two of us in our family, there's not a lot of wiggle room. Without the added focus of kids and husbands, she and I didn't give each other much room for error.

When she got me home, she walked me to the door, holding my arm across the driveway like I'd aged before her eyes.

"Mom, why don't you sit in your recliner while I draw a bath for you? Then I'll heat up some soup."

I knew Sharon wanted to help me, and it would be a kindness to let her, but I had a powerful need to take care of myself, in a slow, pokey way, with no one else around. I wanted to be sure that even though I felt fragile while sitting on the van's bumper earlier that evening, I could bounce back to my normal self with just a little time. Time, a hot bath, and then to bed. That's what I needed.

"Sharon, there's an old Irish proverb that says 'A good laugh and a long sleep are the best cures for anything.' I don't feel much like laughing, but bed sounds good, and I can find my own way there. And if you hurry, you won't be so late for your date."

She didn't argue, either for her own interests or for mine. Though her reason wasn't clear, it was welcome.

When she turned to leave, she hugged me and whispered, "Mom, we still need to talk, but I'm proud of you."

Once inside, I stood in my living room and let the quiet and familiar comfort me. In the years since Tom's death, I had made only a few changes in our trailer. When he was alive, he didn't like change much. If he liked something, he liked it forever. He didn't see the point in updating or switching around or in any of the other phrases I used to nudge him to be more flexible. He liked what he liked, and that was that.

Mostly it wasn't worth fussing with him to redecorate, but since he'd been gone, it had been fun to shop at yard sales for bargains. Finds like the big brass lamp in the corner I got from a sale over in the rich part of town made me happy. Now I switched it on and admired the welcoming glow. Most of the rest of the furniture had been there long enough that when I looked at old family photos, the room behind us still looked the same. Tonight it gave me comfort to know that Tom put his feet on this same couch when he slept during ballgames, and that Sharon spilled nail polish on the rug by the table. I felt like an archeologist, enjoying the sniff of dust from old times.

Still, despite my nostalgia, the couch needed recovering. The slipcover on it had slipped a notch from shabby chic to just plain shabby. The overtime pay from tonight's escape would make a nice bonus in my next paycheck. I thought I might get a floral print for the couch cover, with cabbage roses and peonies. The JC Penney's catalog had one like that featured on their cover. But I worried it might look too old lady-ish. Of course, at that moment, I felt like an old lady.

I never admitted to Sharon, but these work adventures were kind of tiring. I was all right in the middle of the action, but afterwards, whew, I felt pooped. And pretending to be fine was even more tiring. During the escape, all I wanted to do while sitting on that bumper was cry and shake and be a mess. Thank heavens, I limited it to just shaking.

Leaning against my raggedy couch, I slipped off my shoes. The dried mud would probably scrape off so I could salvage them. Just then, the doorbell rang. I thought it must be Sharon, coming back with some food. But through the window next to the door, I saw Joe Brown.

"My, my, my. Now I see you twice in one night. It must be trouble that brings you around. Anyway, come in. I just got home."

"Yeah, I know. I called the hospital as soon as I finished the interviews and read the report. They said you'd been released. I'm glad you're all right."

I led him from the door to the living room, where, from behind his back, he drew out a bouquet of mums. "I thought these might be nice for you. I hope you like red. It's all that was left at the Pig this late at night."

For a second, I worried my blood pressure had disoriented me and that I was rambling around in my daydreams, only wishing this was real. But then the lamp light shined on the Piggly Wiggly cellophane wrapped around the flowers, and their dumb pig mascot on the sticker was smiling in my living room.

"They are beautiful. This is so nice of you. It *is really* good to see you again." I said this sincerely, but then worried it might sound sarcastic. "I mean, I wondered where you'd got to these last months. Then when you showed up tonight with the escape team, I was really surprised."

"Well, we need to talk about that." As he spoke, he fiddled with his key ring. "Here's what happened. Just as the riot ended, the central office sent me out of state for an undercover job. A prison in Maryland had their own big contraband problem, with the local sheriff involved in smuggling in drugs. So I had to be his new best friend in order to get proof to indict him. The operation there went fine, but the whole time, I felt bad because usually after a disturbance, I get with the people who helped me and fill them in on what all happened with the investigation."

He still stood in the middle of the room. He had a look on his face like he had a piece to say, and we couldn't get comfortable or casual until he got it said.

"It's always personal for me when staff risk themselves to help me do my job. But when I transferred out of state so quick, I didn't get a chance to get with you. I knew that other Internal Affairs staff would meet with you, and I told them to be sure to reassure you about Ernest. Then, I wanted to send a personal message to you, but each time I scribbled a note, it sounded like a printed Christmas card a politician sends, 'Thanks for your help. Will be in touch next time I need something.' So I put it off, and put it off, expecting to make it home earlier than now, and I could see you in person to thank you. But the Maryland deal kept getting strung out with delays, so I couldn't pull out. Anyway, I'm sorry to deliver my thanks so late. And I'm sorry to be so clumsy about it."

"I did wonder what happened. I appreciated you looking for me in the riot, but then after you grabbed me, you slipped away and were gone. It was puzzling."

He put his keys in his pocket and seemed more at ease. "When I pulled into town today, just getting in from Maryland, I heard about the escape on my radio scanner. Since I was in the vicinity, I called into the office for more details, and to see if they needed my help. When they mentioned your name as one of the staff involved, I about ran off the road." He kind of laughed.

Then he got serious again. "I hate that you got caught up in this escape, but I'm glad you're still in the prison business. A lot of good people work in prisons, and you're good with inmates. I thought maybe you moved on after the riot."

By this time, I had moved us into the kitchen. I asked him to pull down a vase from the top cupboard for the flowers. As he talked about his undercover work, we kept interrupting each other, talking too fast, filling in news about events over the last few months.

He said he didn't want any tea since he couldn't stay, at the same time he took off his jacket and hung it over the back of a kitchen chair. Then he gulped the tumbler of tea he said he didn't want and held out the glass for a refill.

When we settled at my small breakfast table, I said, "Fill me in on the escape. What's going to happen to Joshua? And what about Faith Miller? Was she involved with him?" To my ears, I sounded like I was jabbering to a friend to fill me in on soap opera episodes I'd missed.

He got that stern look I'd seen before and said, "I'll tell you what I know, but of course, it's totally confidential." His serious look removed any hint that this was an exchange of gossip about an adventure. I sat across the table from him and tried not to fidget with the ruffle on the placemat.

"Do you remember what I said about interviewing inmates who are in trouble? To them, I'm not just their only friend, but a friend with connections who can help them out of their mess. Most inmates will tell anything for ten candy bars and some chips."

It wasn't the time for me to joke that for me, he could skip the chips if the candy bars were Almond Joys. Joe Brown was in his all-business mode.

"So after you and Mel left in the ambulance, I told the escape team to take the inmate to the medical clinic to get his fire ant bites treated. We have to do this routinely after an escape - have the guy checked out so he can't sue us later - but I made it seem like I was doing him a favor. So when I met with him later at the clinic, he was feeling better and figured I was a softie since I'd got him to medical. He said he knew he had to do some time for the escape, but he wanted to shave some of the time off by giving me a dirty staff person. So I gave him my usual spiel about not being able to promise anything, but if he gave us solid information, we would include it in our report."

He paused before going on.

"This is the part that is still under investigation, so it is totally confidential. If it got out, it could ruin any chance for a conviction."

I didn't take offense at Joe's reminder to me to keep this secret. I respected the seriousness of this business and felt proud that he trusted me.

"So here's what he's saying. Inmate Joshua, I forget his last name, claims that the librarian, Faith Miller, left the gate by the library open for him. He said that they went to high school together. He recognized her when she fell in the cafeteria, which you saw happen in real time. Supposedly, afterwards, he went to the library to chat with her about old times. But he also admitted that he hoped their "chat" would be friendly enough for them to have sex, just for the fun of it."

When he mentioned the inmate's sexual plans, Joe Brown paused a minute and looked kind of squinty-eyed at me, as if asking if I was familiar with the concept. When I didn't melt in a puddle on my kitchen floor, he continued.

"But here's where it got interesting. The inmate said she didn't want to have sex but that she had another business transaction in mind. He claimed she was interested in making more money than sex with inmates could generate, and she offered another idea. According to him, she offered to leave the gate open if he paid her a thousand dollars. in cash. She planned to claim she lost the key, so we would then think he found it and let himself out of the gate."

Well now, I sure wasn't expecting to hear this. I asked in a hushed voice, "What do you think about her? Do you think she's that dumb?"

"Well, when I interviewed her, she said she lost the key to the gate, and that's how the inmate escaped. Which is what the inmate said she would claim. She said that because of her status as a new employee, she knew she'd be fired if she reported losing a key. So basically, she denied that she did it on purpose."

"What was she like when she said this? Was she upset?"

"Kind of upset, at least when she remembered that she was supposed to be upset."

"Oh, dear, this doesn't sound good."

"She is a very strange person. She presented herself as a wilted violet, an innocent new employee, who made a terrible mistake. But she didn't look faint, and she didn't really cry - just kind of sniffled. She didn't appear to be greatly upset that she made this big mistake. It was more like she knew she should be upset, and she tried to make herself look upset, but I don't think she was. Does that make sense?"

"I can see what you are describing. Except when she told me about her family's choir, she was upset in a trance-like way. She wasn't crying and carrying on, but she definitely had emotions about it. Did you get a chance to read the notes from her diary yet?"

"Yes, I did read them before my interview with her. They assigned the case to me since I was there at the scene. And by the way, the staff were impressed that you were alert enough to link them with her possible role in the escape. I told them you were trained in super max, so you knew all the tricks now."

He smiled and I smiled.

"When I asked her about the inmate suggesting sex, she was all prim and said she would never think of doing such a thing and turned him down. But when I asked her why she didn't report the inmate then to the staff, she just said at first that she didn't know that she should. So I pointed out to her that it was a disciplinary issue for an inmate to ask a staff person such an inappropriate question, but then she said again that she didn't know she should report it. So I pushed her a little and reminded her that this was covered in her employee training. And it was at this that she got pretend teary and said she didn't want to get the inmate in trouble since he was just 'joking' and that she was too uncomfortable talking about sex to a staff person."

"What part of her story do you believe?"

"From the diary notes, it is clear that she came into her job with the intention of taking advantage of any chance to make money on the side. I think she sees herself as smarter than all the rest of us, and because of her exploitation as a child, is somehow entitled to work money schemes. But I think that things moved a little quicker than she expected. Since she and Inmate Joshua knew each other, and he had the money available, I think she got too greedy too soon. She put out the plan to help him escape before she had really studied the layout and knew how to cover herself better. As it was, the unlocked gate led directly to her. And since she admits she failed to report a lost key, she's out of a job, with only a thousand dollars to show for it."

"Did Joshua actually have someone pay her the money? Or was he supposed to do that once he was free?"

Joe laughed. "Oh, no, the money part was the only piece she seemed to get right. The inmate said the gate was opened only after she got the money."

"How did that happen? I thought inmates couldn't have cash money."

"The inmate said that his girlfriend met with Miss Miller in the mall parking lot last night to hand over the money for the escape. The girlfriend confirms this and even showed me a photo she took with her cell, which supposedly proves the pay-off."

"Does Miss Miller admit to taking the money?"

"Not exactly. She admits to meeting with the girl friend and says that they were classmates also. And she says that the photo shows the friend returning some money which she owed to Miss Miller, but says it was only fifty dollars, not a thousand. Our Miss Miller says she sold the girlfriend some jewelry about a month ago, so this was a debt which was being settled when the money was handed over."

"I don't know what to believe about all this. What do you think will happen? Will you be able to charge Faith?

Joe crunched ice from his tea and said, "Unfortunately, at this point, I probably don't have anything to charge her with. Her claim that she lost the key is enough to fire her for negligence, but of course is not an admission that she did it on purpose. To try to prove her word against the inmate's is basically a 'he said, she said' deal, which won't hold up in court. Even with the photo of the money exchange, a good lawyer would just claim that it's exactly what Faith Miller said, a pay-off of a debt. And of course the girlfriend will soon realize that it is in her own interest to agree with Miller's claim since the alternative is the girlfriend admits to financing an inmate's escape. It's early in the investigation, of course, but I think it's going to be a problem getting enough proof to charge Miller with anything."

He frowned and went on. "Our Miss Miller may be a librarian, but that girl has serious problems. There's something twisted about her. It wouldn't surprise me at all that this isn't the first time she's tried to make money off inmates in some kind of way. All through the questioning tonight, she acted cool and kind of snotty. She tried to sound like a new employee worried about losing her job, but it came across mostly as her being annoyed that she lost her job, not embarrassed or sad. I wish I could lock her up, but at this point, there's just not a case. At least the prison policy of failing to notify officials about the lost key is enough to keep her from working again in the prison system. That's something, anyway. And, like I say, I definitely plan to follow up with her, asking around the community to see what she might be tied to. I'll probably get a warrant to look at her bank account, see if the thousand dollars. is sitting there, but I doubt that it is. That money is either spent or under her mattress. She's too smart to run it through her bank account. And of course, even if it was there, it's not proof that it was a pay-off."

Then we talked some more about Faith's exploitation as a child, which Joe agreed had been sad. But, as he said, "Plenty of people with sadness in their life don't think it gives them a right to break the law."

With that, I thought I knew the whole story. But then Joe stretched and stood up to take his glass to the sink. He spent a minute there, either looking out the window into the dark, or studying the blue gingham valance. When he spoke again, it was with his personal voice, not the voice he used when he described the case to me - the voice with professional distance in it. This voice was really sad, and really mad.

"The other girl involved in this, the inmate's girlfriend, she's the one who really shocked me. After all my years doing criminal work, I don't shock easily. It's expected that inmates try to escape. That's logical. It's also expected that dirty staff will do bad things for money, just like what caused the riot that you got caught up in. But this girl, Joshua's girlfriend, not only is she stupid enough to have this fool as her boyfriend, but she is studying to be a teacher. A *teacher*! Can you imagine? She used her tuition savings to pay for the escape, yet somehow she still thinks she's worthy to teach children. When I heard that, I about threw up."

Joe shook his head like a sad Labrador we used to have and walked over to get his jacket from the chair.

"Don't mind me getting so upset. I'd rather tell a crazy story to a normal person than let it give me an ulcer." He shrugged into his jacket and grinned at me, as if asking if this was all right.

"That's a real extravagant compliment, that you consider me normal," I joked. But then I wanted to make something very clear. "In fact, I'm glad you're so upset about that girlfriend. It is really depressing that behind the inmate, behind the dirty librarian, is someone pretending to be like the rest of us. It upsets me, too. And I'm glad you told me how you feel."

We moved together toward the front door. "Maybe I could pick you up later this morning for breakfast at the Cracker Barrel, and then I'll drive you to get your car."

"Sure, that would be great. You mean, like we need to have another official interview for my report?"

He smiled. "I'm not very good at this personal stuff. I wasn't good with it when I was married, and it may be why my wife left me. Not the whole reason, but it made it easier for her to go. But I had time to think while I was in Maryland. I want to do things differently now. I'm tired of holding back like some walking robot. If I can go undercover and pretend to be not me, then I could be not me in real life. So this would be like a date, you know, like people do."

As I was smiling and nodding, he leaned over to give me a kiss, which ended upside my nose. I couldn't tell if it had been meant for my forehead or my mouth, but it was definitely a kiss. Somewhere between a peck and a smooch. My head bobbled like a Hawaii doll on a dashboard, so I couldn't be sure where he aimed. Then he hurried down the steps to his car, and as he drove down the driveway, we both waved and he beeped the horn twice.

Oh, my goodness, how can this be? I thought to myself, "*I really like Joe Brown. Tom would like him, too. Sharon kind of liked him, but it was hard for her to not be so picky.*"

Thinking of Sharon, I wanted to call her, but I didn't want to interrupt her date again. Hopefully that red ruching worked its magic for her tonight. I didn't want to interrupt the conception of a possible future grandchild on her living room couch. I'd call her first thing in the morning.

There was no longer time for a long soak in the tub. I had to figure out what to wear for my date. For my last first date, forty some years ago with Tom, I wore turquoise capris and a yellow halter-top. But I think for tomorrow, I might want to be a little more, umm, *subdued*, as they say. Maybe something red.

Devil's Food

Faith Miller's Story

The search for truth: shuck it down to the cob.

One

All night I replayed my interview with Investigator Brown. He called it an interview, but it felt too much like an interrogation. Despite my tears and whispered admissions of shame, he did not seem convinced that I simply lost the key to the library gate and an inmate found it and used it to escape. Again and again, he asked why I didn't report the key missing right away, why I hadn't reported the inmate's sexual remarks, all questions, which if I answered truthfully, would have me in jail instead of just fired.

I almost admired his stubborn focus, his refusal to be fooled by my false tears, kind of like a chess player admired his opponent's attacks on his own queen. But I was stubborn, too, and I knew that if I kept focused on the fact that while he might be smart, he had no evidence. Which meant I was going to be all right once he gave up on his hunch.

My challenge was to stay strong, to not give him any entry to disproving my story, and to quiet my tumbling tummy, my irritated intestines, my damn diarrhea. I hated that my nerves showed in such a dumb, obvious way. I prided myself on being strong and stoic and smart, and I resented my body for not cooperating. Even a more private migraine would be better, if I had to have some stress-related malady. It just wasn't fair.

So when I pulled into Jasmine Rose's parking lot to get my fortune told, and splashed into a deep mud puddle, it was no surprise that straight from the car wash, my beautiful Mustang was so quickly messed up. "Damn, Faith," I told myself, "this whole week had been just one thing after another."

I parked in front of her shop, which was next to her boyfriend's tattoo parlor. Aside from the work needed in the parking lot, the two shops, Jasmine Rose and Frankie's Place, both looked kind of worn down. Rosie had a big potted fern at the front door of her shop, but Frankie's front only had black painted windows. At least he had a Harley logo stuck to the door as a little décor.

I checked the fenders of my car. Sure enough, there was mud splattered in several spots, which meant a second trip back to the car wash later. With quality cars like mine, it's not wise to let toxins eat into the paint.

But as soon as I walked into my best friend's store, my worries fell away like wilted petals. Jasmine Rose had a signature scent of incense, a blend she prepared herself. She used a mortar and pestle to mix the incense, just like a chemist. She used the same precision to grind her marijuana buds nice and smooth.

When she got ready for the Grand Opening of her store, she explained to me, "Faith, it's important for a business to be unique. I want my customers to think of me whenever they catch a floral drift in the air."

She gave me some examples, "It's the same reason the iPad company uses an apple in their advertising, and why you have that cute little horse on your imported Ford. Don't you remember us studying that concept of 'branding' in class?"

Jasmine Rose and I had been friends since high school. Her name used to be just Rose, but she thought that was too plain for her business. We both loved our Future Business Leaders Group since we both loved money. I still called her Rosie, unless we were in a business setting.

Rosie envied me when I went to college. Since her grades weren't so good, and she didn't get any scholarship money, she couldn't go. She was disappointed, but she chimed in with my sisters, all telling me, "Get the hell out of here."

Besides, Rosie's plan for our future had a twist. She wanted me to come back to be her business partner after I finished my courses in economics and marketing.

"I figure with your smarts, and my creative flair, you and I can be this town's Martha Stewart. We can have several businesses running at the same time."

She added, "We already know not to trust anyone except each other."

Our plan came together pretty well. I got a dual degree in Business and Library Science. The Business degree taught me what I needed to know to draft our business plans. The main focus of our model was to have several revenue streams flowing in at once.

When we got real busy filling orders, Rosie and I always chanted, "Diversify, diversify, diversify," which guaranteed one of us would laugh. We made a great team.

My second degree in Library Science was my fall back option in case our business ever had a slack period. Besides that practical aspect, I always loved the quiet and privacy of libraries. At the time I worked on it in college, it seemed like a personal indulgence, but when I returned to town, I saw how the degree could be a major help in developing another revenue stream for our main business. But then I made my big mistake this week, which was why I was so mad at myself.

When Rosie and I talked business, she frequently told me, "Sweetie, I have never met anyone as smart as you." No matter how often she said it, I loved to hear it.

Rosie herself was not as gifted with book smarts. Her tendency to get facts twisted amused me, and she would laugh along with me when I corrected her. But Rosie's huge gift was that she understood people. She knew how to be comfortable with anyone, she was charming, and she was fun. I had none of those gifts. But I was smart, and I wasn't shy about showing it. Of course in the business we were in, sometimes I had to pretend to be sweet and simple. At first it took some practice, but given the rewards, dumbing down myself was just another financial tool.

So having Rosie as my partner and my friend gave my life enormous happiness. I loved that Rosie was so free with her love, so easily affectionate. She understood me, and I felt safe with her.

While I was away at college, Rosie had two babies with Damien, who was a year ahead of me at school. He started serving time last year for driving the get-away car for two buddies who robbed our local credit union. Unfortunately, the get-away car blew its engine when Damien floored it out on the bypass.

When Rosie called to tell me about it, she cried, "I wish I'd thought to tell him to rent a car instead of using his beat-up Corolla."

I agreed with her that sometimes business expenses were key to financial success and reassured her that she'd be all right without Damien. After all, she could bring the kids to visit him in prison.

"Rosie, life goes on after bad things. It's dysfunctional to just fall apart. I'll be home soon to start our plan, and you'll be so busy, you won't have time to miss Damien."

By the time I graduated last spring and came back to town, Rosie had already opened her palm reading store. It happened so easily, we felt it was meant to be.

Rosie put it well. "Faith, I won't pretend that Frankie is my only love. I'll always keep a special love for Damien as the father of my children. But Frankie came into my life as a gift. He is sweet and easy to be with, and he follows directions well."

We laughed together, and though I knew her remark about Frankie was a joke, we both knew it was true. Rosie had definitely assessed his strengths correctly.

Frankie had the good fortune to be the only child of a local real estate developer. Frankie made it through high school all right, a year behind us. His biggest talent was sketching cartoons. In school, he doodled in the margins of all of his text books, very intricate drawings of dragons and angels and devils.

When he graduated, his father understood that Frankie wasn't inclined to work a regular job. So his father sent him to Charlotte to apprentice the tattoo trade from a friend of a friend.

Some months later when he got back, he and Rosie ran into each other at a party. Within days they knew they had a special relationship and became a couple. Frankie tattooed Rosie's name on his leg, right above the knee. It was one of the few patches of skin still available for ink.

Rosie put off getting Frankie's name done, but then a wondrous thing happened.

In one of those convenient occurrences, which in Rosie's world she would call 'cosmic', Frankie's parents liked Rosie for her practical side, a trait which they had noticed was lacking in Frankie. The parents thought they made a good couple together, which was fine. But what was great, well, okay, *cosmic*, was that it seemed that there was a small strip mall of two stores that Frankie's dad had trouble renting since it was in such a rough part of town. Behind the two stores, but part of the same parcel, was a very large storage building.

The parents invited Rosie and Frankie to the Cracker Barrel for lunch, where his dad presented a plan.

"These buildings have been vacant too long. I don't want to spend money to upgrade them, since paving the parking lot alone would cost a fortune. But, Frankie, you could use one shop for your tattooing service, and if you wanted, you could loan the other shop to Rosie for her fortune telling business. I have no idea what you'd need the storage building for, but you could just leave it empty or store junk in it."

Rosie said she stopped breathing. Frankie's father went on. "Now, Frankie, here's the challenge for you. We've done our best to educate you, and now it's time for us to step back. You kids can have the stores rent free, but you have to cover all your other business expenses."

Rosie said she poked Frankie to smile and nod, which he did.

"Son, this is a leg up, not a hand out." Frankie didn't seem to know what this meant, but Rosie said she nodded for both of them.

According to Rosie, Frankie's mom didn't say much during their lunch. She mostly stared at Frankie's ink sleeves on both arms. Rosie said she thought his mom was not such a fan of tattoos.

So the deal for the property was agreed on. Of course, Frankie's father didn't know Rosie spent her childhood monitoring the sprinkler system and grow lights for her parents' marijuana plants on their three-season porch. The primary site for their larger acreage was a few miles out of town, south of the bypass. Her family didn't make a lot of money from the weed.

Her dad still worked his landscaping jobs, and her mom worked at Wal-Mart, but the extra money kept them comfortable.

But Rosie and I had our plan to grow the business. And now we had a perfect corporate office in her fortune telling store, with the packaging plant in the storage building behind Frankie's parlor.

She and I were equal partners in the business. I handled sales development, and she was in charge of production and distribution. Frankie had designated duties, but no separate share of profits, which was fine with him.

As he put it, "As long as Rosie's my girl, I know she'll do me right. Just being with her is my share."

Her parents were our primary supplier. Rosie maintained strict quality control standards over each shipment, which amused her dad.

"Rosie, you think your old man would sell you trash and twigs?"

One night recently, Rosie and I drank too many gin and tonics. I told her, "You are so blessed to have parents who encouraged you and taught you the family business. They showed you how to make it in this world. And look at Frankie, his parents probably wished for a different kind of son, but they didn't leave him stranded."

We both teared up, Rosie from gratitude, me from anger. Then we went back to watching "Dancing With The Stars."

My agreement with Rosie covered our partnership of the marijuana sales. But she did not receive a percentage of my plans for side prison projects, like leaving the gate open. Nor did I share her profit for her fortune-telling business. My whole purpose for taking the prison job was to have close access to customers. I thought I could learn firsthand how to maneuver around the security procedures that tried to restrict contraband from coming in. The end goal for me was to increase our prison sales. And using my library degree to get me into the prison system was a perfect fit.

Then, like an idiot, I botched my first project and lost my prison access. Now I would again have to coordinate sales through other people. And it was like they taught us in school: it was never a good business plan to have too many points of contact between the customer and the provider.

I made a mistake with the deal with Joshua, so I felt bad as well as stupid. I let Rosie down.

When I came in the shop this morning, after splashing up my car, Rosie shouted out, "Hey, girl, it's good to finally see you in person again, instead of just talking on the phone. Fill me in on what's happened since we last talked."

I sank into her customer's chair. "I will, but first I need a reading to settle me down. I'm mad, and I'm sad at being so stupid. So don't be too nice to me, or I'll slobber and cry."

Two

We discovered Rosie's talent in middle school. Whenever we played with the Ouija board, the spirits responded to her. For me, I heard no voices, but with Rosie, spirits shouted over each other to be heard. Of course, being Rosie, she was not content. She took her talent to the next level. She studied books at the library on palm reading until she understood all the nuances.

I look back on those days as a good memory. She and I would get a table in the back of the library, surrounded by silence. Rosie studied diagrams in big books, some with ornate bindings from decades past.

"Faith," she'd whisper. "Stop staring into space, and give me your hand." She would grab my hand and lay it alongside her own. For minutes, she stared at our two palms, comparing similarities and analyzing differences.

Lots of times, I would just be back from a prison singing gig and would be pretty much bummed out. In the library, I sat very still, enjoyed the silence, and stroked the silky finish of the mahogany table top. I stared across the big room at the librarian and envied her job that didn't require much smiling or talking. To my eyes, the librarian's concerned frown was the height of professionalism.

If I had the energy, some days I'd read alongside Rosie. Next to her fancy palm reading books, I'd stack a pile of *Readers' Digests*, all turned to the 'How To Improve Your Vocabulary' section.

Rosie had little interest in big words, unless I found ones related to palms. Then she practiced pronouncing them until she had them smoothly.

"Bi-fur-cated," she drawled it out.

I whispered, "It's like the line that branches several ways out of the palm."

"Sounds like what my Uncle Manuel does after Thanksgiving dinner," she answered.

We giggled until the librarian glanced our way.

For me, vocabulary words felt like dollar bills. For every new word I learned, I bought my way to a different life. I wanted people to know I was smart, that I had a life beyond shaking a tambourine in a dark prison chapel. I wanted my words to advertise me.

In my head, I wanted to hear others say, "Ah, here's an educated, intelligent girl. I need to listen to her." Big words made my voice louder.

Later, in college, other students in my business classes teased me. "Faith, you don't need to show off your vocabulary to earn your first million."

In my grown years, I realized that my sisters found their own ways to advertise their specialness. Patience finally stopped cutting herself and instead used tattoos to shout her messages. She had almost as many as Frankie, except instead of dragons or monsters, she used words. 'Born to Be Free' bragged on her left bicep; 'Enjoy Life' on her right breast; and her own name surrounded with fireworks spread across her back. All of her inking told some part of her story. When I saw her last, about a year ago, I teased her, "Patience, if you keep going, you'll be surrounded by your autobiography." She was a little zonked on her Ecstasy indulgence, so she may not have understood my compliment.

I haven't had the chance to talk with my other sister, Chastity, about our advertising traits. The last I heard, several years ago, she was stripping in a big hotel in Las Vegas. Maybe the cash bills she collected were more real than my fancy dollar words.

All of these memories from the past were stored in my 'Rosie' file. Without her as my best friend, I don't think I could have salvaged a normal life. Like for Patience, her life so far had been spent in a series of psych hospitals and rehab facilities and half-way houses. And as far as Chastity's life, Rosie teased me that I couldn't follow her to Vegas since, "Faith, honey, you may be smart and know big words, but you cannot dance at all."

Seeing Rosie today at her shop after my rough week at work was such a relief. She smiled at me as I collapsed in her chair.

"Good, I'm glad you want a reading. I haven't had a chance to do one on you for a while."

She sat across from me and opened my right hand. She stretched each finger slowly, almost to the point where I felt uncomfortable. Then she rubbed the base of my thumb, over and over with a slow rhythm. Finally, she picked up a crystal salt shaker, and dribbled scented water on my palm from it.

"Now we can begin," she said in a low voice.

She bent over my hand and reached for a magnifying glass, which had a long silver handle, carved with flowers. After a few moments, she said, "I see anger and frustration. And it looks like a simple mistake caused you a problem." With her other hand, she shined a small pen light onto my palm. The magnifying glass scattered the reflections like sequins on the table between us.

"But I also see new opportunities ahead. I see the line signifying your personal strength bifurcating the cross hatch of current problems. I see that strength line dominating all the other movement in your hand."

She bent closer. "And see, right here? This means that in order for the new opportunities to develop, there will be new people entering your life. This will initially be stressful for you, but eventually, productive."

My friend smiled as she finished my reading and picked up a long hat pin tipped with an ivory pearl. She pricked my thumb and then dribbled a few drops of blood onto a rose petal. She gently placed another petal on the prick and whispered, "This is nature's band aid."

Rosie took the petals and burned them in the flame of an incense candle in a small crystal votive vase nearby.

"May the spirits bless you in the new opportunities that have opened for you." With this, she ended the reading.

Rosie slumped back in her chair. "Wow, I am exhausted from that. Your spirits were shouting to be heard. I feel as weak as a kitten."

She opened the top button of her smock and reached over to the counter beside her for the Chamber of Commerce directory to fan her neck.

"There's some chili in the crock pot in the back workroom. And I think there's a package of shredded cheese in the fridge. You look as hungry as I am. Then I want to hear all the prison news. The local station mentioned the escape, but of course didn't have any details." Rosie kept fanning while I put together our food.

Over lunch, I filled her in on the whole mess, including my poor planning.

"So, basically," I sighed, "I let the customer dictate my terms. I didn't want to make a move so quickly, but Joshua absolutely would not wait. He said he was so sick of being locked up, he planned to climb the fence at midnight that week if I didn't leave the gate open for him. I didn't want to lose my sale, and his girlfriend had the cash, so I went ahead and gave him the key. Then I played my fluster act about losing the key to that Investigator Brown, which was my cover story."

Rosie scraped the last bit of chili from her bowl and licked the cheese off the spoon.

"I remember Joshua from school. His voice could slick the skin off a snake. Do you think the investigator believed that you lost the key? When you called me in that quick call right after it happened, you seemed to think they would only fire you. That is not good, but it's not a crime. Of course, I'm sure Joshua wasted no time naming you as the villain. In fact, knowing Joshua, he probably tried to claim that you pushed him out the gate and wouldn't let him back in. I can hear him now, crying in the swamp where they found him, "Thank God you rescued me. I was headed for the front gate and got lost.""

We laughed at her joke, and I gave her hair a pull as I collected the lunch things. Rosie's friendship was a treasure. She knew I made a stupid mistake, but she wasn't interested in making me feel worse.

"That Investigator Brown worries me. I tried to convince him I was just young and dumb, but I'm not sure he thought it was that simple. He pushed me about the meeting with Joshua's girlfriend, and I admitted I knew her from school and that we saw each other recently. Since she paid me in cash, nothing went through the bank, so he'll have a dead end there. But I don't know about him. He just makes me nervous."

"It's not like you to be nervous," Rosie remarked. "Usually you don't show nerves at all. Well, except with your stomach. Maybe you're just feeling mad about the mistake. You're such a perfectionist; you haven't had much experience of making mistakes and feeling yucky."

I shrugged, but she wasn't done with her pep talk.

"Maybe you should work around here for a couple of weeks. Frankie could use some help with packaging. Sometimes I worry he's not careful enough. It's best if we change up the look of our deliveries, so the contraband investigators don't realize how much volume actually comes from our place." She interrupted herself to ask me, "Hand me that manicure kit on the cabinet, would you, please? I want to change out this gray polish for something lighter. There's a Chamber prayer breakfast in the morning, and I don't want to look too Goth. They're already curious about me since I'm their token palm reader. Not too many of us are Chamber members."

We laughed, and Rosie went on, "Imagine if they knew what really generated most of our income. They would absolutely freak. They'd be rushing to tell each other, 'I knew gypsies couldn't be trusted.' Just like all gardeners are Mexicans, only gypsies can read palms. My dad and I provide a real public service, being such convenient stereotypes."

It was fun to have the time to hang out with Rosie at her shop. Taking the prison job didn't let me drop in to see her as much.

"Don't let me forget to get back to my packaging worry, but I just had a good idea."

I raised an eyebrow. Rosie sometimes had some wild ideas.

"Since I'm already hooked up with the Chamber of Commerce, how about you join the Rotary Club? You have the open time now, and it would provide more cover for you. Who would be suspicious of an unemployed librarian who heads up a project to read to little kids at an orphanage?"

I frowned since I'm not much of a social mixer, but Rosie had a good point.

"Let me think about it. I do need to expand my contacts. I think we need more sales from in-town. The prison market is really good, of course, but they're disproportionate. If we had to slow down our throw-overs for security reasons, we would feel it in our cash flow. In fact, that's what happened right after the riot at the max prison. They moved out a lot of our inmate vendors, and we are still not totally back to our previous volume. It would be good to have stronger sales in town to act as a cushion."

Rosie said, "Now that we're back talking about distribution, it's the throw overs I'm worried about. I'm not sure Frankie is mixing up our deliveries enough. He doesn't seem to understand the difference between reliable delivery and predictable delivery. I mean, we can't be like Fed Ex with a logo, so everyone knows which packages are ours. I had to take the camo tape away from him. Frankie thought it was cool, and he was using it too often. It was like he created our own damn logo."

Rosie and Frankie were a good team, but she did have to monitor his piece of the business. But he didn't seem to mind.

"No problem," I agreed. "I'll spend more time with Frankie. I also have a new contact at the jail that I need to visit." Rosie didn't know when she read my palm that her vision of a new contact for me was already in the works. It was just more proof that she had a real gift.

She asked me, "I thought you were barred, or restricted, or whatever from the prison system. How can you make sales calls at the jail?"

I know that Rosie only asked that for information, but her question made me feel mad at myself all over again. It reminded me of my stupid mistake, which left me banned from the state prison system. It also made me feel vulnerable for future stupid moves. And a big part of my job was projecting confidence when I was carrying contraband. Insecurity fueled mistakes, and Rosie should know that.

"Well, Miss Palm Reader, for your information, the prison problem is totally separate from my jail access. The jail system is run by the county, so none of their visitor lists overlap with the state's. Of course, I doubt the county would ever hire me for a job since I'd have to name the prison as my last employer, but I do still have access to visit. And also, now that I think about it, maybe I could become a volunteer at the jail. That would be a productive sales source to look into. But anyway, my access is still good, and my new contact has given us some decent orders this past month. So I need to pay Ted a visit for an 'atta-boy.' His cellmate, who used to be my contact, just got released and is working somewhere in town. So Ted might be feeling lonesome."

When I finished, Rosie looked at me, as if she had another crazy thought.

"Faith, you know how much I like to cook?"

"Yes, and I'm glad to share the results."

"What if we offered a new product in our line? The other day my mom was laughing about all the hoopla in Colorado about their legalization of marijuana sales. She remembered from back in the 60's when she baked brownies with marijuana mixed in. According to her, the only problem was keeping the brownies moist since the weed tended to dry them out. I think it would be fun to add that to our inventory."

I laughed and shook my head as in, *What next?* "Sure, that sounds like fun. We'd have to bake it fresh right before delivery, but that's manageable. I wish prisons still let food come in as gifts, since that would be a big market. But I can definitely see it selling to our old rock and rollers. It would be like a novelty item. I wonder if we could package it differently, in a vintage style, like with a psychedelic twist?"

We laughed together about the possibilities. Our best ideas have come from brainstorming together.

"I think I'll ask my mom to make the first batch with me. She'd enjoy passing a family recipe from one generation to the next."

Rosie admired her new polish and said, "So, enough about business. This is my other great idea. Since you'll be around more, we could work on a disguise for you."

For years, Rosie had been trying to channel my inner yuppie.

"We'll take you out of those dumb clothes you wear that make you look like you're headed to a leper colony for a book club meeting. You would look so hot in denim leggings with sequins on the butt pockets, and kick-ass boots with a high heel. Oh, yes, I have my work cut out for me."

"There is no chance at all that you have me as a rehab project. I like dressing comfortably. It suits me fine. Although I did see a new lingerie line in the Victoria Secrets catalogue. Now for that, I'd spend some of Joshua's money."

This was a comfortable and familiar battle between us. She thought I dressed too matronly, but I thought my look was elegant in its simplicity. And Rosie's always had more interest in fashion.

I did like nice things, but I didn't like to draw attention to myself, or for that matter, I didn't really like to mix with people. This was, of course, a contradiction, since my business is sales, and most sales people are flashy. But I found that if I told people what they wanted to hear, most times they'd think we'd had a good conversation. And if they thought that, they were happy with our terms, and the sale was done.

I felt blessed that my intelligence allowed me to think ahead of my clients, so ultimately, our sales agreements were to my benefit. Which was why misdirection with the Joshua project was so embarrassing. I let him set the terms, which was something I was trained to avoid.

After I left Rosie's, aside from my reoccurring regret about the prison project, this had been a good day. To drive my shiny car, to visit with my only friend in the world, to eat and laugh and plan with her, and then to go home to my own place, all in all, it couldn't get much better.

I planned to broil a small lamb chop for supper and have it with a baked potato with real butter. I'd watch the business news on PBS, then take the Victoria Secret catalog to bed with me to finalize my next order. I had new, seven hundred thread count, lavender sheets, so my bed was a safe, luxurious oasis.

Three

Doing business with Ted was low key. He was neither smart nor ambitious. He only wanted access to the product for personal use, plus cash in his canteen account for his Mountain Dew addiction. In return, he smuggled in the package I left in the ladies' rest room in the visiting room of the county jail.

This morning when I came to the jail's visitor's gate, the usual officers were on duty. The staff was used to seeing me come through, and I was always careful to never present a problem or draw attention to myself.

"Good morning, Miss Miller. You're starting your visit a little early today."

I gave a polite smile and put my identification card on the desk. "Just a little early, I guess."

"Just walk through the metal detector, and we'll get you processed in."

Of course, I carried nothing on me to alert the detector, so I walked through quietly. My long cardigan matched my skirt, which hung just below my knee. For a little color, I had on a white blouse. The staff seemed to appreciate the simplicity of my outfit, since they frequently had to turn away visitors who wore tight jeans or scooped necklines. I don't care how Rosie teased me, my simple wardrobe was classy. It also in no way brought the attention of the officers to me. I made their job simple, which was my goal.

"You have a nice visit, ma'am."

"Thank you," I answered, still with my low voice. But I was careful to look at the officer when she spoke, so she wouldn't think I had anything to hide.

She waved me on, not feeling the need to pat me down physically. If she had, she would have found a quart bag of marijuana in the bottom of each bra cup, and another bag tucked under my blouse, held secure by the elastic band of my skirt. But I gave her no reason to worry. My procedure worked every time.

Once inside the visiting room, I headed straight for the ladies' room. I unloaded the bags and put them in the bottom of the trash barrel, under a bunch of wet paper towels. From a quick glance, it just looked like a soggy mess.

I always felt relieved when I off-loaded the delivery. It felt good to not have physical responsibility for it anymore. I imagined a museum curator felt the same way after carrying a donor's statue from storage to a display case.

Sometimes my anxiety made me glad to have such quick access to the restroom for personal reasons as well, but today my tummy was fine.

Ted's jail job was to clean up the bathrooms after the weekend visits. It could be nasty work, but obviously it had benefits. His access to the dropped off packages allowed him to move them into his cellblock. Depending on the size of the delivery, he carried it either in his hollowed out Bible or the crotch of his long johns. Neither area was usually searched very thoroughly.

Once in his cellblock, Ted turned the packages over to an officer we paid directly. She had been on our payroll for almost a year and was trustworthy. Since all of our deliveries were prepaid by the inmates, she touched no money, which was a safeguard for her and for us. She had never mixed up who got what quantity.

"Hey, Ted, how are you doing?"

"Morning, Miss Faith, it's good to see you. I was surprised when they called me out for a visit." Ted's arms were corded from the time he spent in the inmate gym. I was sure he would have been happy to show off his abs, too, but the presence of the visiting room security officer mercifully precluded that treat.

"Why were you surprised? This is my normal visiting week."

"Yeah, I know, but I heard you had trouble on your prison job. I thought you might have got locked up."

"Oh, my goodness, no. Prison rumors get so crazy."

I tried to laugh it off, but inside I was so furious, my stomach started churning. I hated the notion that my name was gossiped about by stupid inmates. The only role I wanted them to see me in was as a business woman - not some criminal on their level.

"Part of what you heard is true. Unfortunately, I made a mistake on my job and, of course, there were a lot of questions I had to answer. But there were no charges against me about the situation. So nothing has changed about our arrangement here."

"No offense, ma'am. You know how rumors go."

"Sure, no problem. I guess Steve's release came through. You probably miss your old cellmate already."

"Yeah, him and me did all right together. I heard he found a job at some mobile home dealership here in town."

"Well, that's good. Do you know which dealership?"

Our little town used to be known as the Mobile Home Capital of the World, but that was before the recession.

"I think it's that one past the bypass. Sanders is what I heard."

"Good for him. I wish him luck."

Ted smiled. "You're right; it will take luck for him to stay out. That boy ain't got much planned. You might want to pay him a visit. Maybe he'd be interested in helping you out again or something."

Our delivery routes were not shared information. We did not encourage our contact people to mix together, like some happy sales club. Ted could assume whatever his little mind allowed, but he wouldn't get confirmation from me about the extent of our business network.

I smiled, "I'm just glad he's out. And I'm glad he trained you before he left. But I guess you'll be out, too, before too long. Are you going back to your family here in town?"

Like a flash, Ted's mood changed. It made me wonder if he had found a source for some performance pills. Those muscle-building drugs made a person flash from mellow to monster, with no warning.

"You leave my family out of this. I do my thing; you pay me, that's it."

"No problem, Ted. I meant no disrespect."

I knew how to do humble real well. While it was common for some inmates to keep their families totally separate from their jail time, it also sometimes meant there was something unusual going on. And in my business, unusual was never a good thing. I didn't know anything about Ted's family, but I thought I might need to at some point. Particularly if Ted started acting squirrely.

To cool Ted down, we talked about the weather, and the bad food in the jail cafeteria. I checked the clock on the visiting room wall and saw with relief that I'd spent enough time with our pleasantries.

"Ted, you are a big help, and I appreciate you taking over for Steve. I included a little extra in the package for you this time."

We parted in a friendly way. It was important to keep delivery staff happy, so Ted's bonus was toward that end. But his pill use was a concern as far as his reliability. Ted would need watching.

I figured I'd make one more stop before finishing work for the day. But I wanted to hurry, because I had something nice planned for later. There was a serious sale at Nordstrom at the big mall a few miles south on the interstate. Nordstrom carried some gorgeous silk robes. Yes, silk. Not shiny polyester, raw silk. When I saw them on display a few weeks back, before they were reduced, the Nordstrom personal shopper saw me feel the texture of the fabric. She smiled. "Yes, Miss Miller, real silk. Made by the busy worms in our special basement." I smiled politely at her little joke, but not so much that she would think we were buddies.

The purchase would be an extravagance, even on sale, but I so needed it. The embarrassment Joshua had caused me to feel had not easily faded. When he named me as helping him escape, he exposed me in a very personal way. I felt violated. My favor to him when I gave him the key helped him and me both. It was a shared act of trust. But he disrespected that trust.

A little self-indulgence would definitely help me seal that wound.

But first, I wanted to check out Steve. What Ted didn't know, because Steve had the good sense to keep his mouth shut, was that before Steve got his jail time for a DUI, he had already worked for us.

Steve and Ted were a lot alike, which was probably why they got along well as cellmates. Their criminal histories were petty stuff, but they had both spent lock up time more than once. And they both liked to keep their bodies strong.

While Steve was not necessarily smarter than Ted, he presented himself better. He wasn't blustery or narcissistic, which was why I liked doing business with him. Plus, he had a very strong throwing arm.

He liked to brag, "If I wasn't so dumb, I could have got some college money. My arm is that good."

Before his last lock up, Steve was one of our go-to guys for over-the-fence throws at our local max prison. When he was no longer available, I had to use someone else. Someone who wasn't near as satisfactory. In fact, for most of his throws, I made it a practice to be on the scene to make sure it went smoothly. Frequently, I parked behind the tree line and observed his throw. Me watching was part of the principle in business called 'management by walking around.' I called it taking care of my investment.

One night, I made a mistake while leaving the area after a throw. Instead of turning left onto the highway, I turned right and ended up in the prison parking lot. No one stopped me, so I guess I wasn't seen, but it scared the hell out of me.

As soon as I found my way out of the parking lot, I was on the phone to Rosie. "I'm scared. What if someone saw me?" Even though I didn't have contraband on me, I didn't want to have a witness who could tie me to the scene of the throw over.

Rosie used her common sense voice. "You're all right. Don't worry. If you're stopped, just say you got lost on your way to the Cracker Barrel."

Just talking to Rosie settled me down that night. And I did go to the Cracker Barrel for my cover. The manager, Chris, was there, doing his own out of hours walking around. He introduced himself. He made a convenient alibi if I'd needed one, but I wasn't interested in following up with him like he suggested.

With Rosie as my friend, I didn't need another friend.

The entrance to Sanders Motor Sales was nicely landscaped. It had three of those expensive Palmetto trees clustered together. I knew business must be good since there were several models on display, in a range of prices.

When I stopped in the parking lot, Steve saw me and came over to my car window.

"Hey, Miss Miller, it's good to see you. Are you here to buy your dream home?"

I laughed with him. "Hey, back at you, Steve. I'm glad to see you out of those stripes. Do you have a minute to talk, or is this a bad time?"

"It's cool. The owner, Mr. Sanders, went into town for a Chamber of Commerce meeting. Everyone else is out on deliveries. Why don't you pull behind that big unit there? Your car is so sharp, it might catch some eyes. I can take a break from patching up this foreclosure here. I swear, once people get behind on their payments, they let everything go to shit."

Steve and I talked a while, and he was definitely interested in resuming his route at the max prison. I bumped his delivery fee up a little to keep him motivated.

"Steve, you were so reliable before, it's a pleasure to have you back."

"Thanks, Miss Miller. I hope I can stay out long enough to buy a car, so I appreciate the work. What about the guy who's doing the throws now? Is he going to be a problem?"

"No, don't worry about him. I'll put him somewhere else."

We made our plans and waved goodbye. Steve's concern about the other guy was legitimate, and a sign of Steve's job experience. But I didn't want him to get involved in what could lead to a fight. My plan was to keep the other guy in place, but decrease my use of him. I'd just tell him that since the riot, business was down. The gangs still hadn't gotten re-organized enough for steady sales. They needed to get some strong leaders back in there, so we could all make a living.

As for me, I was off to Nordstrom's to spend some more of Joshua's money on the rough slub of raw silk.

Four

A few days later, I pulled into Rosie's parking lot, and the blue Crown Victoria stayed right on my bumper. He didn't flash his blue lights or chirp his siren. But he didn't need to. I knew he was following me.

For a moment, I was tempted to drive on toward an empty lot down the road before stopping, but I didn't want to look evasive. I needed Investigator Brown to think I had nothing to hide, and I wanted him to think my greatest fault was stupidity.

When I got out of my car, I stood at the back bumper. I kept my voice smooth when I greeted him, but inside I felt my nerves. In fact, I was so nervous, I wished I could dash into Rosie's and head straight for her bathroom. Instead, I tucked my hair back into its bun and straightened my shirt collar.

I wanted him to see me as shy, not anxious. It was not a good sign that he came to talk with me again. I had hoped we were finished with the prison key investigation. But now it looked like we were not quite through.

"Hi, good morning." I stood by my car with a timid smile.

"Good morning, Miss Miller. I'm glad I ran into you. I saw your car a few blocks away, and followed you to a more convenient stopping place. I've got the certified copy of your written statement for you to go over. Shall we go somewhere for coffee while you take a look at it?"

"Sure, I'm glad to sign it. I'm certain there are no changes. Let's go into my friend's shop here. She always has coffee brewing."

"That sounds great." He didn't seem rushed or distracted. He acted as if he had nothing else to do and nowhere else to go.

I let him open the door for me and ducked my head a little as if unfamiliar with the courtesy. Brown knew me as a timid librarian, and this is who I wanted him to continue to see.

When we walked into Rosie's, the chimes on the door handle announced us. Rosie was on the floor, unpacking a shipping box of costume jewelry. It was a new line she ordered: kind of Southern Girl meets Gypsy Goth. The gold coin necklaces were guaranteed to leave green grime on the neck, and the smoky gray glass stones looked like bits of chipped asphalt. I agreed with Rosie that they would sell like crazy.

"Good morning, Rose," I said to her. "I came in for another lemon scented candle and brought someone with me. This is Investigator Brown from the prison where I used to work. I promised him some coffee."

Rosie stood up, gave me a quick hug, and shook hands with the investigator.

"It's good to meet you. Faith told me about her dumb mistake with that key she lost. She feels awful about it."

I relaxed a little. Rosie was so cool.

Investigator Brown nodded a little toward each of us, as if acknowledging that Rosie knew about my situation.

It was one of my operational rules that when a person had things to hide, it was best to avoid unnecessary lies. Trying to remember how much is included in a lie can be a way to get tripped up.

"Good morning," he answered back to Rosie. "I don't want to put you out about the coffee. You have a nice shop here."

"Rose, Investigator Brown said I needed to look over some papers. Is it all right if I spread them out on your reading table?"

"Of course, that's fine. Maybe while he's at the table, some left over spirits could convince him to have his palm read." Rosie smiled at him like a carnival barker.

"What do you say, Investigator Brown? Are you interested in looking into your future?" Rosie asked directly.

"I have enough trouble with the past and the present, so I better pass on the future." When he said this so easily, I got a twinge again in my stomach. This guy was not going to be easy to fool.

He glanced around the shop, and I followed his eyes, worried that Rosie had left signs of our other business out on the counters. The only thing I saw was a carton of baggies, but that could be easily explained. I reminded myself that, even though he was smart, we were, too.

Once we were seated at the table, Rosie brought us mugs of coffee and a plate of oatmeal cookies. "I wish I had some brownies ready to offer you. It's a new bakery product we're going to have available soon for our customers."

Watching Rosie was a tutorial in Advanced Bluffing. I ducked my head to keep my smile from showing. Rosie was a genius.

"Thanks, just the coffee is good. Miss Miller, if there are any parts of the statement that you'd like to change, we should probably schedule a time when we can talk in private."

"No, sir, I'm fine talking in front of Rose. We've known each other since middle school, and she's heard all about my terrible mistake with the key." I gave a nervous laugh, and said, "I'm sorry, I guess she just said that."

Brown nodded again and glanced toward Rosie.

I picked up the papers and read them slowly. Then I dug a pen out of my purse. "The copy looks fine; there's nothing I need to change about it. Of course, I'd like to add how sorry I am to cause everyone so much trouble, but I guess that doesn't go into an official report. Where do I sign?"

Brown showed me the place for my signature. While I signed, he remarked casually, "Yes, I understand your regret. But I still don't quite understand why you didn't report your lost key sooner. And, I have to say, if you had reported the inmate as soon as he made those inappropriate sexual suggestions, he would have been put in solitary right away. It's kind of puzzling why you waited."

I placed my hand to my mouth, as if embarrassed at his reference to Joshua's suggestion for us to have sex.

Rosie put her mug down and asked me, "Faith, is it all right if I share my opinion about your delays with Investigator Brown?"

I nodded, not knowing her plan, but trusting her entirely.

She settled in her chair with the erect posture of a prestigious psychologist testifying in court. "See, Mr. Brown, Faith has serious problems from things which occurred in her childhood. Two results of those problems are that first, she absolutely hates to make mistakes, or even be wrong, about anything. Even trivial things, much less something as serious as a lost key. She tries to be perfect, which of course isn't possible. That's part of why she's so shy and careful how she speaks." I made a fake grimace, as if ashamed to hear these things.

Rosie picked up her mug and took a sip. She touched her lips with a gingham napkin. "The other problem with Faith is related to S-E-X." She actually spelled it out, with a straight face, as if I were a traumatized child, ease-dropping on concerned adults. "She is uncomfortable with any reference or discussion about it."

I again grimaced and took a deep breath. "Investigator Brown told me that he saw my diary pages, and I filled him in on my parents' prison ministry. I believe he's also interviewed Mrs. Kelly about what I shared with her. So, please, maybe we don't need to talk about it again."

Rosie went on, as if I hadn't spoken. "You see how she dresses. I've tried for years to get her to dress her age, but she feels best when she's dressed like an old lady. So for her to not report the inmate's sexual solicitation is as understandable as her failure to report her mistake with the key. I'm certainly not saying her behavior was acceptable in a professional position, but it is consistent with her normal behavior. That's who Faith is."

Rosie told no unnecessary lies; she just didn't include some necessary pieces of the truth.

I put my face in my hands, as if this was just too much to hear.

Through my fingers, I watched as Brown gave Rosie a look with a half-smile and stood to leave.

"Well, I guess that wraps up my business for today. I'll file this report, Miss Miller, and you'll get a copy in the mail."

He walked toward the door and then paused and looked around again. "Your shop is larger than it looks from the front. Is the tattoo place next door also yours?"

Rosie answered, "It's my boyfriend's store. They're operated separately, of course, but it makes it easy for us to visit."

"When I pulled into the parking lot, I saw there's also a big building behind his store. Is that used by you, as well?"

Rosie and I both knew that we didn't have to answer this question but to refuse to do so would be a huge red flag.

If Brown didn't leave soon, I was definitely headed for Rosie's powder room.

"It is his, but we both use it for storage. Although, I do admit that he's a bit of a pack rat. He keeps things he should get rid of, but he likes to hang on to odds and ends. For instance, he's got several old motorcycles and their parts scattered around in that big dusty place."

"Really? I'm an old gear head myself. Do you suppose he'd let me take a look at what he's got? He might have just the part I've been looking for. I have a beat up bike myself."

Rosie kept on, as if she was invincible.

"He's out of town for a couple of weeks right now, but I'm sure he wouldn't mind me letting you in to look around. Let me just get the key."

Rosie went behind the counter and pulled a small box from under the cash register. "Let me see here, I know he gave me an extra key some time ago. And I think I labeled it." She poked around in the box, pulled up some keys that had no labels, and then said, "Nope, not here. You know what? Let me check my purse, maybe I just dropped it in there." She dug into the bottom of her big satchel and then shook her head.

I watched in awe as she pretended to regret not having the key.

"I am so sorry, Mr. Brown, but I guess I don't know where that key is after all. But as soon as he's back, I'll let him know that you're interested in checking it out."

"Oh, well, there's no rush."

He moved further toward the door. "I'll just leave my card for him. Ladies, it's been a pleasure. Thanks for the coffee. And if there's anything else that occurs to you, Miss Miller, you also have my card."

"Good meeting you, Mr. Brown. Come back sometime and try one of my brownies," Rosie hollered as the bells chimed the door's closing.

Rosie and I looked at each other. Neither of us smiled. We looked as if we were thinking the same thing, *Is he satisfied?*

But before we could talk, I rushed for the bathroom.

Spoiled Chicken

Faith Miller's Story

scratch (n): satisfaction for an irritant
scratch (n): to withdraw from a
competition
scratch (n): without resources
Scratch (n): Satan, the devil

(Random House College Dictionary)

One

"Hey, hija. Step all the way back to the barn door to see if anything is showing past the tarps."
Rosie's dad finished stacking bundles of pine straw in front of tarps hung from the ceiling of the barn, just as Frankie's truck pulled up with the final load of product from our old warehouse.

Rosie moved over to do as he asked. She checked from different angles, then said, "Si, Papa Padre, esta bien. It looks like the storage shed of a cheapskate gardener who hoards the straw stolen from his customers' trees." She threw her straw hat towards him and added, "And you're such a smart business guy, that you sell it back as special organic straw, hygienically processed. You were a green, recycling hippie before it was ever trendy."

Her familiar laugh made me remember our fun times. It gave me hope that maybe we could still be all right, despite our current crisis. I wished we were laughing around the table in her shop instead of out here in the country at her father's place.

"Watch your sass, Miss CEO. I might be a hippy gardener, but I'm not on the run from the po-lice like you. Show some respect to your old man." They laughed together, then Rosie kissed the top of his head as she carried another tray of plants past the tarp curtain.

The barn was drafty, but not dirty. It looked like it could have held a cow or two at one time, but by the clean smell of the place now, no animals had lived here recently. The best thing about the barn was its location. It was far enough into the country that there was very little traffic around Rosie's family's property.

I stretched my back and tried to get comfortable in the rusted folding chair Rosie's dad had found for me. For the last several days, worry about our situation had given me terrible stomach cramps. I hated that my stress-related IBS was so visible. It's hard to hide diarrhea. On my last trip across the yard to the bathroom in their house, I tripped over the damn cat and fell on the gravel path. So now my leg hurt, my stomach spasmed, and my palms burned from the scrapes. As I tried to relax on this rickety chair, I saw big palmetto bugs crawling out of the pine straw. I scooted away, worried they intended to crawl up my leg.

I hated nature, but because of my mistake at the prison, we had to move our entire packaging division to the country into this old barn. I didn't like sharing Rosie's laugh with her dad. Hearing them tease each other was like listening to a foreign language. In my world, my sisters and I would have needed prayers for forgiveness if we'd spoken so casually to our parents. We may have even needed a coat hanger whipping to be sure we got the message.

Logically, I knew I should be grateful that Rosie's folks had come to our rescue. With no hesitation, they had offered a solution. "Come on," they said, "Get your plants back to our country air before that guy comes back snooping around."

Investigator Brown made it sound like he only wanted to admire Frankie's cycles in the locked warehouse, but we were certain he really wanted to poke into our lives. If he couldn't get me on selling the key for the prison escape, he would mess me up some other kind of way. It wasn't fair, but he was that kind of person. He was one of those guys that want to prove themselves smart. If he could get a search warrant for our warehouse, he would know about our business.

My poor stomach knew it was my fault. If I hadn't been so greedy with the prison key deal, if I hadn't moved too quickly, our business would not have been disrupted. Rosie acted like it was no big deal, and of course, Frankie shadowed Rosie. Still, I knew the truth.

I'd known since we were kids that Rosie was close to her family. But now that we had to mix with them, I knew I didn't like sharing her. Listening to them today, I thought they sounded like the stupid Waltons.

"Frankie, once this last batch is unloaded, my mom has hot enchiladas for us." Rosie wiped her face with the bandana she wore around her neck. She looked cute with her face flushed. "Where's Ron? I thought he was going to help with our loads."

Ron, a friend of Frankie's, sometimes made deliveries for our business. He was about our age, taller than Frankie, with lighter hair. Kind of blonde. He didn't have as many tattoos as Frankie - at least that I could see. I never spent much time with him, but Rosie trusted him, so to me, he was just part of our overhead costs.

"Oh, never mind, there he is, pulling into the drive now. Frankie, you and Ron carry the rest of the plants behind the tarp, and then we are done here. This worked out great." Frankie nodded and smiled back at Rosie, like a kindergarten kid praised by his teacher for washing his hands.

As Rosie's dad passed by, he asked me, "Miss Faith, do you need help getting to the house? An arm to lean on?" I checked his smile for another meaning, but he seemed normal. In my mind, it paid to be paranoid, even about the Waltons.

"Thanks, no, sir, I'll be fine. I'll just take it slow."

Then Rosie called out, "Come on, everybody, Mama's got food and iced tea for us, and she's tired of keeping the kids out of the salsa. Let's call it a day."

She grabbed Frankie from behind and shouted, "Are you hungry, Frankie-o?"

Ron stood close by me and mumbled, "Too much love around here for me." He put a twang to 'love,' as if he was singing a country western song. He turned to me and said, "Let's go, Fussy Faith, little lady. I missed breakfast."

I gave him my 'I don't want to play' look, but as I stood, my leg gave out, and I landed against his arm.

"It kills you, doesn't it? Imagine, socializing with the help. What outrageous behavior." I wasn't sure if he was flirting with me or being sarcastic. After all, he was just the delivery guy. But his arm was already around my shoulder, so we limped toward the house.

My leg really did hurt, and I definitely didn't care about staying for lunch, but I needed my purse from the kitchen. Then I could get back to town.

"You're glaring at me with the same look you gave those water beetles," Ron laughed.

"Palmetto bugs."

"Whatever. And stop showing off. I already know you're a librarian, as well as a drug dealer."

I tried to pull away, but he held on. In a fake innocent voice, he asked, "Don't you like being called a librarian, Miss Fuss?"

Rosie and Frankie came up behind us. They were holding hands and laughing along with Ron. Rosie tugged my hair and said to Ron, "Don't tease Faith just because you haven't read a book since high school. If it's not spelled in computer code, you don't even look at it. You're both too smart for us regular people."

I smiled like I was having a good time, too. "What kind of programming do you do?" I asked.

"Right now, it's just basic runs. But someday I'll be really good. I finished my degree at tech last month. Now I'm waiting for a call-back from that big distribution center that opened last year off I-95. I'm trying to get on there in a starting slot. In the meantime, I make deliveries for Frankie when he's busy at his ink shop. It pays me enough for my truck payment."

I didn't let him know it, but I found Ron's humility refreshing. It seemed real, although it could be part of his 'nice guy' disguise. Some guys in our business liked to do the whole gangster personality. Other guys hid out in a pose like an Eagle Scout. But with Ron, it was possible he was simply a nice guy. At least he wasn't like those people who pumped themselves up as the smartest or richest or sexiest or whatever.

So I gave him a polite smile, "I hope it works out for you."

"Thanks, Miss Fuss, your ebullient enthusiasm warms my heart." Ron squeezed my shoulder, and we limped into the kitchen. My stomach tightened, but not in a bad way.

When Rosie's kids ran to greet us, her youngest smeared tomato sauce on my jeans.

"Oh, Chiquita, your hands are sticky. Tell Miss Faith you're sorry." Over her shoulder, Rosie added to me, "I'm sorry, Faith. Her hugs can be messy sometimes."

"No problem, I'll just throw them in the laundry when I get home."

I pretended that this was no big deal. But everyone knows red stains are hard to get out. So with that hassle facing me, along with the bugs, the fact that their house toilet was slow to flush, and the prospect of major stomach problems if I ate even one enchilada, I was definitely ready to leave. Not to mention the headache building the whole morning from all of their noisy laughter.

As I grabbed my purse and said my goodbyes, Ron looked toward me. He was at the lunch table, holding one of the kids, with a plate of food in front of him.

In his look, it seemed as if he knew exactly how I felt. I thought I even saw a hint that if he could, he would leave with me. Of course I wasn't sure, since I didn't know him that well. Not that I cared, but he certainly seemed friendly to me today during this ordeal.

As I closed the kitchen door, he looked up again, and I heard him shout, "Drive carefully, Faith."

Everyone else in the kitchen was busy feeding kids or filling plates. It felt unusual to have someone concerned about me. My stomach tightened again. This time I was sure it was not from my IBS. It felt like a flip, just like in a cheap romance novel. I hurried away, embarrassed I was such a cliché.

Two

A few days later, at her shop, Rosie and I were tallying our new orders. Her round table was cluttered with spools from the calculator she used, along with scraps from our chicken salad lunch.

"Rosie, I can't believe you would ask such a thing of me."

I stared at her, not sure that she was kidding. Always before, her suggestions to redo my clothes and hair was a running joke between us. She knew I liked plain style, and I knew she wouldn't push me too hard. But now her plan was too specific.

"Faith, this is business. It's as much business as these account invoices we're going over. Think of this Chamber of Commerce dance as just another business deal. Since I'm on the hospitality committee, I have to go. And if you come, too, it's a chance to show we have nothing to hide. When Brown asks around about us, we need to be known as struggling entrepreneurs. Of course we're on the quirky side of the Chamber roster, but a tattoo parlor and a palm reading shop are not illegal. That's the message we want to stress."

"I do understand that. I'm glad you're involved with the Chamber, for the same reason I joined the Rotary last week. But I don't need to be at the Chamber dance. Right now I'm an unemployed librarian, so it's fine for me to keep a lower profile than you. Let's not argue about this. You go to the dance, and tell me about it afterwards."

Rosie pulled the run tape from the calculator and attached it to a batch of invoices. "Faith, I need you. Since I'm on the hospitality committee, I'll be busy with the tickets and the buffet. You know that Frankie can't handle conversation or mix with those people. He'd look dumb sitting at our table all by himself. But he'll be fine with you and Ron there."

"Wait, how did Ron get into this plan? He's just a delivery guy. Plus, you know I can't go to a dance with some guy. You know that's not what I do. I'm sorry, but absolutely not."

"Faith, we need to protect our investment. We need to be seen just as normal as that ditzy girl with the hair salon who joined recently. Who, by the way, just got voted onto the Civic Pride Committee."

"You mean Lisa? I thought she ran the pill sales traffic. I see her at the jail visiting inmates fairly often."

"Hurrah, you just made my point. You and I think she has a business on the side, separate from doing hair. But to the Chamber, she's just a former cheerleader with a full service hair and spa salon."

We frowned at each other, wondering who was going to break first. Then Rosie giggled.

"Oh, yes, that spa definitely has full service. With a couple of pills or some powder, I bet those fancy new chairs at the wash station can flat-out recline." We both laughed, picturing the possibilities.

I put on a pretend pout. "I don't know why I let you abuse me this way. But all right, I'll go with you and Frankie. But that's all I agree to. We don't need Ron to go. Plus, I get to wear whatever I want."

"Please, Faith, let's keep this simple. You know you can't wear your nun's habit. People will think you're either a Charles Manson groupie or a foreign terrorist. I'll do the shopping for you. You can think of it as a costume, not a statement about the 'real you.' Besides, this gives you an excuse to order something new from Victoria Secret." Rosie knew that I dressed differently in my secret, non-public life.

"Fine, whatever. You shop, I'll go. But not with Ron along."

Rosie looked sideways at me as she got up from the table. "You know he likes you."

"You know I don't like to talk about that high school kind of stuff."

"All right, fine, I won't tell you what he said. But it is definite that Frankie will not go without Ron along, too.'"

I put the list of pending orders in my file box, along with the bank deposit slips and Rosie's stack of invoices. I double locked it, put my key in my purse, and handed Rosie's back to her. I'd stop at our safety deposit box at the bank on my way home.

"So, what did he say?"

Three

I looked nice. The navy blue halter dress Rosie chose fit perfectly. When I first put it on in her shop, she teased, "Faith, you look like a naughty librarian. And if you'd let me add suede boots with bronze hardware, all the men at the dance will think you left your whip in the car. This outfit has the potential for some serious dominatrix speculation."

Of course, I rolled my eyes at her, but snuck another peek in the mirror as Rosie finished fussing with my hair.

Without my baggy khakis and long cardigan, I felt exposed, surprisingly, though, not anxious. Rosie's explanation that this dress was a costume made perfect sense to me. I did feel confused about whether my true self was the pile of crumpled beige tossed on the chair, or if it was even my secret collection of lingerie in my bedroom drawer. Both of those styles were familiar friends for me. This new look was confusing. But I liked it. I decided not to worry about which was my true self, and for tonight, I would enjoy being disguised as a model in a catalog.

A couple of hours later at the party, Ron grabbed my arm. "Come on, Faith. Let's join the line dance. I haven't done the 'Boot Scootin' Boogie since last summer's Peach Festival. And then I was so drunk on peach brandy fizzes I about upchucked right there on Main Street."

"How charming." I glanced over at Frankie, expecting him to frown, not wanting us to leave him at the table alone. But he waved me off. He was talking with the commander of the local VFW chapter. They had a sketch for the guy's new tattoo scribbled on a napkin between them.

The whole awkwardness of having Ron at the dance with us was avoided since Rosie and I arrived early to help set up the buffet. Frankie and Ron came in later, so loose and laughing, it was obvious to me they'd smoked some of our product in the parking lot.

"So, Faith, Faith, Faith, please dance with me." Ron put his hands together as if in prayer. People around us smiled, as if we were a cute couple. Their attention seemed friendly but felt strange.

"Oh, all right. But don't be too showy."

When Rosie told me earlier that Ron 'liked me,' it made me nervous. Of course, I had to ask for details. Rosie was counting money from the till when I asked, and she didn't even look up.

"It's not a big deal. He thinks you are interesting. He doesn't get why you act stand-offish, but he said he doesn't need to know. His view is that if Frankie and I like you, that's enough for him. Basically, he likes hanging with us all."

At that point, she looked up from the stack of cash. "Faith, it's not complicated. He likes us, he likes you, we're all good. It's not like he's seeking a love partner and a picket fence. He's just a guy who likes to have fun."

Ron led me to the dance floor, in the back row of the crowd. I had never done line dancing before, but I tried to act like I spent my teens dancing to the Electric Slide like every other girl raised in the south. I almost forgot that instead, I had been on stage in smoky prison chapels, banging a tambourine while strangers imagined things about me.

The lady beside me smiled when we got in step with her. Her sequined jacket sparkled under the lights, and she strutted like a Rockette. When she stumbled and brushed my arm, I simply smiled at her. I thought it was ridiculous for a woman her age to be so tipsy and flashy, but I put those thoughts aside. Surprisingly, my critical thoughts didn't try to push through. My head stayed quiet, and I danced like it was a regular Saturday night. Ron looked over at me, and as if he read my mind and yelled, "A girl's just got to have fun on a Saturday night!"

I felt dizzy, wondering how he knew what I was thinking. Usually Rosie was the only one who could read my thoughts. I looked back at Ron and shouted, "That's for sure," and did a little kick like the lady next to me.

When the music cut to a slow dance, Ron and I headed back to our table. On the way, a guy stopped in front of me. He was our age, smiling, and only a little drunk. "Hey, don't I know you?" he asked me.

I looked at him, honestly puzzled. Ron must have read my expression, since he moved up next to me.

"You probably don't recognize me out of uniform. I'm one of the front gate officers at the jail. Don't you visit the jail sometimes? You look different tonight, but I'm sure I've seen you there."

For a moment, I froze. I crossed my arms across my chest as if protecting the payload in my bra. It startled me to realize that I had no drugs on me. I had no bra to hold the drugs. Tonight I was free of all that. I dropped my arms back down. "Sure, I do recognize you now." I didn't say my name, just smiled. "And you're right; I have been there to visit a few times. My cousin's an inmate there. It cheers him up to see family."

The guy leaned in closer to me. I smelled fresh beer and strong cologne. "Sure, I'd do the same for family." He put on a serious look, like he was saying something profound. "Family's all that matters. Like tonight, I'm here with my sister 'cause she didn't want to come alone." He paused to think. "Not that coming to a dance is the same as a jail visit."

At that point, Ron moved even closer. "You're so right, buddy. So, excuse us, we need to get back to our table. If we leave our friend alone too long, he might drink our beers."

I smiled and nodded to the guy as Ron led me away. As we walked together, Ron said, "I thought I better get you away from him before he asked too many questions. Besides, if you told any more lies, your cousin would have been the head of his school's Christian Athletes' group who was locked up for shoplifting a Mother's Day card."

It was easy to smile at Ron's nonsense. And I liked being rescued from the awkward meeting with that guy. As we sat down at our table, Rosie waved from the door of the service kitchen. She mouthed, "Come help."

On my way across the floor, my high heels tipped and tapped. I liked feeling flippy and fragile. In my usual oxfords, I hugged the ground, ready to take care of myself. But in my strappy heels, I felt lighter, looser. I felt that the world was a nicer place - that not everyone was waiting to trip me.

The fun of feeling free lasted the rest of the evening. I laughed when Ron teased Frankie about running out of skin for more tattoos. It was touching when he spoke about his truck. "It's the first vehicle I've ever owned. I know it's dumb to love a truck, but if it wasn't such a girlie thing to do, I'd give my beautiful truck a name."

So we all toasted Ron's truck. "Cheers to your Chevy," Rosie said, starting a drinking game. We each took a turn suggesting a name for his truck, followed by a chug from our glass. My idea was 'Sebastian.' But Ron said, "Sorry, Miss Faithful, but I'm too drunk to pronounce it."

When Rosie opened her purse for lipstick, she found the most recent Victoria catalog. "This came in the mail as I left the house," she laughed. "Come on, Faith, you and I will have a contest to see which one of us owns the most of them."

I shook my head like it was too dumb but joined in with her. "This one is pretty in turquoise, but not very comfortable." Ron grabbed the catalog, and he and Frankie penned in crazy tattoos on the photos of the models. Neither of the guys seemed surprised that I had a secret hobby. They were too busy being gross. I felt a little dizzy that my two lives were getting blurred, but I didn't worry about it.

When the lights blinked to signal the end of the party, we crowded onto the floor for the last dance. Ron and I smiled as Rosie and Frankie kissed each other, and Ron gave me a hug. "It's been a fun night," he said.

I smiled at him on the way back to the table and added a swish to the tip tap of my heels.

Four

When I woke up the next morning, I didn't feel anything ridiculous like 'happy.' I did look forward to getting together with Rosie to talk about the party. And I thought Ron might drop by her shop.

I started to put on my usual khakis and sweat shirt. But then I thought better of it. With a shrug, I pulled on some tight jeans that had never been outside. I usually wore them only at home. I posed in front of my closet mirror, admiring the curve at the hip. My hip. Today I added a silky purple tank. I didn't look back at the mirror because I didn't want to give myself time to change my mind.

At Rosie's, she greeted me, "Hey, girl, come sit with me." She was slumped over her reading table. "Help yourself to some herbal tea. I have such a hangover, I can hardly move." She slurped from the mug in her hand and inhaled the steam with a noisy snort.

As I fixed my tea, she glanced up. "Look at you. Why are you dressed like a normal person? Did you get your secret closet mixed up with your sack cloth and ashes, martyred-nun collection?"

"They're just jeans. It's no big deal."

Rosie heard me mutter and shrug off my change. But she knew me well enough to not push for an explanation. I joined her at the table and moved her crystal ball and tarot cards out of the way. Even though she preferred to simply read palms, some of her older customers still liked the more elaborate props.

She put the stuff onto the floor and said, "I don't care how bad I feel right now, I had so much fun last night the pain is worth it. It's been forever since Frankie and I have been out in a crowd."

She bit into an oatmeal cookie. "He never would have gone without Ron there."

A raisin dropped from the cookie onto the table. She carefully wet her pinkie finger to pick it up. Just as carefully, she said, "It looked like you had a good time, too." With equal caution, she went on, "You looked great."

Rosie did know me well, but I knew her just as well. She wanted to talk about my clothes and Ron, but she stayed safe. "People really liked the buffet."

I laughed and leaned toward her. "Don't worry, I'm fine. I just decided to stay in costume for a while. Do you think purple makes me look fat?"

"I think you look terrific. Like a fashion model. Compared to you, I feel like a schlumpy wannabe gypsy." She gulped more tea.

"So, what part did you like best?" I asked her.

"When you told me about that conversation between you and that jail officer. I was so proud of you, like you were a full package partner. I like having a partner who is smart, and pretty, and who can mix it up with both jailers and chamber wives. I felt proud to be your friend."

I hadn't expected Rosie to give such a serious answer. "Thanks. I learned from watching you."

She ate more cookie and wiped her mouth. "I think it helped that you wore a costume."

"You're right. All this time, I hadn't figured out that normal clothes are costumes, too."

We were still smiling at each other when Ron came through the shop door. "I sure hope you have coffee."

Rosie told him, "There's some in the back that Frankie made. He can't stand tea."

Once he joined us at the table, he stretched out his legs and leaned back. "You ladies were spicy last night. That was a fun party. Some of those chamber people outlasted us."

He reached across me to the cookie plate. "Hey, Faith, I like that purple color. It matches my eyes this morning." Rosie and I both smiled, and he went on, "And as for you, Missy Rose, I sure hope these cookies are from your special recipe and not ones for your kids' lunch boxes."

"Sorry, Ron, my stash was empty. These are just regular cookies. Which reminds me. I need you and Frankie to drive out to the farm today to bring back some product. I've got orders I need to get packaged for a big delivery later this week."

He pulled in his legs and sat up straighter. "Sure, Rose, no problem for today. We can go early and be back in time to watch Atlanta lose again." Then he paused and fiddled with his cup. "But later in the week, you're going to need to get someone else to make the deliveries. I'm leaving town."

Rosie was so surprised; she sloshed tea into her saucer. "What? You're kidding. You didn't say anything last night about leaving."

My stomach suddenly felt tight and uncomfortable. I didn't say anything I didn't look at either of them.

"No, it's a sudden thing. Last night when I got home, my old girlfriend Elsie called. We got to talking, and she suggested I stay with her over in Myrtle Beach until the company calls with my start date." He smiled a little. "Elsie's real easy to be with, and she's got a place of her own. She says I can get a temporary job as a bartender at the club she waitresses in, which would be enough to keep my truck payment going. And she gets that once I start my coding job, I'll have to move closer to work."

"Well, damn, Ron, we just got you trained right." Rosie reached over to thump his hand. "And you didn't even rip us off too much." They laughed a little. I smiled along with them.

"Rose, you are the best boss a bum like me could ask for. And, Miss Faith, you are the smartest drug dealer in the county. I'm going to miss teasing you."

He stood. "Let me go get Frankie on the road, so we'll be back in time for the game. You both take care." I watched Rosie smile at his back as he walked through the door connecting Frankie's shop with Rosie's. I tried to smile, too, as I wondered if I needed to rush to her bathroom.

"Damn, I hate that he's leaving," Rosie said. "It was fun having someone we could trust that we all got along with." She looked at me. "I thought even you were starting to feel comfortable with him."

"Sure, Ron was a good guy. But, you know, people come and go. It's no big deal. It's part of the business to get along with the staff." I meant everything I said, but I didn't have words for the rest of my feelings. I did know my stomach hurt, and I was tired of smiling.

I gathered up my purse. "Sorry to run, Rosie, but I've got some errands to get done. I'll call you later."

Outside her shop, I stood by my car and felt the cool breeze of the morning on my bare shoulders. I rubbed my stomach with one hand. With the other hand, I dug in my purse for my car keys. From the trunk of my car, I got a long trench coat. I buttoned it, tied the sash, and pulled the collar close to my neck. The beige coat covered the purple of my tank and most of my jeans. I pulled on the brown leather gloves from the pocket.

Ron's truck was next to my car. When I pushed my key into his fender, I pushed so hard it hurt my finger. But I didn't let that stop me. I knew how to do hard things. I remembered the hurt of my fingers from gripping my tambourine so many years ago. My key left a deep scratch from the rear bumper to the front headlight.

At the front of his truck, I looked back at the scratch and admired the straightness of my mark. It was as if I'd used a ruler. But of course, my good posture kept me from wobbling.

I rounded the truck and paused. I said to myself in a soft voice, for my ears only, "A girl's just got to have some fun. It's only fair."

When I finished my work on the other side of his truck, I walked back over to the passenger side door. I rubbed the scratch. I felt soothed by the depth of it, proud that I had pushed through the pain on my finger.

Then I walked over to my car and shivered a little as the breeze picked up. The morning sun created a sparkle on my glossy black Mustang. I drove away.

Burnt Sugar

Wilma's Story

Give God a chance to show up and show out.

One

The guy that drooled on my neck was not the love of my life. He was in my bed by invitation, which proved one more time that my string of bad choices was still unwinding. But he wasn't a rapist, or a bully, or a traveling salesman. He was just Travis.

We've known each other since fourth grade. Even though we've never had a time together that lasted longer than a week, he's always stayed a friend. Travis and I dated off and on in high school. After we graduated, we almost got serious about each other. But then I met Ted and fell over the moon in love.

Being sweet and understanding as he is, Travis stepped aside 'with no hard feelings' as he put it. He went on to work with his dad in his car repair shop, and I went on to mess myself up with Ted. By the time I started to miss the steadiness of Travis, the corn was off the cob with Ted and I was pregnant with my sweet baby Richie.

Travis now owns his own body shop here in town, which was part of the reason he came home with me last night. He fixed the quarter panel of my car that got caved in by Ted at Walmart. We sort of traded with each other, my parts and labor for his parts and labor.

The second reason I'm here next to Travis is because he brings me back to the memories of being young. It felt good to still be able to negotiate a deal with him. The older I get, the more I worry that my butt looks wider than Oprah's. Of course, Travis showed his years, as well. I remembered when he first got his tattoo on his shoulder. Over the years, it had stretched so much that instead of "Mom", it now read "MOOOM". It had faded, too, even with the shine of morning flashing on it.

I needed to get up to start my day, but my knee was stuck under his big hairy thigh. I thought if I could slip out to the shower and get coffee started before he woke up, he wouldn't expect us to have another go at it. By my figuring, we had an even trade, with no gratuity needed for this deal. But I was sure Travis wouldn't agree, since he'd always been a little over-eager. He would probably hope for a surcharge for parts deterioration or maybe a house call.

It was my day off from my job at the prison, and Ted's parents had my two kids for an overnight visit. Delores spoiled them with pancakes in the morning and her permission to watch cartoons all day. She even carried their lunch of fried bologna sandwiches with chips and soda in to the living room, so they wouldn't miss any of their cartoon marathon. They liked to sit on each side of her on the couch while they all munched away. Delores bought the fancy bologna without the string on it. She claimed it was healthier. Their grandpa Wilbur had to go to work during the day. He managed the Dollar Store close to the bypass, but Delores didn't work due to her diabetes. I knew when I picked them up that afternoon, she most likely would have a casserole of cheesy macaroni and a package of sugar cookies for us to bring home, for no reason except to stretch the specialness of the day.

Most times when I picked them up after a stay over, they were still in their pajamas from the night before, with their eyes in a trance from watching television all day. Due to her sugar problem, Delores shouldn't eat all those good things, but she sacrificed that way for the kids.

I never worried about the kids being at their grandparents' house. If the visits happened when Ted was drinking, his parents would never let him close to the kids. We did try to make it together, but Ted's terrible temper didn't get better. He kept feeling the need to hurt me, and I didn't like the kids seeing my black eyes. When he stole from his dad and got so mad because I told his mom about it, I was relieved when he was arrested and sent back to jail. Him being locked up was too bad, but I'd be lying if I pretended it wasn't just fine with me. Him gone makes me less jumpy.

He's in the local jail, not at the big prison where I work. My prison is the super max that got built a couple of years ago. Our local politicians got them to build it here instead of in the upstate by offering for free this big acreage out by the swamps. The area had been empty for years. The plan was that the prison would be a cash cow for our town. It would have jobs for all the people laid off when the cotton mills shut down. Then the paycheck money would slosh around town for our new prosperity, as they put it. It hadn't quite worked out that way since most of the contracts for food and maintenance got snatched up by big companies in the next county. We did get a new motel built for the prisoners' families to stay at when they came to visit on weekends. What I heard was that some of them inmate families had gotten to know each other real well. They had weekend parties together after visiting closed on Saturday. Kind of like tailgating at football games.

Anyway, it was never the plan for the prison to hire so many of us ladies from town. It was always assumed that the men would want the macho jobs. But around here, most of the applicants who passed the reading test were girls. They even offered special reading classes for those who flunked to give them another shot at the test, but we still didn't get many men who qualified.

I was real happy to get a job at the prison, being as the work is steady, and it had great medical insurance. The last couple of months, I've been assigned to the roving perimeter post. This means I drive around the fence line in a truck. I drive for my whole shift, around and around for hours. I have two big responsibilities. First, I have to be sure no inmates get over the fence to escape. This is a pretty basic deal. If I ever see someone climbing over, I am supposed to shoot them. Since it hasn't happened to me yet, I don't know how I will respond. But I feel important carrying that responsibility. Frankly, I am surprised I am trusted to shoot someone.

Travis just shifted over, so now my knee is free. I should get up, but I feel so comfortable I hate to leave.

When they told me the second part of my job, it was more complicated. I was supposed to watch for anyone coming out of the woods who tried to throw contraband packages over the fence into the prison yard. If that happened, I was supposed to stop my truck, call over the radio to the control room for assistance, and then grab my shotgun and tell the thrower to lay on the ground. I've never seen a thrower on my shift, but one time I did spot a package. I wish I had seen the person who threw it. This contraband problem was important because there was so much money involved. When the inmates got a package, they sold the stuff in it to other inmates and made a ton of money, even after paying the cost of the thrower. Usually the packages had cell phones, drugs, or alcohol in them. The thrower cushioned the bottles as careful as a UPS shipment.

Aside from those two parts of my job, the rest is pretty boring. Just driving in circles. One time a guy on another shift got so bored; he fell asleep and drove into a light post. He claimed the monotony hypnotized him. Nice try, but he still got suspended.

The driving in circles did give me time to think, which I've always loved to do, like now, lying here so peaceful. All through my school years, teachers put notes on my report cards about me spending too much time daydreaming. Even after all these years, I find it easier to stay in my head while shit happened around me. Lately I've tried to be more proactive, as they said in my training classes at work. That means not just waiting for the next bad thing to happen, but taking control of situations. That idea of controlling things was new for me, but I liked it. Still, I did love my daydreaming hobby, which was why I still hadn't moved out of bed, daydreaming while MOOOM rises and falls.

Before I pick up the kids this afternoon, I have two things planned. The most fun will be lunch with my friend, Miss Kelly. She lives in a nice doublewide only a mile or so down the road. She used to be at my prison before the big riot, but then she was promoted to a smaller prison nearby. She was with me the day I found the contraband package. Of my recent Good Luck Days, that was a great time. Having Miss Kelly with me made it more special. She is old enough to be my mother, but I think of her as a friend. She doesn't think I was stupid for marrying Ted.

"Wilma, honey," she told me one day, "there's no controlling who we're going to love. And it might not be a very good choice. But it only makes us stupid if we let the person stay when we don't need them anymore. Maybe what we needed when we're young is not the same thing we need when we get some years and some sense. If our needs change, then love is not enough reason to hang onto somebody." I thought of that a lot when I got to missing Ted. I didn't need him, and I didn't want him around, but I did still love him. I was just glad he was gone.

Miss Kelly had been a widow lady for a lot of years, but lately she'd taken up with the investigator at work. He spent a lot of time out of town for work, but when he was around, they had cook-outs and went to the flea market. I doubted they had too much fun, if you know what I mean, them being so old. But I had seen them holding hands. Miss Kelly's daughter, Sharon, graduated ahead of me in school. She was stuck up, but Miss Kelly was never like that. She was a lot like I'd want a mom to be, if I ever had a choice. I haven't seen her in a while because we'd been on different shift schedules so it will be fun to meet her at the Cracker Barrel to catch up over lunch.

My own mom was gone. First, she killed her liver with drinking, and when it got so bad she couldn't drink anymore, she shot herself dead. I kind of understood why she didn't want to live. But I wished she'd picked a nicer place to die, like a pretty garden with a fountain or even a comfy recliner. Instead, she went out by a dumpster and pulled the trigger. Like her version of trash to trash, instead of dust to dust.

I had a little mystery errand planned for today also. My father-in-law passed a message to me from this man, Mr. Sanders, who owned a mobile home dealership, with the fancy kind of trailers. Supposedly, he had a job I'd be interested in. I was going to talk with him, but most likely, the job was cleaning out repos, which I wasn't sure I wanted to do. Still, the extra money would be a good idea. That was the 'planning ahead' thing kicking in.

Well, Travis just stirred again so I guess I better get going and start my day.

Two

Mr. Sanders carried his self as you'd expect, him being last year's Businessman of the Year. He'd been honored at a banquet the Chamber of Commerce held out at the Holiday Inn. A friend of mine helped with the catering and brought me some leftover ham.

When I walked into his office for our appointment, his certificate hung in a big gold frame on the wall behind his desk. Sitting on the desk itself, right in front, he had a photo of his wife and son, Bill. It must have been taken at the beach some years ago. Mrs. Sanders wore a straw hat and had a pretty smile. But Bill still had braces on his teeth and was skinny, with long legs and arms. In the photo, he only looked a little like the picture in our newspaper some months ago. That picture was taken after his accident.

Like an important man, Mr. Sanders gave me a big smile and a handshake, and he told me how much he admired the changes my father-in-law had made at the Dollar Store. Still holding his smile, he said, "Wilma, I hear you have been keeping them straight over there at the prison." He laughed like he was the first person to say this.

"Thanks, Mr. Sanders. I'm glad the Chamber helped get the prison built here. It's a good job to have." I may not belong to the Chamber, but I knew how those kind of people talked.

"Yeah, it's been good for the town. Listen, we just got in our newest doublewide model. Do you want to come check it out with me?"

As we walked across the big asphalt lot, he explained that in the manufactured housing business, trailers were now called models. He said he kept some of the more simple models for young couples just starting out, but for the last year, he'd carried more of the luxury editions for families with two paychecks.

"Yes, Wilma, I do believe the economy is coming back. Couples feel more comfortable spending a little more than they planned to. Now take a look at this model. The transporter just brought it in this morning. It has three bedrooms and three bathrooms, one with a jetted tub. It's called the Southern Supreme. You'll never guess why."

He looked at me like I was supposed to really guess. "Because it was made in the South?"

"Good guess, Wilma. You have a very logical mind. But, no. It's made for our southern market because the kitchen has a cabinet fitted out with slots just for storing frying pans. Isn't that something?"

I couldn't tell if he was joking or if he was for real, so I just kept smiling along with him.

The tour of the Supreme would have been more enjoyable if I could picture myself ever living in such a place. But being as I'd just traded sex for a new quarter panel, I didn't feel particularly focused on trends in the trailer park industry. My frying pans dumped on top of each other in a bottom drawer worked just fine in my kitchen. So when he suggested we look at another new model, the Darlington Dream, I said, "Mr. Sanders, not wanting to be rude, but I need to be getting on my way soon. I heard you might have a job opening."

He stopped smiling and ran his hands over and over the shiny Formica counter, as if stroking his dog's head or wiping up a spill. He started to stutter a little, like he wasn't sure what to say next. It was clear that he thought like a businessman and was used to taking care of business deals. But whatever job he had in mind for me was not as simple as wiping grease from the ovens of repos.

Everybody had read in the paper about his family problems. His son, Bill, went to college in the upstate on a track scholarship. He came home for the summer after his freshman year, lived with his folks, and helped out in his dad's business. For fun during the evenings, he hung out with a couple of guys from his high school class. Some of them went to college also, and some were a little older. One of the guys had a date to be deployed to Afghanistan. One night they made the rounds of their usual bars, and on the way home, Bill's Chevy ran off the road onto the soft shoulder. He grabbed the steering wheel too hard, the tires lost traction, and the car flipped over several times.

The guy going to war got killed, and Bill got charged with killing him because he'd been drunk.

Even the dead boy's parents said they didn't want to press charges, but the prosecutor said he had no choice due to state law. That's how Bill ended up with an eight-year sentence. Our paper ran lots of articles about the trial, and they always showed two photos. One photo showed Bill's mug shot, his eyes huge in his thin face. The other photo showed Bill's face buried in his mom's shoulder, with Mr. Sanders' arms around both of them. The background of the photo showed a sheriff's deputy, waiting to cuff him and lead him out of the courtroom to prison.

Like everyone in town, I knew about the situation, but not in a particular way, since I didn't personally know the people involved. It wasn't like our families knew each other from lounging at the country club pool together. Bill's story sounded like a lot of our town's news, bad stuff just happens. I'd pushed it to my daydream brain, in a large file of bad luck stories.

Mr. Sanders finally looked up from the Formica counter and said, "Wilma, Bill moved to your prison a few weeks ago. He's been through all the processing stuff, and due to his long sentence, the requirement is for him to be at a max prison." He looked at me hopefully. "I don't suppose you've seen him in one of the housing units?"

"No, Mr. Sanders, I haven't seen him. Mostly I'm assigned to the perimeter - not in the housing units." I thought Mr. Sanders probably wanted to ask me to watch out for Bill. But as he went on, I found it wasn't that simple.

"Right, I'd heard that's what you were assigned to. See, Wilma, Bill is not having an easy time of it. Some of the white guys in his cellblock offered to watch out for him, with him being so skinny and looking so young." When he said this, Mr. Sanders' voice shook a little, but then he went on.

"He'd been thankful for their help and kept them supplied with candy bars and sodas. His mother and I felt relieved that he had this arrangement, so we put extra money in his prison bank account for whatever he needed to buy for the other fellows when they went to the canteen. But recently things changed, and now his friends keep pushing him for something else. When Bill called the other night, he was crying."

Three

Our orientation training included a segment where an inmate's family asked us to watch out for their loved one. But if "watch out" involved anything more than a referral to the prison chaplain, our instructions clearly said that we could not talk about prison business.

I started to explain this to Mr. Sanders, but he talked over me. It had been hard for him to get started with his sad story, but now it came in a gush.

"These friends are not friends. They are threatening Bill. They say they don't just want his canteen stuff anymore. They want him to finance the upfront cost of sending a package of tobacco over the fence."

Inmates liked to smoke. But several years ago, the state prisons started a smoke-free policy. So right away, contraband cigarettes became big business. The canteen doesn't carry tobacco products, so the profits of selling smuggled cigarettes could be more than selling drugs or alcohol. For the minimal cost of a couple pounds of loose tobacco and some wrapping papers, inmates cleared a profit when they sold it.

"Mr. Sanders, you need to call the Warden. Tell him what's going on." I told him this with a sympathetic frown, wishing that my suggestion would end this conversation.

"Wilma, I already talked to the Warden. Since I'd met him earlier at a Chamber meeting, I felt sure he'd straighten out Bill's situation. I thought I only needed to call him since he seemed to be a reasonable guy. But he only offered to put Bill in isolation, on protective custody. For that, Bill would have to stay there for several months, but what's worse, he'd have to name the guys who threatened him. Wilma, you know he can't give any names. He's got eight years in front of him. He can't even qualify for another prison until he gets his time down. Going on protective custody won't help at all."

Mostly Mr. Sanders's voice stayed calm while he described Bill's problem. But when he talked about the Warden's refusals, he got more agitated.

"This mess seems just another example of how big government complicates the lives of us regular people. The only reason they stopped selling cigarettes was because congress made such a big deal about the rights of non-smokers. Well, smokers have rights, too. Not that Bill smokes, him being an athlete, but he wouldn't be in danger if those other boys could just buy cigarettes like before."

As Mr. Sanders got more excited, it seemed to make him feel better. He stopped stroking the Formica, but slapped it a time or two for emphasis. He didn't use a shouting voice, but he spit a little, like he was giving a speech.

"We talk about 'Big Government' all the time at our Tea Party meetings, and now we have another example, right in the prison in our own town."

I figured Mr. Sanders wanted me to talk to the Warden to try to convince him to waive the requirements in order to get Bill transferred. "Mr. Sanders, I'd help if I could, but the Warden wouldn't listen to me. He's too high up the chain; he doesn't even know who I am. And even if I tried, I'd get in trouble suggesting special treatment for an individual inmate. I'd help if I could, but I'm sorry, I'm just not important enough."

Mr. Sanders took out his wallet and laid five hundred dollar bills on the Formica.

"Wilma, you are such a sweet girl. It seems like you understand about bad luck. As a mother, if you heard my wife crying herself to sleep each night, you'd understand even more. We're not bad people. Bill's not a criminal. If he'd had five beers instead of six, he'd be back on his college campus by now. He wouldn't be afraid to take a shower, or walk by himself to the cafeteria. We're in a bad luck situation."

Mr. Sanders spoke the truth about bad luck. I did understand it. It was the one thing about life that I did understand. There were two things they covered a lot on Dr. Phil. The first was money. For some people, money made their world. Either they tried to get more of it, or they had fun spending it. But for me, I'd never had any money except a paycheck. I didn't have a clue how to get more of it, or make it grow, or any of that financial stuff. I get a paycheck, and then it's gone. I had never been interested in buying stuff, so being broke was not so bad. I mean, if the kids needed shoes, we went to Walmart and we're done. But other people, like my friend Mrs. Kelly, shopped for a hobby. She loved feeling clever in finding bargains. But for me, shopping meant having to be in crowds and feeling stupid since I couldn't buy whatever caught my eye. For me, spending money was not a hobby or a sport.

The second big deal Dr. Phil talked about was sex. He said some people fixed on sex as their "driving force". They loved the thrill of the chase and sweet romance. Well, I'd had love sex. After Ted and I had our arguments, lots of times we ended up in bed. Sometimes we had to be careful how we did it, since sometimes he had hurt me before the romance part kicked in. But Ted made it all right by whispering how much he loved me. Sometimes he even cried, he loved me so much. So even though it may sound weird to other people, I counted this as love sex. And of course, I knew all about quarter panel sex, which to me, in the long run, was like bargaining down the price of something expensive.

So Dr. Phil's two categories were big motivators for a lot of people. For me, neither of them were worth much thought or energy.

In my world, bad luck got my attention. It was what brought people together, since most all of us have bad luck in common.

I looked Mr. Sanders in the eye and told him straight, "I would love to take your money to talk to the Warden, but I don't want to do you wrong. I couldn't rightfully earn your money since I could never convince him about a transfer."

It was then that Mr. Sanders explained the details of the job he had in mind for me.

"Yes, Wilma, I do understand that. And I respect your integrity for not wanting to rip me off. That's not seen so frequently in the business world. But there is a job that you could help Bill with, without talking to the Warden."

I started to smile at the compliment he gave me. Hearing the word "integrity" in referring to me was a bit unusual. But the compliment lost some of its fizz when he went on to explain what he wanted me to do.

"Since your job is to drive the perimeter, I understand that you're in a position to know when a package comes over the fence. Usually you would report it if you saw it or if you saw people throwing it. And normally, you would do your job to try to stop the throw over. All I'm asking is that you not see those things on a certain date and time."

So that's why he invited me to come to his business to talk about a job. Just like it didn't have anything to do with how well I could clean repos, it also didn't have much to do with my precious integrity. It was about Mr. Sanders knowing that my job put me in the right place at the right time. It was no different than him knowing the Warden and trying to convince him to bend the rules. I bet he used the integrity word when he talked to the Warden, too, as a way of making it all right to do something wrong. He asked the same thing from both the Warden and from me, to change how we did our jobs. I was in good company.

Mr. Sanders went on to explain that he already arranged for someone to throw the contraband package over the prison fence, and Bill's protectors had a plan in place for picking it up from the prison yard. All they needed to complete the plan was for me to not see the package after it was thrown. At the timing of my choice, the thrower would come out of the woods, and I wouldn't see him as I drove by. Mr. Sanders talked about these details as if he'd moved past the difficult decisions, and he was delegating duties.

He promised that there would be only tobacco in the package. He said he respected me too much to include marijuana or pills or cell phones or weapons. Those things were illegal, and as he said to me, "Wilma, I would never ask you to take part in anything illegal. That package will only have loose tobacco in it, and that shouldn't be against the rules anyway."

And for not doing anything, just because I understood their bad luck situation, the five hundred dollars should be considered a gift for me. An appreciation gift. Mr. Sanders tapped the bills into a neat pile and slid it across the Formica.

His use of those sweet words, 'bad luck,' left both of us tearful. We didn't have much else in common, but bad luck was a powerful bond. As he handed me the bills, he gave me a quick hug. We didn't feel awkward together, and it didn't feel like I had a job to perform for a boss. It felt like I had a favor I wanted to do for a friend down on his luck.

Once I got back in my car and headed out of the parking lot, I called Miss Kelly to let her know I was running too late to join her for lunch.

"Wilma, hon," she said, "late is no problem. The Cracker Barrel serves all day. Come on ahead. You and I haven't had a chance to chat in quite a spell."

"Thanks, Miss K., but I'm late to pick up the kids, too. It looks like this day is not going to be as easy as I thought. Why don't we plan for sure on our next day off?"

"Sure, Wilma, whatever works best for you. I know it's hard to juggle your schedule and the kids. Take care of yourself, and call me soon."

I felt bad about lying to her, but I just wasn't in the mood to hear Miss Kelly's kind words and upbeat energy. Her life had been going so well, she might have forgot about bad luck.

Four

When my high school guidance counselor described my plans for the future as "a spinning top going 'round and 'round and 'round with an occasional wobble," she spoke the truth. It described perfectly how I earned a living. My job was to drive in circles, 'round and 'round the fence line of this damn prison. Sometimes I reversed direction, just to mix it up a little, but I was still going 'round and 'round. No North, no South, just 'round and 'round. I wondered what my job looked like on a GPS map.

The air that night looked mostly yellow up around the glaring flood lights. My shift started out like a normal one. At our staff inspection, the captain gave us his usual prep talk about staying alert. With us lined up in rows across the room, he reminded us as he did every shift, to watch for contraband coming over the fence.

He sucked in his beer gut to stand taller, and said, "All right now, we know the inmates have their spotters out, waiting for the packages to land."

He looked over at me and raised his voice, "If you perimeter rovers see anything moving, get on your radio to let us know. And remember to watch out for yourselves. People get weird when money's involved. It's bad enough the stuff is coming in; we don't want any of you injured by one of the throwers." Then he shuffled some papers, smiled, and said, "Let's go to work."

Well, hell, yes, I'd be watching all right. Tonight I'd definitely be watching. During the muster, I'd checked out the new girl assigned with me to drive the other truck around the perimeter. She'd only been on the job a few weeks, and she already looked bored. Plus, she'd already taken shortcuts with the rules. During tonight's uniform inspection, she rolled her nails into her palms to hide her red manicure with half moon gang signs. The sergeant saw her do it, but surprise, surprise, he didn't give her an infraction or even challenge her about it. Whatever. Everybody had to make a living. As long as she didn't mess with me, we were cool. Besides, the sergeant saw me noticing his favoritism toward her, so now he owed me. Hopefully, I'd never need any favors from him, but it was nice to have him understand I watched him just like he was supposed to watch us.

When I climbed into my truck, the seat still felt warm from George's big butt. George was the guy on the day shift. It smelled as sweaty as a twelve-hour shift could leave it. I also smelled a hint of garlic in the upholstery. George must have had a sub for dinner. As I stretched the seat belt, I bumped my head on the shotgun hanging behind the driver's seat. The gun was dull black except for the shiny wood stock. The dark color of the wood kind of looked like the kitchen cabinets in the Southern Supreme doublewide Mr. Sanders had been so proud of.

Carl, our armory sergeant, prided himself on maintaining our weapons. He kept them oiled and clean, and he made sure we got to the range on a regular schedule in order to keep our shooting skills sharp. He took his job seriously, one of those ex-military guys. It felt good to be able to trust a co-worker. He didn't ask me out or nag me for my phone number like a lot of these guys.

This prison had so much sex going on with staff, it felt like high school. And that wasn't even counting what happened between staff and inmates. I bet my co-worker got herself that gang manicure because of some inmate inside the fence she had a thing with. Well, too bad. She was stuck on the outside perimeter with me. Unless her honey jumped the fence, he wouldn't get to admire her nails tonight. And if he did jump the fence, I got to rack that shiny shotgun and shoot his ass, just like Sgt. Carl taught out on the range. I smiled at the thought of the spark that would put in this long twelve-hour shift.

But to be real, I was not about all that Rambo shit. Since I had traded sex to get my car fixed only a few days before, I needed to back off my high horse. I wasn't Saint Mother of God, after all. Just a woman trying to get by.

My head talked to itself so much that night. I wasn't wanting to think too much. Besides the 'round and 'round of my job, tonight there was going to be one of those wobbles my counselor predicted.

Tonight I knew I'd be earning my five hundred dollars from Mr. Sanders. I was not going to see a guy in camo come out of the woods. I was not going to see the package fly over the fence. I was not going to see it land on the ground. I was not going to see it roll across the clumpy grass. I was not going to see it, any of it, at all.

Five

"Rover One, what's your location?"

The radio startled me out of a nice daydream of my wedding to Ted. We married in one of those tourist chapels in the Smokey Mountains and had us a honeymoon in a cabin close to Dollywood. Ted's parents paid for everything as their gift to us. I brought back a big jar of apple butter for them as a thank you present. To this day, Delores keeps the empty jar on the shelf in her kitchen to hold spare change for presents for the kids.

Our honeymoon cabin was high up in the trees. It had a big soft bed, but the television didn't get good reception. It didn't matter because the hot tub on the cabin's deck was our favorite thing. In truth, being three months pregnant, I wasn't supposed to use a hot tub, but Ted persuaded me that it would be all right. He wanted us to mess around in the bubbly water, drinking bubbly beer. Ted always knows how to tempt me with not such good ideas.

"Rover One, repeat location." I grabbed the mic to answer the control room operator.

"Control Room, this is Rover One. I'm alongside the chapel on the west yard," I answered.

"10/4. Someone's making a dinner run to Hardee's. Do you want anything?"

"Negative," I answered, "but thanks for asking."

As I put the mic back on the dash, the truck lights caught the glint of a possum on the side of the road up ahead. Since this road I drove was outside the prison fence, animals from the nearby tree line frequently wandered by. The possum stared at me as I drove past it, watching it close to be sure it didn't dart in front of the truck. I didn't want to run over it. I used to have a perimeter partner who purposefully aimed at possums or rabbits, swerving at the last second. He thought it was funny to see the scared animals twist around to get away from the truck's tires. It was a happy day for me when he quit his job. Somebody said he went to work in a slaughter house, but I think they were joking.

Just after I checked the rear view mirror to be sure the possum was safely behind me, I scanned the road ahead and saw a guy carrying a package dash out from the tree line. When he got up to the perimeter road, he drew back his arm and gave a big swing. The package went up, and then up some more, until I could hardly see it through the windshield. As the runner turned and jogged back into the woods, I heard a big swoosh and then a thump. I put both sweaty hands on the wheel and kept driving. Within seconds, I drove past the package lying on the ground, right up next to the fence. But, Sweet Jesus, it was on my side of the fence.

"Oh, no," I muttered to myself. "You were supposed to throw it over the fence, so I couldn't see it. I wasn't supposed to be able to see what I just saw."

I pounded the steering wheel but kept moving on down the road. In the rear mirror, I could see the package still lay where it landed. No miracle had happened to pick it up from the weeds and fly it over the fence into the prison yard.

Well, shit, now what? There was no way I was stopping to throw it over, even if I could, which would not be physically possible. Besides, the inmate spotters were watching from their cell windows. If they got caught bringing it in from the yard, naming me to the investigator would be their free rides. And Mr. Sanders hadn't paid me to guarantee delivery. He had only paid me to not see the thrower. So, I did my part. It wasn't my fault the thrower had a weaker arm than Mr. Sanders's money paid for.

Turning the corner by the cafeteria building, my partner, Rover Two, made the same turn, headed right toward where I had just been. This put her on the stretch of road right by the package. If she saw it, she'd get big time credit with the Captain for "interrupting contraband."

The time I saw a package lying in the cafeteria yard, I got recognized at our staff inspection for being so observant. I even got a certificate, which I framed and hung over my kitchen sink. It was one of the happiest times of my life. Even better, I shared my good luck time with my friend, Miss Kelly. I felt like I gained entry to a club of ladies who can do things, and do things right. Ladies who don't get so down during rough times that they just give up. My mom couldn't be one of those ladies, but I sure did want to join their club. Finding that package made me feel like a new member.

I was smart enough to know that it was not just random luck that caused good things to happen. My first weeks on the job, I paid close attention to learn what they tried to teach us. So when I found the package, I had earned my good luck.

But it sure felt like random luck brought bad luck. And what had first felt like a good deed for Mr. Sanders's random bad luck, suddenly didn't seem like such a good deed after all. And I was pretty sure the cramps starting up in my stomach were telling me that for sure.

As I watched in the mirror, my partner drove past the package. She didn't see it. She didn't even slow down. She was probably too busy admiring her damn nails.

I couldn't believe this was happening. What was I supposed to do? I already earned my money by not seeing it, and then I did see it, lying there like a roadside bomb. If I didn't report it, my supervisors would ask how I missed it. If I did report it, Mr. Sanders would be really mad.

I kept driving. It wasn't possible to give the money back to Mr. Sanders. The five hundred dollars had all been spent. Most of it went for my trailer rent, and some for lottery tickets as an investment, which as usual, didn't work out. And then Ted called from jail. He needed a little money for his canteen account for soda and stuff. He didn't ask for much. Actually, only a little, like it was a test to see if I'd send any at all. Even though we were apart, he was the kids' dad, and he had sounded so sweet and sad when he called.

I kept my speed slow, although I felt like I was racing. After another turn, I came around the corner and came up on the package again. It was still there. Damn, I wished what's her name would just do her damn job and see it. It wasn't fair that my partner was so lazy she couldn't even find shit when it was right in front of her. I couldn't do everything by my damn self. It wasn't fair.

Then, in the darkness, I heard the radio. "Control Room, this is Rover Two."

"Come in, Rover Two."

My partner's voice finally echoed loud and excited over the radio. "You better send the Captain out here right away. There's something on the side of the road that don't look right."

"10/4, hold your position, Rover Two. Rover One, do you copy?"

"10/4, Control," I said in my most professional voice. "I'll keep driving while Rover Two waits for assistance. I haven't seen anything from my position."

Thank God. Please, Jesus, let them believe me. I wiped my sweaty hands on my pants leg and kept driving. 'Round and 'round.

Six

"Could you please slide that avocado dip over this way?" I asked my mother-in-law, Delores.

"That stuff is so good; it's hard to believe it's a vegetable."

Delores was such a sweetheart. She topped off my soda from the two liter bottle on her kitchen table and opened a new bag of potato chips. We drank diet cola due to her diabetes, but it was still tasty. I do love me some cold Coke. Relaxing with Delores in her kitchen was one of my favorite things. I felt safe to tell her almost everything going on in my life.

Through all these years, and despite all the drama with Ted, Delores stayed by my side. She knew about Ted's problems, but as his mother, she also knew how easy it was to love him when he was between his bad spells. She was that way with me, too, loving me no matter what dumb stuff I got mixed up with. If ever I'd been lucky enough to have a close friend in school, it would have been someone like Delores. She was different from Miss Kelly, although they were about the same age. Miss Kelly was like the English teacher I had who stayed on me to say my grammar right. It was good to have Miss Kelly in my life, but nothing beat sitting at Delores's table, taking comfort in her sweet forgiveness of my careless ways.

When I told Delores about the contraband package problem, she shrugged and said, "Weren't your fault that guy in the woods messed up." Her saying this so quick made me smile, since that was exactly how I saw it, too.

When Mr. Sanders called to say I owed him another chance to get a package in, I told him, "Mr. Sanders, I tried to do you a favor, but it didn't work out. So I'm out of this deal."

He gave a big sigh. "But, Wilma, the package didn't get in. So we need to try again."

I answered kind of snotty, "Well, I did my part, and that's all I can say."

He didn't answer that directly, just gave another sad sigh and said, "I'll pray on the situation."

I didn't know what that meant, but I knew I didn't owe nobody nothing.

This afternoon at Delores's, I talked with her about my son Richie's trouble in school. The third grade counselor had called me to meet with her, and that's never a good deal. It wasn't like we were meeting to discuss Richie's application to Harvard. And as soon as I walked into the school for the meeting, I wished I'd had the sense to wear my work uniform. I could have pretended I was just getting off shift, with no time to change.

Complain as I did about my job, that uniform did make me look like I was somebody. It had as much insignia sewed on the shirt as a five star general, and so many pockets in the cargo pants that I could carry a damn nuclear warhead. And I was really good at keeping my boots polished shiny black.

But, dumb me, I showed up instead looking like girls do at Walmart at the first sign of spring. I had on a tube top, spandex leggings, and a belly ring to direct the eye to the prize. I looked like a can of biscuits that just popped open. My flip-flops slapped too loud in the hall on the way to the counselor's office.

"Come in and sit down. I'm so glad you could come in, so we can talk about Richie. I'm Sally Monroe."

She welcomed me into her office with a quick smile. She had a lamp on her desk like a therapist on *Sex in the City*, as if the glaring fluorescent overhead was not enough. Or maybe it was supposed to mean that her office was a warm, special place, more special than a regular office. Well, maybe that worked for the kids, but not so much for me. I didn't think Sally Monroe and I were going to get along. It didn't look like she had a clue about bad luck.

But the posters on the walls were about going to the library, doing homework, and shooting for the stars - all the things I wanted for Richie. It was just that the damn lamp was too special. Truly, Sally Monroe did dress nice. She had on a navy pantsuit. Her navy pumps were low enough that she could wear them on the playground, so maybe she didn't stay in her office all day. Looking at her, I wished again that I had worn my uniform. This meeting would have definitely gone better.

What a stupid shit I could be. In my uniform, I looked like a member of the "Ladies Who Do Right" club. Also, I would have been able to listen better to this counselor since in my uniform, my ears didn't ring so loud with an angry buzz.

"The reason I wanted us to talk is that Richie has been having problems with a boy in his class. Has he told you about it?" she asked me like this was a quiz, and there was only one right answer.

Of course, I lied and told her that Richie had filled me in on the whole thing. I didn't want her to think I was one of those parents whose kids don't talk to them. I was sure Richie would have told me; it was just that life had been busy lately.

Smart Sally must have figured that I didn't pass the quiz, because she went on. "A boy has teased Richie more than one time. He made Richie cry by calling him 'fatso' and 'blubber boy.' Twice after recess, Richie hid his face in his hands and cried, but when his teacher offered him time to go to the office to calm down, he got angry at the teacher."

As she described the hurt that had been done to my precious son, I just stared at her. She kept glancing down at my foot that was bouncing up and down so fast the flip flop dangled and was coming off. She stared like she was hypnotized by the flashing sequins on the straps.

She went on to tell me that the boy had been in trouble for bullying other kids also, and that the school was working regularly with his parents. When I asked for the name of the bully, she quoted the school policy that wouldn't let her tell me his name, probably knowing that my next stop would be at his parents' house to knock the shit out of him and them.

We agreed that I would keep talking to Richie about any problems at school, and if I thought he needed counseling, she would arrange it. She seemed sincere in wanting to help Richie, but she was polite to me in a way that made me gag. I imagined that her dealing with me fit into a line on her resume about her specialty in working with parents with cultural, non-academic differences. It would also fit the category of reaching out to parents on the margins of the spectrum who didn't feel comfortable with the school system, or some other damn thing which would have been avoided if I'd worn my damn uniform. I hated it when I was stupid.

So now at Delores's house, I teared up as I whispered to her about Richie's problems. She got mad too, and then put her frosted pink fingernail to her coral pink lips and whispered back in her Paula Deen imitation, "This calls for some serious southern comfort. Maybe I have some of those cute little powdered donuts in the cabinet. But don't let the kids see 'cause there's not enough for them."

She stretched up to reach the cabinet over the fridge and waved the package like she'd found a brick of gold. I peeked into the living room and saw Richie still laid out on the sofa watching Sponge Bob reruns, with Susie asleep on the pillows next to him.

Delores and I laughed as quietly as we could at how silly we were behaving, and then we laughed more when the donuts' powdered sugar stuck to our fingers, glued by the grease from the potato chips.

We tried to figure out the identity of the bully, but we didn't know many kids in Richie's class. We both agreed that since Richie didn't want to talk about the problem, we wouldn't bring it up to him. Being a boy and all, we didn't want to embarrass him.

As Delores wiped crumbs from the table, she asked, "Do you know yet when Ted gets released?"

"It looks like it'll be delayed until next week," I told her. I explained that he got in a little trouble for drinking in his cellblock, and some disciplinary days got tacked onto his sentence. It wasn't exactly his fault since the liquor didn't actually belong to him. He had just been drinking it to be social. In fact, part of the money from Mr. Sanders that I'd put in Ted's canteen account had been to pay back the owner of the little bit he'd drunk. His share cost him a can of shaving cream and a jar of instant coffee. I'd hated to give up the money for it, but Ted said the other guy would beat him up if he didn't pay. And Ted had asked so sweet, I had to agree.

Talking about Ted made me teary again, and I looked across the table at Delores.

"You know, I guess I'll let him come back with the kids and me when he gets out. I mean, Richie needs a man around to help him with this bully problem. I know we've had our problems, but Ted needs to be there as his daddy."

Delores took another sip of her soda. "You don't have to do that if you don't want to. I've been watching over that boy all his life, so he'll always have a home here. You know how his moods can get hard on you. I don't want anything bad to happen again."

I appreciated her support for me and remembered how bad I looked with two black eyes. I couldn't go to work until the color faded enough for makeup to cover it. But seeing Richie curled on the couch, the cartoons flashing like neon across his face, I leaned over to Delores and whispered, "You know, I've heard that boys who get bullied grow up, you know, kind of girly. That's why I think he needs a daddy, to teach him to fight back and stick up for his own self. I don't want to look back ten years from now and see my son with bells in his pockets, or jingle in his tank, or however they say it. So, yeah, I'm going to tell Ted that he can come home."

After loading the kids in the car for the ride home, I thought about having us all together again. Sure, Ted would fit fine in the bedroom, but the rest of the trailer got crowded for a man with moods. We'd just have to see how it went. I knew this, though, Ted had best not go flaring his nostrils even a little bit, or he'd find his sorry ass back with Delores. I'd hate to put the burden on her, but I couldn't miss any more work because of some injury to me.

That rash of crap had to stop.

Seven

"Wilma, I need to see you right away."

This was the second call from Mr. Sanders in a week. The first had been to tell me that I owed

him a do-over. When I refused, he said he'd pray on it. So I guessed he was calling to tell me the result of his prayer.

"Mr. Sanders, I have not changed my mind. I am not going to 'not see' another package."

"Wilma, I can't talk about this over the phone. Please come out to my office as soon as you can."

Of course, I was worried that someone had found out what we had done. Or maybe the thrower was threatening to talk if he didn't get more money. I worried that Mr. Sanders wouldn't handle blackmail very well.

When I got to his office, he was slumped into his executive chair with the high back. He rolled it back and forth behind his desk. If he'd had the energy to stand, he'd probably be pacing. As soon as I walked in, he told me his idea for payback for what I supposedly owed him.

"Mr. Sanders, I can tell that you don't really want to do this."

His fingers fiddled with the frame of the family photo on the corner of his desk next to the fake green plant. The leaves on the plant showed more dust than when I'd first visited his office.

He didn't look at me. "Wilma, I do want to do this. It's what any man would want to do. You owe me money, and this is a good trade. I'm a businessman. So just hurry up and get those jeans off."

Well, now, if that wasn't the most romantic invitation I'd heard in a while, I thought. Even before Travis and I had our quarter panel sex, he'd still made some effort to include a little socializing. He'd said to me, "Wilma, I like you a lot. I always have. How come we lose track of each other?"

"I don't know the answer to that, Travis. I guess having Ted in and out of my life is too much drama. Having you around more would just add to the drama."

"Girl, you know I'm too boring to add drama. You and Ted make your own noisy drama. I'm one of the 'last man standing' type of guy."

"You're right, Travis. Let's not fuss. I really appreciate you fixing my car."

"I'm glad to help you. You can ask me for help any time. What kind of fancy perfume are you wearing? It don't smell like that Avon my mom sells."

"It's Ivory soap, Travis, from the shower we just had." I poked him on the arm and laughed, "And don't talk about your mom, she's already here in bed with us," I said and pointed to his tattoo.

But, now, in Mr. Sanders's office, not only was Mr. Sanders leaving any romance out of his suggestion, he didn't seem to have much heart for it either. For a man who supposedly wanted sex so bad, he certainly was taking his sweet time about it. He hadn't even gotten up from behind his desk. He looked old and sad.

"Mr. Sanders, you are a nice man. And from her picture, your wife looks to be as nice as you. She's got a big smile, and her beach hat is cute. Think how bad you'll feel holding her and calming her worries if you have the memory of our five minutes of secret sex stirring in your mind."

Frankly, I didn't think he would even make it five minutes, but I didn't want to hurt his feelings.

He slid lower in his chair and closed his eyes. I could barely hear his voice over the noise of the air conditioner.

"She won't let me comfort her. Ever since Bill went to jail, she can't be herself. She stiffens up and says to leave her alone when I go to hug her. Every night she sleeps in Bill's room, in the bed he's had since he was a boy. Even our old poodle, Sammy, sleeps in there with her. That damn dog. It's like they blame me for Bill being in prison."

He swiveled in his chair and looked out at the parking lot from his office window.

While he admired the view, I slumped in my own chair, thinking about this whole sex thing. I understood the nuances of quarter panel sex with Travis, and Lord help me, I've been a giver of "please don't hit me again sex" with Ted. So this new version of sex from Mr. Sanders shouldn't have been a surprise. His suggestion that I owed him for seeing what I wasn't supposed to see when the contraband came over the fence was made with so little energy, it was like Mr. Sanders asked just because it seemed like the thing to do. But he didn't seem really interested in the idea.

I was curious about the payback he expected from the guy in the woods with the used up football arm who couldn't make a good throw. I'd bet the payback for him didn't involve sex. He had probably arranged with that guy to clean the gutters on the Sanders's house, or maybe slow cook some ribs in his smoker. Given a choice between payback sex and payback gutter cleaning, I guess the sex would get finished quicker. *But, damn*, I thought, *how come I didn't get the option to make Mr. Sanders a payback casserole? Or to scrape grease out of the ovens in his repos?*

Of course, in a fair world, I didn't have to pay back anything to him. It wasn't my fault the delivery failed. And besides, his son's quality of life in prison was his problem, not mine. How come I couldn't be a used up option like the Warden when he'd turned down Mr. Sanders's request?

I wanted to fuss about all of that, but then Mr. Sanders swiveled back to face me. He wasn't crying, but he wasn't looking like his puffed up Chamber of Commerce Man of the Year self, either. His sadness was the most real thing about him. I leaned over and patted his hand.

In a low voice, I told him, "If my boy Richie was in the same mess as your Bill, I'd be messed up, too. But you need to realize, if the package had gotten in, you'd still be worrying today about the next one the gang would demand. It ain't going to end. You're the Golden Goose, and your juice has hardly even started to drip. When those boys are done with you and Bill, you'll both be so crispy and dried out, you won't have enough spit left to even take comfort in good memories. You need to be thinking of another way to help Bill. Paying for shit to be thrown over the fence is endless blackmail."

As I leaned back in my chair, I couldn't stop a little smile. That was quite a speech for me to make. I might be dumb about a lot of stuff, but I did know way too much about people being used. I quietly got up to leave the office, and Mr. Sanders looked up. He had slumped so far down, only his balding head and sad eyes showed above his desk.

At the door, I stopped and added one more piece to my speech. "And, you know what, Mr. Sanders? You need to take a sleeping bag into your son's room where your wife is sleeping, and lay your sorry ass on the floor each night, right close to her. Hell, even your damn dog has the sense to stay close to her."

On the way out of his office, I saw one of Mr. Sanders's employees nearby. He had Steve on his name tag. He stared at me like he was trying to remember where he'd seen me before. But I didn't smile back since I couldn't remember meeting him, and I sure wasn't interested in making any new friends.

As I got in my car to drive home, my rear view mirror reflected my big, righteous grin as I replayed my advice to Mr. Sanders. *Damn*, I thought, *just call me Dear Abby.*

Eight

The happiness of facing down Mr. Sanders totally faded the next night when my sergeant gave me a note from Investigator Joe Brown. My instructions said to meet in his office after inspection and not to go out on my perimeter post. Any attention from Internal Affairs is never good, and this time I had no doubt about why he wanted to see me. The rest of my shift members looked at me when I got the note, clearly wondering if it meant I was in trouble. I smiled and shrugged with a little head shake toward my sergeant when he gave it to me, as if to say, "Oh, this. It's no big deal." But inside, I knew that it was a very big deal.

If he had a job other than investigator, Joe Brown would have been a solid fit for the nice guy category. He stood tall, had hair going gray, and always wore a tie on the job. He was also the sweetie of my friend, Miss Kelly.

The mental picture of them being, well, *sweet together*, was not one I liked to dwell on. It was not as bad as seeing vibrators advertised with an AARP senior discount, but it was kind of close.

Anyway, being called to Investigator Brown's office could only be a bad sign. Just a few days had passed since the throw over attempt, which had stayed in my mind like a thunderstorm. To take money from Mr. Sanders, to see what I wasn't supposed to see, had been flat ass wrong. No matter how I squared it with Mr. Sanders, I messed up when I took the money. To pretend anything else, like the bad luck Bill was having, was a reason to do it, but not a good one. But Lord knows, I needed to keep the show going, believing my excuse, or I'd be a crumbled pack of crackers.

On my way to Investigator Brown's office, I checked that my boots were shined. Shining my boots was as much a preparation for work as brushing my teeth. My uniform shirt looked freshly ironed and hung on me with creases from the spray starch I loved to over-use. On the outside, I looked like a good worker.

"Come in, Officer, and take a seat," he said as he opened his office door. His office looked clean, with the walls bare. No pictures of waterfalls or jokey cartoons hung on the bulletin board. Clearly he used his office for business - not just a place to hang out. He wasted no time getting to the reason for our meeting.

He looked hard at me and said, "I've read your report of the last contraband package found near the fence." He looked harder when I didn't say anything back, then went on. "It surprised me that you didn't actually find it. I remember from a while back that you had really sharp eyes in spotting a throw over. Was there a special reason you didn't see this one? It seems as if you just drove past it, and then that rookie officer working with you stumbled on it."

I took a quick breath and told my first lie of the meeting. "I had a bad headache that night, so I guess I wasn't as sharp. I'm sorry I missed it, but now I'm fine." I'd rehearsed this excuse in my bathroom mirror, wanting to keep the lie simple and believable. But now, my face felt as shiny as my boots, and I felt sweat on my forehead. I'm a terrible liar, but two parts of my story were kind of true: I did have a headache, and Lord knows, I was sorry.

Before I could tell him any more lies, Joe Brown straightened some papers in front of him, and said, "I'm asking about the thrower because of a rape last night in one of the cellblocks. The inmate's name was Bill Sanders, and the rape and the package are supposedly related - at least according to the information I've received from some snitches. It was said that a group of guys had been extorting him for the throw over, and when he didn't deliver because the package didn't get in, he was raped. He's refused to give us any more information and claims he doesn't know who assaulted him, but I need to know the background of that package. We transferred the inmate today to another prison for his safety, but I hate loose ends. If any details of that night come to you, now is the time to let me know."

I kept quiet while he told me the details about the rape, mostly because I couldn't breathe. He didn't seem to find my silence suspicious, but then he shifted in his chair and changed the subject.

"Another reason I needed to see you is that the Sheriff's office said your ex-husband will be released soon from their jail. They always let us know about any of their prisoners who are related to our staff. You need to understand it doesn't affect the immediate status of your job here if your ex-husband did come back to live with you and the kids, but it surely makes us concerned. We'll be watching very carefully that he's not, shall we say, influencing you in any activities that are illegal. You've been a good officer, but sometimes family can create problems. You'll want to be careful he doesn't mess up the good record you're building here on the job."

He looked at me as if expecting me to argue, but all I could answer was, "Yes, sir, I'll be careful."

With that, he stood, we shook hands, and he opened the door for me to leave. Part of me wanted to bend over and throw up. Just let the truth splatter everywhere, so I'd be the good officer he thought I was. But doing that was not really an option, since not only would I lose my job, but they'd send my ass to jail. The thought of Ted coming home from his jail time to take care of the kids while I did my jail time was a thought that made me feel faint with panic. It wouldn't be one of those movie situations where the cute, bumbling father tries to be Mr. Mom. Ted doesn't do cute. He would just bumble - or worse. And the very worst part was that he wouldn't really try to do right by the kids. He'd slide them to his mom's care, and while I loved Delores, I worried how long she would be healthy enough to raise kids.

At that point, I realized that while I was correct to forecast Ted's failure as a father, it was more correct that this mess wasn't Ted's fault. It was mine. I'd brought this into my family. I took money to help contraband come in. That's illegal. All of this was my doing. My mom killed herself and left me to raise myself, and I was about to put that curse on my own kids. They would have to do for themselves while their stupid mom sat in jail, sending cute, pathetic cards on their birthdays.

For whatever reason, for at least two generations, my family had not gotten the training manual on how to live life. I never researched our family tree, and maybe a long way back some branch had an Einstein or a King of the World. But based on my mom, and now me, our grandparents must have met at their family reunion. Seems like the best we know is how to scramble out of messes. Lord help us.

With a jolt, I realized my spacing out time still had me standing in the doorway of the investigator's office. He smiled and leaned forward, "Oh, and Wilma, Mrs. Kelly said the other day that she hadn't seen you lately. She sure does think highly of you."

We smiled at each other as if we were regular people ending a meeting, instead of one regular person and one piece of shit person.

As I walked down the hall from his office, my boots made a solid rhythm on the waxed linoleum, like I was in a parade of crisp uniforms, all eyes forward, head high, marching in step with each other.

I thought of a sign I'd seen outside the church over on the by-pass. It read, "Saints are Welcome, Sinners are Forgiven." I wished it was that simple, that forgiveness happened so easily. In my opinion, I'm so full of rotten mess that I need to nail boards over my ass to keep the rats out. And even if by some miracle I got forgiven, it didn't make my criminal act go away. I could be one of those inmates who spends her sentence on her knees in the prison chapel while her family outside wasted away.

Lord help us. I mean, really, Lord, help us.

Nine

When the Lord got busy, his ways were indeed damn mysterious. Two days after my interview with Investigator Brown, Ted came home from jail on probation. The plan was for him to stay out of trouble and find a job, while he lived with the kids and me in our trailer.

Richie and his sister made plans for Ted's homecoming - to make it special for him. Over the front door, they hung paper banners that said, "We Love Daddy." They worked hours to spell it right. They even turned off their cartoons to concentrate better. I made his favorite cake, and at J.C.Penney's, I bought a pretty yellow nightgown with lavender flowers on the bottom.

As I drove home, I daydreamed of the Waltons living in our trailer. *Wilma, you look so sweet. Thanks, husband, I'm so happy you are home with us again.*

But Ted's celebration plans didn't quite fit ours. Rather than lavender flowers sex, his preference was for jeans at the ankle, right inside the front door before the kids got home sex. He hardly noticed the banner the kids made. In fact, by the time they got home from school, he was asleep, so I had to hush their excitement at seeing him.

"Daddy's tired, but when he's rested, we'll have our party."

When he was finally awake and stumbled into the living room, they rushed to hug him and asked right away, "Do you like our banner?"

Richie jumped up to try to touch it where it hung over the door.

"Damn it, boy, don't jump in the house."

"Do you like our banner?"

"Yeah, it's great, but don't be jumping around so much. If your mom's been letting you do that, then that'll have to change."

After dinner, I served the red velvet cake, but he hardly touched it. By that time, he'd had enough beers that the cream cheese icing didn't mix so well.

So the party ended pretty much before it got started. After awhile, Ted left to get together with a buddy. He didn't tell me anything about this 'buddy', and I didn't ask. The kids weren't really that upset when he left the house. I gave them another piece of cake and let them watch cartoons before bedtime.

I couldn't sleep, so when the phone rang at midnight, it didn't wake me up. I think I was expecting it.

It was Delores on the phone. "Honey, Ted's in jail again."

"Oh, Delores, what happened?"

"Well, he and a friend were drinking. Then the friend borrowed a car from someone and while they were driving, they came up on a routine drivers' license checkpoint. Ted said they had to bust through the roadblock because they couldn't be caught drinking since they were on probation. He said the police caught them a few blocks down the road, and the open bottle violated them right off. But then the police searched the car and found marijuana on the dash, and Wilma, this is the worst part..." she paused.

"What, Delores? Just go ahead and tell me. All of it is the worst."

Delores was crying at this point. "Under the front seat, they found a gun. Ted says that it belonged to whoever owns the car, but of course, the police are charging Ted and his friend. So the worst charge is "felons in possession of a weapon in the commission of a crime." Delores' listing of the charge made her sound like a terrible mis-cast on Law and Order. Such words were foreign sounding in her sweet drawl.

We agreed to meet at the jail the next day for Ted's bond hearing. That's when we told him that none of us had money for bond or attorney fees, so he was on his own.

Ted's dad took the lead and said, "Son, we're sorry, but we just don't have it." Delores stood behind her husband when he said this and sobbed into her tissue.

Ted bristled up and said with a sneer, "You all are sure not much of a family."

That hurt to hear, but then he was bundled in cuffs and leg irons and shuffled back to a cell. And then we got to walk out the door. Maybe Ted didn't think we were much, but we were free and together.

When his dad went to bring the car around from the parking lot, Delores and I had a few minutes together. As we waited by the curb in front of the jail, Delores put her arm around me and asked, "Are you all right, honey?"

I was embarrassed that I didn't need the tissue she offered. I had no tears left.

I touched her sweet chubby fingers, and said, "Delores, I know you're his mama, and I mean no disrespect to you, but truth be told, I feel like it's Friday afternoon on the last day of school."

She giggled and hugged me, and then I had tears.

"Wilma," she said so easy, "you are such a good girl. Not having to worry about Ted's problems is going to make your life so much easier. You won't have all that confusion messing up your good plans. Lord knows, you need some peace."

I hated that I saw Ted's prison time as heaven-sent for me. It was like a celestial time-out, delivered down just as I was whooped to my knees. Delores was right. The Lord did know that I needed some peace. With Ted's multiple charges, the kids would be mostly grown before he was released again and I could give serious thought to the divorce I kept putting off.

As I loaded her into their car when it pulled up to us, she called out, "Bring the kids over next week when you have some time off work. They can watch cartoons while you and I try this new recipe for fried donuts." Her husband groaned, and I laughed.

Their car pulled away and I hurried for my own. It was late, and I still needed to shine my boots for work.

Ten

The freedom I felt from not needing to worry about Ted being home freed up my mind to think about the next person on my worry list. When I'd been distracted about Ted coming home and lulled by daydreams of him taking charge as a real father to Richie, I had put aside my own plans for Richie and his bullying problem. But with Ted gone, I needed to get serious about how to help my son.

I kept coming back to the idea of the Boy Scouts. At night, when I drove the perimeter, I smiled at visions of Richie in a uniform. Maybe he'd have boots, too, and I could teach him how to get a good shine.

But the visions were not a plan. I had no resources to make it a reality. But I did know someone who knew how to plan. When I made the call to Mr. Sanders, I was nervous.

"Hi, Mr. Sanders, this is Wilma. I'd like to come see you."

"What? What for? Well, sure, Wilma." He cleared his throat over the phone, like he had allergies. "Can you tell me what's on your mind?"

"I'd rather wait until I see you." I didn't mean to sound rude or mysterious. I was just too nervous to explain well without watching his reaction.

"All right, come on over. I'll be in my office most of the day."

I drove right over. I so wanted this plan to work, and I knew I didn't have a back-up plan if Mr. Sanders refused to help.

Walking into his office was beginning to feel familiar for me. "Hi, Mr. Sanders, thanks for seeing me." He looked some better than the last time we'd met, not so much like a guy waiting for his stroke to arrive. But he looked anxious, like he was expecting me to tell him some bad news.

"Hey, there, Wilma. I've been curious about your call."

"Mr. Sanders, I have an idea for you."

He was sweating and kept darting his eyes, like I was a pickpocket in the crowd at a Braves' game. I didn't understand why I was making him so nervous.

"Sure, Wilma, I'm glad to listen. Sit down." I did. My uniform boots reflected the ceiling lights. Their shine gave me courage.

"Mr. Sanders, it's hard for me to get started. I've gone over and over this little speech, so I'm just going to jump in."

"Wilma, you're making me nervous. Just tell me what you came to see me about."

I sat up straighter. "My son, Richie, needs to join the Boy Scouts."

Mr. Sanders looked puzzled, like he hadn't heard right. In fact, he looked like his ears heard words he didn't understand. I thought he gave a little head shake as if to clear them.

But I couldn't worry about his confusion, I needed to lay out my plan. "See, Richie's had some problems at school. He's a cheap target for a bully in his class, 'cause Richie is a little chubby." I repeated what Sally Monroe had described to me.

"If he had a club of built-in friends, he'd have help dealing with this bully. The school does have a Boy Scout troop, but they don't do much. So I was thinking that you could sponsor it as a tribute to Bill."

Mr. Sanders stayed quiet. But I didn't let his quiet shut me up.

"Also, I have a worry about Richie being in Scouts, even though I want him to be. On the news, they have stories about Scout leaders getting busted for, you know, sex stuff with the little boys. I figure if you're involved, the bad men would be too intimidated by you to try stuff with Richie."

As I talked, Mr. Sanders seemed to become more focused on what I was saying. He didn't seem as anxious or confused. I didn't know what his problem had been, but I needed to make sure he understood how important this was for Richie.

As I paused to see if there was anything else I needed to add to my request to make it more clear, Mr. Sanders picked up the photo of Bill and his mom from its normal spot on the corner of his desk.

When he finally spoke, his voice was soft.

"Bill loved scouting. That was our thing to do together. Even when he went off to college, I'd drive up for weekends so that he and I could camp and fish."

"I'm sorry, I didn't know that. I didn't mean to make your memories more sad. But it makes my idea even better, to honor Bill with something he cared so much about. And at the same time, help my Richie."

"They're good memories. In fact, I've still got a garage full of camping gear. Do you remember me describing how my wife keeps Bill's room the same as when he left? Well, I keep all our camp stuff and fishing rods in the garage, like he and I are going to use it soon. It's the same thing my wife does. We're alike that way, trying to make him feel closer."

He put down the picture frame, but then leaned over to straighten it.

"I don't know if you know this, but Bill went to that same school that Richie goes to now. My wife and I spent hours sitting on bleachers watching him play ball or run track. He and his friends were just little kids, but they loved that school. On the weekends, some other dads and I took them on scouting trips. It wasn't all camping. Sometimes we'd go to a museum or a concert. The whole idea was to show them a bigger world outside our little town."

He laughed a little. "Of course, they didn't enjoy the museum or the concert as much as they did the camping."

He sat up straight. "Wilma, I think you've got a good idea. For me to get back to those happy days would be a relief. Of course, they would never let me name the troop after Bill because of the circumstances, but that doesn't matter. It would still help me feel close to him."

I hadn't started smiling yet I was just waiting for a problem with our plan.

Mr. Sanders' voice shifted into his Chamber of Commerce planning voice.

"The principal of the school comes to the Chamber meetings, so I know him. Let me get with him to see what he thinks about me organizing some more activities with the troop. I'll get back with you after I talk with him."

As we stood together on the way out, he spoke to me again. "Wilma, I've got to be honest with you. I was worried about seeing you again. We've had some, shall we say, unusual business dealings. And the last time we met, I wasn't as professional as I should have been. So I thought today you might be coming back to threaten me. You know, a blackmail type of thing."

I looked surprised because I was.

"Mr. Sanders, I would never do that. I took your money. I broke the law as much as you did. We both were wrong. We both have that hanging over us."

He nodded. "Yes, I know. It feels better to be making good plans about the scouts. I don't think I'm cut out to be a criminal. You know, I think a lot about what we did. I hated feeling so desperate to help Bill, but now I feel such guilt over what I set in motion."

"I heard at work that Bill was transferred to another prison. Is the new place better for him?"

"It is better. It's smaller, and some of the inmates there have short sentences so they try to avoid trouble. And Bill's got smarter about how to do his time. He stays more to himself."

Then Mr. Sanders got that far away look again, as if thinking about something. When he refocused, he turned to me. "I didn't know that Steve knew you and your husband."

"Who's Steve?"

"He's the guy who used to work for me. He's the one that put the plan together for the throw over. I know you saw him here at work."

I remembered the guy staring at me the last time I was at Mr. Sanders's office.

"What does that have to do with Ted or me?"

"He said he was Ted's cellmate before they got out on probation. He's the one who partied with Ted the night of Ted's release. Then they got arrested together. He's that guy."

I felt like my world was too small. Everyone knew everyone. I tried to breathe, but I couldn't quite remember how.

"Wilma, are you all right? Don't you faint on me. I'm sorry to bring this up. I thought you knew about Steve and Ted being friends and working together."

"How would I know?"

"According to Steve, he and Ted had a good business with contraband going on at the jail before their release. In fact, Steve used the same connection when he did my throw over. Of course, Ted was still in jail at the time, so he wasn't around to help, but Steve said he had another guy to help out. I thought Ted might have said something to you about his jail business. And he probably knew about Steve's job for me at your prison. Although, I don't know that for a fact."

"Mr. Sanders, you forget. I'm not that type of person. I only helped with contraband that one time, just to help you. Ted knew better than to tell me stuff that he did. I'd turn him in."

In my mind, I told myself that I wanted to believe I'd turn him in, but I wasn't sure. In those days, I was weaker. Of course, I didn't share these thoughts with Mr. Sanders. I wanted him to see me as having at least a little righteousness.

But Mr. Sanders must have heard my silent, busy thoughts, because he went on. "I wish I could claim that I turned Steve in, but I didn't. I would have lost too much if people knew what I did. The only piece of this I did right was to refuse to give Steve a good recommendation to the judge as his employer. When I refused to do this, I was afraid Steve would blackmail me, but I guess he'd have to incriminate himself in order to drag me in, too."

He stopped talking and looked straight at me. "I really thought that's what you were going to try today. To blackmail me."

"Mr. Sanders, I thought you were smarter about people." I wasn't quite yelling. "I did do wrong. And if anyone else knew, I'd go to jail. You and me, we'd both go. We'd join Steve and Ted. Don't you see?"

He shook his head slowly. "I wish I hadn't got this started."

"I wish I hadn't helped you."

With that, I left since I didn't want him to see me cry. When my boots crunched on the loose asphalt of his parking lot they got a little smudged.

Eleven

For the next couple of weeks, I gave thanks for each day that passed without a piece of the sky falling on my head.

Then the phone rang.

"Wilma, this is Mr. Sanders. Would you be able to come see me tomorrow afternoon?"

"Sure, Mr. Sanders. I hope you have good news."

"I do have news."

So we met again in his office. Two co-conspirators in the glow of glossy brochures of mobile homes, with the Southern Supreme and her sister model, the Backwater Bungalow prominently displayed. *Stop*, I told the mean spirited voice in my head. If Mr. Sanders's sales of the Supreme funded a Scout troop for Richie, I hoped he sold a lot of them.

"Wilma, you have gotten something started that is really good."

I looked at him without smiling. My experience with good luck had been too limited to know how to respond. I was afraid if I smiled, the good news would turn out to be a trick.

"I talked to the school principal about re-activating the Scout troop. He was really enthusiastic, particularly when I told him that he wouldn't have to fund any more equipment. There's another guy in the Chamber, an old friend of mine, whose son is away at college. He would also like to get back into scouting. He and his son were active the same years as Bill and me. So we are doing this together. It should be a lot of fun. We're putting together a membership list to distribute in the next few days, so Richie should be bringing that home soon."

I really wanted to smile.

But then Mr. Sanders went on.

"Now, Wilma, this next plan is not something you and I talked about. And it's not for sure definite. What happened is that at the last Chamber meeting, I told the group about our scouting project and warned them they might be hit up for some contributions. The principal was at the meeting as well, and brought up the problem of school bullying. He said the school district had been concerned about some bad incidents during recess. He said his school hadn't had any injuries, but he started to put more staff on the playgrounds, even though it pulled them away from their other duties."

I remember the counselor, Sally Monroe, mentioning an increase in problems. That it hadn't been just Richie who had been bothered.

"So, Wilma, to tell the short version, the chamber plans to fund a part-time school resource officer. We want a designated person to mix with the kids to be sure bullying is controlled. With a designated position, being very hands-on, the other school staff can return to their regular duties."

He paused and his voice sounded like a bingo announcer.

"Once the position is approved by our state charter, I think you would be great in that job."

I saw Mr. Sanders's big smile, and I heard his words, but I wasn't sure what he just said.

"I'm sorry, Mr. Sanders. Could you please repeat what you just said? I'm not sure I caught all of it."

"It's not a perfect job for you. First, it's not full-time, and I know your income has to support your kids. But maybe you could find a part-time job to fill in the lost hours. And secondly, it has no benefits like your prison job. It's not an official school district position. It's a special position funded by the Chamber. Still, maybe I'm wrong, but it seems like your prison job is not as good a fit as it used to be."

My thoughts were clear about that last statement. My job wasn't such a good fit anymore because I was a traitor. I let my team down. And they didn't even know it. And if they did know it, they'd have to send me to jail. My ethics were tested, and I flunked. I got no "E" for effort.

"Why would I be trusted with children?" Just having to ask this question made me sick. Quietly, I gagged.

"Wilma, please don't cry." I didn't know I had tears in my eyes until Mr. Sanders handed me his handkerchief.

"You and I made a terrible mistake. I thought I could solve my son's problem by doing wrong. You tried to do a kindness by doing wrong. We were wrong to try to do something right in the wrong way. But now we have a chance to do right. We have to try to do right harder than we did before, in order to balance the scale."

He put his hand on my arm like he needed to haul me out of quicksand.

"I have to be selfish, Wilma. If you let this suck you down, it will be another wrong I caused. I really need you to understand, or you might slip away. Please don't let go of yourself."

I understood the urgency in Mr. Sanders's voice, but I didn't really understand his words.

"Wilma, please meet my wife and me at church this Sunday. It might help you think things through."

"I don't know, Mr. Sanders. Your church is pretty fancy. I don't have anything to wear."

Mr. Sanders looked like I had slapped him.

"I'm sorry I said that. I didn't mean to be rude. I just don't think I'd be comfortable at a church with big pillars out front." I tried to laugh as if I were joking, but we both knew I wasn't.

"Mr. Sanders, you have shown me kindness, and I just realized that I can be a snob without a country club membership."

I shrugged a little, "I used to think only rich people judged the rest of us over stupid stuff. But I guess it's an equal opportunity thing."

Looking him straight in the eye, I said, "Please forgive me for being such a jackass."

We smiled at each other in a sad kind of way, as if getting us right was a journey we had not expected. Before this experience with Mr. Sanders, my learning journeys had been short trips. My views about luck and people and making do had been familiar friends. Now I was in an unfamiliar place.

On the way from Mr. Sanders's office to work, my head was spinning. I smiled thinking of Richie's new Scout troop, but then I got nervous thinking about a new job. But all my thinking made me realize again and again what a mess I had made. And thinking about this, I couldn't stop crying.

I pulled into a church parking lot and cried hard enough to make my uniform collar soggy. I found some old McDonald's napkins and cleaned myself up. In front of my windshield was a neon sign advertising the church's hours. The sign was bright and glitzy, not sedate and reserved. This church had no pillars out front.

Because I have always been like a bass fish who liked anything that sparkled, I couldn't stop looking at the neon sign. Then that dumb, crazy sign added a flashing crawl. It read, "God gives second chances, third chances, more chances. God gives second chances, third chances, more chances." It repeated itself over and over. It was still repeating when I was cleaned up enough to drive on to work.

That Sunday, I left the kids with Delores, but didn't tell her where I was going. I wore the outfit she gave me for my prison job interview, the navy khakis with the blue dotted blouse, buttoned all the way to the collar. I didn't have a lot of church clothes. Really, I wanted to wear my uniform, but I didn't want to stand out. My normal street clothes had too much sequins and spandex, and I didn't want to repeat my mistake at Richie's school. I didn't want to send a message I didn't want received.

It was new for me to try this church thing. I sat in the back and listened hard. The preacher went on about our jobs as parents. He reached a level of fervor where he was waving his arms and wiping sweat from his face.

Then his eyes left the good people up front and stared at those of us in the back pew.

"If you can't be a good example, then lead by being a horrible warning."

I gasped out loud when he said it because that would be me. I could be pretty good, but I could be plenty bad. I felt like a spirit of some kind zinged through my body, so strong it might have left scorch marks on the pew. I felt sad and proud at the same time.

The preacher didn't ask me to wrap snakes around my neck to expel my evil. He didn't even call for us sinners to come down the aisle to be blessed with embarrassment. He didn't need to do all that. He knew a truth about me: my own self wasn't such a good person, but I wasn't as bad yet as I could be.

He finished up his sermon talking about courage. "If you are a normal person, you can get up the courage to rescue a child from a burning building. But it takes a different kind of courage to change the boring bad habits of everyday life, particularly if this is your third or fourth time trying to change. But it can be done. And for you newcomers here, we have all struggled, and our only hope is to get stronger together. So we are glad you are here to join us in the struggle."

After the service, I got stuck in the middle of a group of members. I was headed for the exit, and they were going to the basement for coffee. When I started toward the door, a woman grabbed my hand and introduced herself.

"Hi, I'm Sarah. I see you're a back-bencher like me. Come have some cake and coffee."

Usually I avoided things like this because I felt awkward, but I was trying to do things I didn't usually do. The people seemed like normal people, not uppity or snobby. It seemed like they were used to having new faces in their services. No one asked who I was related to or what job I had or even if I had kids. It was as if they saw me as a turtle who trundled in and would stay as long as it was comfortable, but if any hot buttons were pushed, I'd withdraw and trundle on to the parking lot.

I assumed many of them had those buttons, as well as me. I didn't feel like I was the only one there who found my way to this basement by first washing the parking lot with tears.

"Hey, Wilma, I brought you some cake. It's lemon. I think you like that kind." The voice behind me sounded familiar.

I turned around and saw Travis. He had on a green plaid shirt with a collar, instead of his usual Harley t-shirt. His face was sweaty, but so was mine.

"Hey, Travis. I didn't know you went to this church." Actually, I didn't know Travis went to any church, but then ours was not much of a talkative relationship.

"Yeah, my mom's come here for years. I come along with her now and then." He shrugged, "You know, to make her happy."

I smiled. I started to say, "Yeah, moms are good at that," but I stopped. I realized I didn't really know this about moms. So I just smiled some more.

He shoved the cake into my hand and said, "Well, look, it's been good seeing you. I'd like to, you know, stay to catch up, but the preacher's got a low tire, and I promised I'd change it."

"Sure, Travis, you go ahead."

He started to leave, but then he turned back. "Like, Wilma, how about we have dinner sometime this week?"

"What? I didn't think I still owed you. I thought we were even."

He looked puzzled. "Owe me? I don't know what you mean. You don't owe me, at least not that I know of. But it's been a while since I've seen you. I fixed your car sometime back, and then we met for a," he hesitated, "we met for a date. But you had to rush off, so we didn't get a lot of time to talk. So how about it? The Cracker Barrel this week?"

My voice was buzzing in my ear. This was too screwy. I thought we were having quarter panel sex. I didn't know we were on a date. If we were on a date, I'd have worn clothes.

"Sure, Travis, I'd like to have dinner with you."

On the way out, he shook hands with some of the members he squeezed past in the crowd. Some of them patted him on the back.

Sarah, who had led me to this basement gathering, came back over to me and handed me a church schedule.

"We have a lot of services and Bible study classes. Almost all of our members work crazy shifts, so there's lots of choices for times. That is, if you decide to come back. And I hope you do. We've also got a couple of classes for kids, if that is something you might be interested in also. Most of us have kids, although we have a few single members, too." She smiled, "I see you met Travis already."

"I did see him. We went to school together. I was surprised to see him here."

"Travis is on the committee that does car and house repairs for our older members. And our single mothers, too. He's been a member a long time."

"I didn't know that. He's a nice guy."

"I do hope you come again."

"Sarah, thanks for the schedule."

I waited to get out of the parking lot before I started crying again. I didn't want anyone to see me. This time I was lucky. The McDonald napkins I used for tissues didn't have dried ketchup on them.

My tears were from frustration. I didn't want to be a church person. A stubborn part of me didn't want to need a church to be a good person. But the truth showed that I wasn't doing such a good job of being a good person on my own. I needed to learn how to be better. If a church could teach me, without pretending they were already perfect, then that would be a pretty good deal.

It seemed to me the rest of the world knew how to handle things that I didn't know how to deal with. And if I didn't know things, who would show my kids? I felt stupid that Travis had a whole life that I never even guessed at. I felt stupid that I had thought Sally Monroe, Richie's counselor, was not as sincere as she was. I felt stupid that Mr. Sanders was not frozen in place by his mistakes. He could change and make good plans that helped other people. He didn't seem to be a snob who thought he owned the world. I felt stupid that the church people laughed at their need for second and third and fourth chances. I felt like everyone knew secrets to surviving that I didn't know about.

I felt stupid that just because my mom didn't have the "How To Live A Good Life" instruction book, I never thought to borrow it from someone else. Like from the preacher. I was amazed how easy it was for Sarah to hand me the church's schedule, not knowing that she was passing on this secret book. I felt comforted to finally hold it in my hand and proud of myself for realizing its value. I felt not quite so stupid since I had the good sense to take it, and fold it carefully, and put it in the pocket of my blue khakis.

Twelve

A couple of days later, Mr. Sanders called me at home while I was doing laundry.

"Wilma, I just came from the Chamber's executive committee meeting. The plan for the school resource position is fully funded for two years. Since it's funded by the Chamber and not the state or the school district, the job hiring process is not complicated. It doesn't have to go through anyone but our committee."

I had to concentrate hard to understand what he was saying. My mind wanted to whirl through my ears to hear what I hoped to hear. I turned off the dryer, so I could concentrate better.

"In fact, the committee is comfortable acting on my recommendation, without interviewing anyone. They are hot to get this started, so we can have the project in place before our state convention. We want to submit it in the community service competition as our innovative effort to shore up holes in our schools from the state budget cuts. We think it's such a good idea, we could take the trophy this year. Last year, the coastal region got it for something to do with frogs in the wetlands. Anyway, the members and the school principal are eager to get started."

Trophy? Wetlands? Frogs? I wished I could hear Mr. Sanders better. I felt so wobbly.

"I told them that you were a family friend who had already passed a security screening to go to work for the state prison system. They understand that you want to take this job so that you can spend more time with your kids. They know that you are trained to "intervene when situations call for it." Of course, you wouldn't be authorized to carry a weapon on school property."

I didn't have a clue how to 'intervene when situations called for it.' That was what got me in this mess. I kicked the clothes basket in front of me and wanted to cry again. I had been doing a lot of crying lately.

"They want to know your start date, and what type of uniform you think you should wear."

I looked at my black nightgown in a heap on the floor.

"Wilma, are you there?"

"Black. My uniform should be black. This is serious business. The teachers need to wear flowery sweaters and navy suits. I need to wear black."

"Fine, Wilma, that's fine. When can you start?"

"I'll let you know as soon as I figure out what other job I can find to make up the salary difference. And I have to give the prison notice. But definitely before the end of the month."

"So does that mean you are ready to make the change? Wilma, this is a chance for you and me both to make things right. I hope you are officially accepting the job."

"Yes, Mr. Sanders, I do accept. And there is one more thing."

"What, Wilma?"

"Boots, I have to wear black boots."

Thirteen

"Thanks for seeing me on such short notice."

I'd spent days thinking about my resignation. I wanted to do the right thing, but I also needed to keep myself safe. Then, last night, driving around the perimeter in the dark, I decided I was tired of thinking so much about it. It was time to see Investigator Brown.

"Come in, Officer, I'm glad to see you any time. I take it you had a quiet night out there. I didn't get any reports of any problems."

"Yes, nothing unusual. The shift went fine."

"Good. What can I do for you this morning?"

"I'm on my way to the Personnel Office to submit my resignation. But I wanted to trust with
you, I mean, I wanted to *talk* with you about something."

I blushed at my mistake and stopped talking.

Investigator Brown smiled a little and said, "Often times in my business, trust and talk are frequently in the same conversation. What's on your mind, Wilma?"

He made this easy to slide into. I told him about Ted being re-arrested and that he would be transferred soon from jail to the prison system. I also told him about my new job at the school.

"Your new job sounds like an opportunity to help the kids. The school is lucky to get you. But you understand, don't you, that just because Ted is coming into this prison system, doesn't mean you have to resign? We can just make sure he's not kept in a location where you are working."

"Yes, sir, I do understand that. But I do want to work with kids, and so it seems the time is right. But there's something I need to ask you."

I wiped a spot of dust off my left boot. Investigator Brown stayed quiet, waiting for me to begin again.

"If Ted or another prisoner started saying things about me, what would happen?"

"Well, it would depend on several things. First, since you and he have had problems, we would assume the negative things were motivated by a desire to hurt you. So we would be skeptical. But we wouldn't totally discount it. I need to be honest with you, and not mislead you. Sometimes even liars and criminals tell the truth - just maybe for the wrong reasons."

He went on. "Secondly, we would review the accusations against you, and if it was backed up by some proof Ted had, then we would coordinate with local law enforcement to look into it further."

He paused and I stayed quiet.

"Can you tell me what you are worried about a little more specifically?"

"Here's my worry. I think that Ted and his friend Steve helped bring contraband into the jail. And I heard that Steve tried to do a throw over here at our prison. But I don't know for sure. I do know that if they were asked if this was true, they would try to hurt my reputation by accusing me of bad things. I don't know exactly what kind of bad things, but they'd try to use my job against me."

I was determined not to cry, but I had to stare hard at the air vent in the corner to stay focused. If I looked at Mr. Brown, I'd be a slobby mess.

"Wilma, I will try to be as clear as possible in this hypothetical discussion because it is obviously distressing for you. With both scenarios you mention, what's missing is proof. It doesn't sound like you have proof of what you're telling me about them. It's what you heard or what you suspect. But unless you have proof, like a video, then it's basically only your word against them. Of course, it puts us on alert about them, and for that, we are appreciative. We can put them on our watch list, so if they continue dealing in contraband, we can catch them early."

He cleared his throat and continued. "Now, let's say they want revenge against you for whatever reason. If they accuse you of a crime, then we want proof from them, as well. Without proof, or if it's just hearsay, then no action is taken against you. Of course, if your name started popping up in other criminal situations, or if you started driving a Cadillac on your salary from your school job, then those would be red flags. But if you obey the law, we assume you to be a good citizen who has a difficult marriage."

I wanted to be a good citizen. That was my plan.

"Thank you, I feel much better. And you're right, I have no proof. It's just a suspicion I have about Ted and Steve."

If Steve had proof against Mr. Sanders, he would have used it by now. And the only link Steve had between me and the throw over was Mr. Sanders.

"Officer, I wish you good luck in your new job. And in a few years, when things settle down with Ted, maybe you'll want to come back into prison work. It is honorable work to do."

Yes, it was honorable work. I just needed time to regain my honor.

"You are a kind man. Tell Miss Kelly I'll be calling her."

"I will, Wilma. You take care."

I headed down the hallway toward the Personnel Office with my resignation letter. The walk quieted me. My head was clear of buzzing. The only sound I heard was my shiny boots squealing on the waxed linoleum.

Fourteen

A few nights after I turned in my resignation, Delores and I met in her kitchen. It felt as familiar and fun as ever, although I felt older. The events of the last few weeks had pushed me into more changes than I could remember since the births of my children. When they were born, I remember feeling like I had crossed a line into adulthood. But the last few weeks had been huge in terms of change. In some ways, I felt older than Delores. But I wasn't ready to think too much about this change. I had enough going on.

I had phoned her earlier about my new job and the plans for Richie's Scout troop. She had been encouraging, but I could tell she was worried about my new job.

"Sweetie, it sounds like a good chance to help the kids. But you'd be giving up your state benefits if you left the prison. I'm glad you're happy; I'm just worried. You know I just want what's best for you and the kids." Delores does not like change. It is scary for her. And I could certainly relate to that.

We got to Delores's just after I'd talked to my father-in-law about a job at his Dollar Store. I needed to make up the income I'd be losing from the prison, as well as get medical insurance.

"Wilma, I'd be glad to have you join me here. You can work as many hours as you want." Then he turned his head to look both ways to be sure no one heard him as he mumbled, "Your security training will be a real help. Lately shoplifters have become a serious problem. I don't know how to stop it. We're supposed to follow the model from the corporate office about being friendly and casual with our customers. But it's getting harder to know who to trust."

Wilbur shook his head and looked sad. "You'd be surprised at how many people break the law. "

No, I wouldn't be surprised, my voice buzzed in my ear.

Instead, I said with my other voice, "I'll do the best I can."

Once Delores and I settled in her kitchen with the kids out of the way, we spoke only a little about Ted. Both of us were relieved that we'd refused to get on his phone list, telling him the collect calls were too expensive.

"Wilma, it about broke my heart to tell him "no". But those calls do cost a lot of money." She stirred frosting in a bowl and whispered, "Plus, I'm so tired of his whining. It don't seem right for a grown man to be so whiny."

I must have looked surprised at her plain speaking, because as she took cupcakes from the oven, she added, "Wilma, Ted always did like to be where the action was, even if he had to stir it up his own self." She licked lemon frosting off her fingers and went on to tell stories of his school days and her many warnings to him about getting into trouble. She opened a bag of coconut to scatter on top of the frosting and frowned as she concentrated.

"Looking back, I know we should have done more than warn him over and over, but I loved him too much for his own good. I didn't want to make him unhappy, even though he made his daddy and me plenty unhappy."

Some of the shredded coconut fell to the floor. "When you two got married, I thought it was the best thing that could happen to him. But I feel guilty that I was too selfish to warn you away. I mean, what kind of mother tells her son's girlfriend to run from him and not look back?"

It wasn't like Delores to talk much about herself. "And there's just one more thing I need to explain to you before we're to eat these pretty things." She carefully placed a cherry on top of each cupcake, with a focus that didn't seem necessary. Her smile almost looked like her real smile, except usually she didn't need to remember to turn it on. I had always thought of her smile as her acrylic cashmere blankie, reassuring to her and easily shared with the kids and me.

"My shame about not raising him to be a better husband won't go away. I know I wasn't doing a good job, but I didn't try very hard to do better." She turned away to put the jar of cherries in the fridge and used a voice like she was talking of everyday things. "And it's pretty obvious that I've never been too good at this setting limits thing they talk so much about on Dr. Phil. But what I am real good at is just being here for my family that I love so much." She looked directly at me with an almost-frown. "Since it looks like you plan to go ahead with a divorce, you'll be a real, official single mother. You need to know for darn sure that I'll be here for you. I wish I was clever and smart, but I just ain't. But hopefully I can love you enough to make up for what I can't do."

When we stopped crying about that, we started laughing because when I got up to hug her, I spilled my soda. The kids began fussing in the living room about who got to hold the channel selector, and we had to quiet them with more potato chips. Finally, we could talk about my news.

"Okay, now, this is a little complicated."

Delores scrunched up her face into a frown, trying to look like a dumb person who had to concentrate on something complicated. I wadded up my paper napkin and threw it at her, laughing with her.

"Do you remember that counselor at Richie's school? Sally Monroe? She's the girl I didn't like because I thought she was so stuck up?" Delores nodded as she finished wiping up the soda-and-coconut puddle.

"Well, I was really wrong about her. I ran into her at the Sunbeam day old bread store. I had to go in for hot dog buns, and she was getting some of that wheat bread that is supposed to be more healthy than the white kind. Anyway, after we nodded to each other, she started a conversation. She was on a rant about having to check the bottom of the loaves for mold."

I tried to imitate Sally. "It's bad enough driving all the way across town to save a dollar on a loaf of bread, but I hate to get it home and the bottom is all moldy."

So we laughed together, and she went on, "It's a rough start to the day to have to wipe green slime from my teeth from eating toast."

Delores laughed at my story, and I went on, "She seemed like a regular person. She's trying to save money to go back to school for another degree in counseling."

Delores put one of the lemon cupcakes on my saucer next to the chocolate mocha one.

"Then we got to talking about Richie. I agreed with her that it made sense for him to see a counselor, now that his dad won't be around. So she's going to refer Richie to a friend of hers who is good at getting kids to talk. She said it was a sign of Richie's good heart that he didn't want to worry me about his trouble at school. I thought it was sweet of her to say that, so I wouldn't feel so guilty about not knowing what was going on."

I took a sip of soda and glanced up at Delores. "She really seemed to care about putting together a good plan for Richie, one that would fit him. I wish I hadn't judged her so bad."

"Oh, sugar, it's just hard to trust new people."

I knew Delores meant well, to let me off the hook so easy. But my heart knew I'd been wrong, and I could do better.

"I wish you'd seen Mr. Sanders when he got so excited about the Boy Scouts."

Delores stopped eating her cupcake and frowned a little, a real frown, not her jokey one. "Well, I do like the idea of the Scouts. But, Wilma, I got to say I'm a little nervous about how much you're relying on that Mr. Sanders. I mean, he's doing good things, but you're tied to him for both your new job and for Richie, too. How do you know you can trust him?"

"I know you are worried, Delores. But if things don't work out, we'll figure out another way. Besides, there's no way I could keep working at the prison. I feel too guilty."

"Honey, I have said time and time again that you shouldn't spend a penny worrying about what happened. You were just trying to help."

I laughed, "Well, I helped myself into a mess."

Even though I trusted Delores with almost everything, I held back some of the details about Mr. Sanders. Like, I didn't tell her that he cried at the idea of Bill visiting with the Scouts when he finally got released. "Wilma, he'll be a grown man when he comes out of prison. He won't be a boy."

I also didn't tell Delores about the Sanders's marriage problems. When I had talked with Mr. Sanders the other day, he was excited because his wife had agreed to go to a trade show with him in Charlotte next month. They were going to look at next year's models.

"Wilma, we're making progress. We're still sleeping in Bill's room, but the other night my sweet wife suggested that I move my sleeping bag onto a blow up mattress so my back wouldn't hurt so bad in the morning. I thought that was such a sincere gesture on her part."

"How's Sammy doing?" I asked, just to lighten the conversation.

"Hell, that damn dog farts and snores all night long."

Delores looked at me like she was waiting for me to answer. I didn't realize I'd been lost in thought about Mr. Sanders's sleeping arrangements.

"I'm sorry, Mama Dee, I was thinking of something else. What did you say?"

"Did you let Mrs. Kelly know about your job change?"

"I did. I called her yesterday. She was surprised, but then she had a lot of questions. We're meeting at the Cracker Barrel for lunch tomorrow, so I'll fill her in then."

"Good. I think she's a good friend to have."

"Yeah, I wish I hadn't let her slip away from me for a while."

Church wasn't a topic that Delores and I felt comfortable talking about yet. She knew that I'd taken the kids to Bible study, and now when I glanced at the clock over the sink, I saw a picture of Jesus that Richie had colored. Delores had it hung on her refrigerator.

I hoped that at some point I could share with Deloris why I liked church so much. But it was complicated for both of us. For now, I just stayed prayed up, so the devil couldn't slip in sideways.

"Mama Dee, I never feel so good as when I'm here with you, but now I've got to get the kids home to bed."

"All right, sugar. Be sure to let me know when the first Scout meeting is scheduled so I can bake some cookies for Richie to bring along."

"Thanks, you are a treasure. Ted was lucky to have you as his mom. Now hand me one more cupcake before we head out. I do love me some chocolate."

Epilogue

Mrs. Kelly, Wilma, and Faith

Gracious plenty

Wilma stood on the school stage under the Career Day banner. Her uniform looked spiffy, and as usual, her black boots shined. From her utility belt dangled a squeeze bottle of hand sanitizer and a flashlight.

"All right, kids, time to be quiet so as I can introduce our next guest speaker."

The kids got quiet real quick, giving her the attention new recruits give a five star sergeant. I about teared up, watching Wilma at work. That girl had sure traveled a ways. I didn't understand why she up and quit her job at the prison, but seeing her today, it was clear that working at her kids' school was a good choice.

She only seemed a little nervous as she got started. "Mrs. Kelly works at the big prison over on the bypass. She's moved around some to other prisons, but now she's back here in town. She's been a cook for her whole life. Sometimes she's worked in big kitchens like at the prison, and sometimes in restaurants around town. Lots of your parents ate her food before you were born."

At this point Wilma lost the attention of the kids. Their faces scrunched up, trying to imagine their parents so long ago. To my ears, it sounded like Wilma was saying I served fertility food. Of course, I 'm sure it was true that some of the bar food I served was later eaten in back seats at the drive-in movies.

Wilma wrapped it up. "Mrs. Kelly is a hard worker, and is here today to talk to you about careers in the food industry. So y'all clap for my friend, Mrs. Kelly."

It had been hard deciding what to wear for my guest appearance today. I found a real cheery purple pantsuit at Goodwill, which the clerk said used to belong to the wife of our town's new foot doctor. But instead of that, I wore my work uniform since that was the reason I'd been invited to the program.

Wilma smiled real big when I joined her up on the stage. The steps up were narrow and steep, but my knees worked just fine.

"It is good to be here with you today. Even though you are still young, it's important to start thinking about jobs you might be interested in as you move up to middle school and then on to high school."

I wanted to make a pitch for staying around to finish high school, but the counselor who spoke before me already beat that drum. So I talked about the types of jobs open to people who can cook. I left out jobs at McDonald's since employees there mostly use a fryer to defrost the food, not really cook it. Then I got to the important finale of my speech.

"Being a cook is a good, honest job. But, to be honest, what I really recommend for you is a job as a physical therapist. That's the person who treats you after you have a problem like a broken leg. Those therapists are paid a lot of money to hurt you." The kids stared at me like I'd lost my mind, so I hurried on. "But after they spend a while hurting you, eventually you'll feel better. Since our country has so many people getting older every minute, physical therapists will always have a bunch of cracked up knees, elbows, shoulders, whatever, to work on. It don't matter what body part is broke, they are ready to snatch onto it and make it better."

The kids looked like they were getting a little bored, so I hurried to the end of my remarks. "Remember, what's important is to stay in school so you can make more money than your folks."

Wilma hugged me when I joined her off the stage. "Miss K, you did a great job. Them kids really listened when you got to talking about broken legs and such." We chatted for a while about her kids and my Sharon. I didn't ask about Ted, figuring today's get together was too nice to taint it with bad memories. We moved over to the refreshment table that the PTA ladies had put together. To me, it looked like the deviled eggs had sat out for so many hours, the bacteria were free-styling through the paprika sprinkles. So instead, I just had a cup of punch.

Just as Wilma served herself, her boss, the principal, came over to us. With him was Faith, the very strange librarian.

"I understand you ladies used to work together at the prison," he said, including both Wilma and me in his big smile.

"However, Miss Faith decided to leave prison work and starts next week with us here in our school library." Since he obviously expected us to make the proper noises of pleasant surprise, he looked confused by our silence. Wilma and I were both too busy sipping warm punch from our paper cups to respond to his enthusiasm. Of course, I could have snorted out a spray of punch, but I was there as a visitor.

Without our expected smiles, the principal just stood there. My expression must have been similar to the look I'd given the eggs. But my good manners reflex surfaced, and I answered him. "Yes, we did work together." Today Faith wore a different version of the droopy beige outfit I'd last seen her in on the day of the escape. Except, instead of oxfords, she wore red patent high heels.

"Mrs. Kelly was a big help to me when we worked together. Her experience and advice were very valuable." Faith directed her remarks to the principal. She hadn't actually looked at Wilma and me yet.

Then Wilma spoke up. "Mrs. Kelly set a high standard of behavior when I worked with her." Wilma's tone made her words sound like a challenge to Faith, like "not so fast, you sharpie, don't you be claiming my friend as your friend."

The principal swung his eyes at all of us. He knew he'd stepped into a hot pile; he just didn't know what the mess was. But he stayed on message. "I'm sure you ladies will have a lot of catching up to do. Wilma, Faith will be leading some special reading classes your kids are in. So you'll work with her both as a colleague and a parent."

It wasn't clear if he meant this as a warning to Wilma to play nice, but Wilma played it safe and smiled back. "The kids like going to the library."

Before he led Faith over to another group of school staff, he thanked me for participating in Career Day. As soon as they moved away, Wilma whispered to me, "What the hell? I thought she got fired for losing that gate key. How can she work here if she was fired?"

Even though I wanted to fill Wilma in on the full extent of Faith's involvement in the escape, I had promised Joe Brown to keep his suspicions between us. He had no proof she did more than lose a key, but he still kept an eye on her. Joe Brown thought Faith was dirty, and he was a patient man.

I could only answer Wilma with my best guess. "They probably let her resign instead of firing her, since mostly they just wanted to get rid of her. Since prison jobs and school jobs are separate deals and since she wasn't charged, she didn't lose her librarian's license. So it looks like you'll get a chance to get to know her better - just like I did."

Wilma drawled, "And look how good that worked out." Then she went on, "Did you see her red shoes with that outfit? She looked like she belonged to a weird group of Wizard of Oz freaks."

I smiled, "You never did like her, just from that one time at the recruitment meeting."

Wilma grinned back. "My judgment of people is not always off. Just when it comes to choosing a husband."

I agreed with her, but since Ted's long prison sentence had just started, I didn't want to sing over his corpse so soon, so to speak. But, truth be told, Wilma's future looked a whole lot brighter without that man around to mess her up. And I for double damn certain knew that Wilma had no intention of getting pulled into Faith's strange world.

Then it was time to go. Wilma and I hugged and agreed to meet at the Cracker Barrel next Tuesday when they had chicken and dumplings on the menu. As I reached the door, I turned back and saw Wilma's kids hanging onto her while she scrubbed their hands with sanitizer goo. Then she used the same tissue to wipe their noses.

About the Author

Jean Bell writes from experience. She worked for more than twenty years in the prison system dealing with issues that dominate the news today: risk-assessment of pedophiles, tracking gang activities, and escape prevention and apprehension. In her last job before retirement, she was in charge of security at her state's largest maximum security prison.

An award-winning writer of essays and short fiction, Bell's *Prison Grits* is her first collection of short stories. She is currently at work on her second book, which also has a prison setting.

Bell and her husband, a retired college professor, live in South Carolina. They have two grown children and one grandchild.

www.ingramcontent.com/pod-product-compliance
Lightning Source LLC
Chambersburg PA
CBHW020742250626
47155CB00003B/885